WARDS OF THE ROSES

MYSTERIOUS CHARM: BOOK 4

CELIA LAKE

ALSO BY CELIA LAKE

The Mysterious Charm Series
Outcrossing
Goblin Fruit
Magician's Hoard
Wards of the Roses
In The Cards
On The Bias
Seven Sisters

Find a complete list of all my books at celialake.com/books.

Sign up for my newsletter to be the first to hear about future books and learn about fascinating bits of research. Happy reading!

Collaboration and curiosity can get through the thickest thorns.

Giles Lefton has an excellent life. He enjoys his mathematics, his teaching at the University, and his cryptography assignments. When a manor missing for centuries suddenly reappears in the middle of Oxfordshire, Giles is glad to take on the project. Figuring out magical puzzles and patterns is one of his specialities, after all. Blinded during the Great War, he knows he needs an assistant to help. One who meets his standards.

Kate Davies can be relied on to do her duty without complaint. A full member of Albion's Guard, she is glad to serve where she is assigned. While she is glad the Great War is over, she quietly misses the greater range of duties she had while so many men were overseas. Now limited to portal duty and seeing to minor scuffles about the local river traffic, she isn't sure what to make of her new assignment. Or the fact she keeps failing at what Major Lefton expects of her.

Together, Kate and Giles tumble into a maze of historical investigation, obscure folklore, and more than a touch of magics neither of them understand.

Face the roses with Kate and Giles in 1920 Oxfordshire, and discover the mysteries of the manor.

ONE

JULY 1920 IN TRELLECH (IN WALES)

"Davies." Edgarton's aide appeared in the doorway to his office, moving almost silently.

Kate had been sitting at attention on the bench just opposite. She stood promptly, walking into the office. She stopped the prescribed three feet from the desk and saluted. "Sir, Guard Davies reporting."

She could feel the way her hair had come loose during the day, untidily, and how the sweat pooled in the small of her back, under the uniform. Kate did her best to stay calm, wondering why he'd called her in, taking comfort in the formalities.

"At ease, Davies." Edgarton gave her an easy wave. "What's your current duty?"

Kate was certain he knew, but when the officer asked, the officer got a reply. "As assigned, sir. Last week it was that barge problem on the Severn." This week, it had been routine coordination of traffic around the portals and several rounds of uneventful patrols.

He nodded. "Would you have any difficulty taking an extended assignment outside of Trellech?"

She blinked. That was not what she'd expected. It didn't take her long to answer, "No, sir. I live in Guard housing. I'd just need to pack."

"No pets or small children, then."

His casual tone didn't fool her. Kate was certain he had the life stories of every Guard in his service memorised, indexed, and colour coded.

"You went to Schola, didn't you?"

"Yes, sir." Why they were going through things he must know, she had no idea, but if that was the dance he needed, she would oblige.

"House?" Which he also must know.

"Bear, sir." And then, venturing a little more than he had asked directly. "Martial specialist, sir. House bohort team four years, and school team my last two." She'd begun playing as soon as she had been allowed to.

That earned her an amused cough. "Those were my next questions, yes. Your team won the apprentice league, your last year, didn't you?"

She nodded. "I was in that match, yes, sir." She could still remember the exhilaration of keeping her team safe through it all. They had been buffeted by all kinds of magical traps and devices, including a splash of glue that would have ruined their best delicate charmworker's dexterity. She had been the one to figure out the puzzle of the last chest, the one that won them the game. She'd only managed in the last moments before it went off in an explosion of coloured powder.

"You've been bored here, since the men came back."

Yes, she had been, but it wouldn't do to be rude. "It's grand to have them back home, sir, but I enjoyed the greater range of duties when we were short handed." Women hadn't been able to serve openly in the Great War, and she had wanted to be neither Healer nor driver.

She'd been fortunate that she'd finished her apprenticeship before the War. By the time the men went to fight, she'd begun to be assigned a wider range of tasks. Of course, there wasn't much choice, at times. But then the living had come back, and they had shunted her to necessary but boring tasks, none of which involved the remotest chance of exploding chests. Or even interesting puzzles that didn't explode.

Edgarton nodded. "I believe I have a task that will suit your skills."

"Sir?" The proper mode was polite curiosity, so she gave it her best.

"There is a small manor house, in Oxfordshire. It has been missing since around the time of the Pact and has recently reappeared."

That was not the type of problem she expected. "Sir?" When in doubt, politely ask for more information. It was all in the tone, as her uncles had taught her.

"We need someone able to collaborate. Someone competent at solving puzzles. Creative thinking." Edgarton was circling around something, she could tell. He was a subtle man most of the time, but he wasn't bothering to hide his discomfort with something here. She couldn't tell if it was due to the possible influence of the Fatae, or something else. If the Pact had anything to do with the house in the first place.

"The house, sir?" At least she could prompt him.

"Why the house was hidden, why it reappeared now, and, ahem," he paused, flicking his fingers. "And how to get inside."

"It's locked, sir?"

"Thoroughly warded. Likely also locked, but we haven't been able to get close enough to find out."

Kate considered. "I'm no lock specialist, sir. I only know the common Guard techniques for that." Opening doors that were locked was sometimes necessary, of course, to save someone in an emergency or to stop a crime.

Edgarton waved a hand. "We suspect some kind of puzzle. Mathematical. Cryptographical."

"Sir, I'm afraid that is even less within my skills." Kate was truly confused now.

"Can you collaborate with someone?" This time the question was clear and quick.

"Sir, I am glad to give it my best." Even if she hadn't been, the chance of getting out of portal duty was too much to resist.

Edgarton nodded, then said. "Sit there." He gestured at the table. "I have some charts."

Kate blinked, but obeyed at once, shifting the chair he'd indicated to sit at the worktable. Edgarton took the chair next to her, unrolling a large roll of paper and setting a paperweight on each end. There was a map, with a sketch of the house in a corner of the large page.

"This is the house. Based on the architecture we believe it dates from the 1200s."

Kate frowned. "Henry II, or thereabouts?" She reached out a hand to touch it.

"Good eye." He saw her slight hesitation, and murmured, "Do speak freely, Davies, ask what you need to."

"Is that when it disappeared?"

"We have a few records referring to it in the later 1400s, but it is difficult to identify precisely when something stopped being mentioned. It could be before the Pact, or after."

She grimaced. "Sir." She considered, peering at the map, the layout. "What did you have in mind, sir?"

As smooth as Edgarton was, he still could not hide his perplexing discomfort. She could see that in how the tension in his jaw shifted, the way he kept pausing to choose his words carefully, that the next thing must be part of that discomfort.

"There is a specialist, someone who may be able to solve the wards. But he will need assistance to do so." Which made her certain his discomfort was not about the Fatae, or at least not them alone.

"What kind of assistance, sir? Protection, a pair of hands? Something else."

Edgarton frowned. "He's one of the war-blinded. Talented mathematician, before. Still." It wasn't a grudging response, but she could hear the glitch of hesitation.

Kate paused, not sure what to make of that obvious discomfort. It was unlike Lord Edgarton. Then she figured out her way through, for the moment. "What kind of assistance does he need, sir? From the Guard?"

"He has an aide, a distant cousin who sees to his personal needs and correspondence." Edgarton said. "But the aide, Vale, has no background in either protective magics or puzzle solving. A literal thinker, is how Lefton put it."

Kate nodded. "So - it is thought that someone who did well in bohort might at least have an idea what to ask about, what to describe?" She would not venture to assume it was Edgarton who'd come up with this idea.

"Precisely." Edgarton looked pleased she'd come out with that herself. "And you have done well, in your apprenticeship and since, in a variety of tasks." He paused. "They tasked me with finding three people. Lefton insists on interviewing a range to find someone he can best work with."

Kate couldn't suppress her smile. "Man of strong opinions, sir?"

"Rather, yes." Edgarton clearly had done a round with him, given how that came out.

"May I ask who else you are suggesting, sir?"

That earned her a broad grin. "Byles and Peck." He waited a moment, then added, "They didn't ask."

Those two wouldn't have, no. Anthony Byles was an arrogant bastard who thought every good thing was his by right. He was very skilled, there was no denying that, but the attitude made him difficult to deal with. Theodora Peck would be interested in the puzzle, Kate was sure, but she didn't always do well working with people.

Kate considered this, then risked a little more, "What else didn't they ask, that I should know?" She was certain there were things no one would tell her, but surely people were interested in a house appearing out of nowhere? She couldn't begin to think through what was going on by herself, she didn't have nearly enough information or experience, but she could at least make the effort and ask.

That earned her a broad grin, and a "That's what I like about you, Davies. You think to ask." He gestured at the map. "You will need to be close to the manor, to investigate it. There is an old manse, here," He tapped the page. "It is large enough for you to have your own space. There will be a housekeeper, and a horse and carriage if you need it."

"Does..." She almost asked if Lefton rode, then realised. "Does Lefton - pardon, sir, I don't know how to refer to him properly - have any specific requirements I should know about? To give proper assistance?"

"He'll explain that if you're chosen," Edgarton said. "He

didn't tell me, I presume so he could use it as part of the interview. And it's Major Lefton, though I suspect he'll ask you to use his surname."

Kate nodded. She suspected given his rank he'd been quite competent, since she didn't recognise his last name as being from the sort of family who would get a sinecure. "May I ask..." And then she stopped, because her first question had been about the cause of his blindness, and that actually wasn't relevant. "Is there a profile of him I might read, before speaking with him? Public background?"

That earned her another approving nod, and Edgarton leaned down to the end of the table, handing her a folder. "Profile of Lefton, and what we know about the house. You have an appointment with him at five this evening, and you are off duty until then to prepare. Report back to me whether he accepts you or not. I will be in the office until at least nine."

She recognised the dismissal for what it was, and stood, claiming the folder, then saluting. "Sir, thank you, sir."

Kate made her way briskly back to her quarters, not stopping to speak to anyone on the way. Once inside, she shrugged off the uniform jacket, coiled her hair out of her way for the moment, and sat down to read.

The brief on the project was only two pages, and labelled with the notation in the Guard's Tongue that indicated it was to be kept confidential.

There was little new information beyond what Lord Edgarton had told her. A manor had reappeared in Oxford-shire in mid June, there were roses and walls; early attempts to access the property had not succeeded. The brief made it clear that she could not discuss the specific location or the magical aspects of the reappearance with anyone not properly authorised. That left some room for general research, perhaps, since it looked like no one had done any general review of the territory involved.

The combination of the paltry information provided and the secrecy baffled her. Surely a house reappearing would have spread through the surrounding villages like a flood. There must be some sort of local folklore and speculation, even if it wasn't at all accurate.

The profile on Lefton was thorough, until his discharge from the Army. His first name, apparently, was Aegidius, which told her everything she needed to know about his family. He was a younger son of one of the First Families who tended toward civil service and military roles. He'd grown up with money and plenty of opportunities for the taking, since the profile mentioned his family had multiple country homes and a townhouse here in Trellech.

As she suspected from the name, Aegidius Lefton had been in Fox House at Schola. It must have polished those assumptions about how the world worked, all tidy and neat and under control. He was four years younger, so they'd overlapped, but she'd not paid much attention to first years. He'd played bohort, nearly to her standard, which was intriguing, and gone straight into an apprenticeship in mathematics and related magics once he got out of school. That last part was not at all what she expected. Nor, she thought, what his family would have preferred.

His War record was exemplary, several minor medals for injuries or heroics in action. Then there was a brief and uninformative note that he and his battalion had been in the line of a magical gas attack in the trenches in Flanders, and he had been invalided out. A third of the men with him had died, but he'd got many of the others to safety.

They had sent Lefton to somewhere called St Dunstan's. From context, it had to do with the blindness, some sort of training in how to manage. From there, he'd worked with someone, retraining some magical skills, at something called The Refuge, then settled into a family-owned townhome in Trellech.

It was not nearly as informative as it might be.

TWO

TRELLECH

Just before five, Kate presented herself at the townhouse. It was in a well-to-do section of Trellech, near the row of clubs.

The door opened, revealing a tall angular man in a tweed suit with his dark hair slicked back. He looked her up and down, the kind of look that made her certain that her uniform was muddy, her hair was escaping, and her boots were scuffed. None of these things were true. She'd even got Adria's help to pin her hair up so it would stay in its tight bun at the nape of her neck come fog or fire. "Yes?"

"Good afternoon, sir. Guard Katherine Davies, I have an appointment with Major Lefton."

The 'sir' earned her a small nod, not approving, but at least not quite as forbidding. It had something of a faded military manner about it, if one with all its crispness worn off at the corners, but of course a man his age would have been in the War. "This way. I'm Phillip Vale, his assistant. Did they warn you?"

Kate blinked, unsure what to do with the phrasing. "That Major Lefton is blind, yes, sir." She paused, then murmured, "Is there anything I should know, sir? For his comfort?"

That earned her a snort and no answer, just a brisk walk to a room at the end of the hallway. At the door, he leaned into the room and announced, "Last of the Guards to see you, Giles," in a manner that was very informal indeed, particularly by comparison. He waved a hand at her. "Go in."

There was no response from the room. Kate paused for a second on the threshold, just long enough to get a sense of the space. It was a generously-sized room, a trifle under-furnished. There were no rugs on the floor, just bare wooden boards, and a wide desk at a broad window that looked out into a walled garden.

The desk had a pile of rather large books on it, and a device that looked like a typewriter at first glance, but with many fewer keys. It was a masculine space, all leather and dark wood, with deep green walls. Two chairs sat facing each other in front of an unlit fireplace. She could just see a man's head over the top of one.

"Sir, is this still a convenient time? I'm Guard Davies. Captain Edgarton suggested I might suit the project."

The man turned in his chair to better face her once she spoke. He was roughly her age, mid-thirties. He kept his dark hair noticeably longer than the Guard permitted, brushing his shoulders, but he was clean-shaven. His dark round glasses hid his eyes, but the frames picked up the burgundy of the silk smoking jacket he wore. Something about what she'd said appeared to amuse him.

He gestured. "Sit." His voice was brusque, but clear.

Kate came over, paused for a moment in front of the indicated chair, then sat, with another "Sir." It seemed sensible for her to say something, after all.

He folded his hands in his lap, facing her precisely, and she realised he must know exactly where the chair was supposed to be. "Tell me about yourself. Name, house, family." There was a tiny pause, then, "Appearance too, please." The tone suggested it was a concession he disliked making.

She nodded, then realised that was not much help, while she tried to figure out what might interest him. "I am Guardswoman Katherine Davies. I'm the youngest of five, and the second daughter. My parents run an inn near Cardiff, and my brothers are in various coastal professions. I'm aunt to several young nieces and nephews."

He nodded and inquired, "Your sister?"

"Married, widowed in the War, working at the inn." She wondered, briefly, what he made of her leaving that out the first time, then continued.

"I was in Bear House, at Schola, and specialised in protective magics, under Master Trenton. He recommended me as an apprentice to the Guard when I left school. I finished my apprenticeship in 1912. I've had a range of duty assignments, but I've been in Trellech for most of the past decade."

"Your War?" The question was almost off-hand. She was having a hard time getting a good read on him, and she found it increasingly frustrating.

"Women weren't permitted to serve in combat, sir, as I'm sure you're aware. I filled in here wherever they needed someone. Protection duties for officers and dignitaries, some anti-espionage work under close supervision, as well as the usual civil defence coordination. Reinforcing shelters, mostly, on the magical end."

That earned her another nod, one that had her leaning forward, trying to figure out what he meant by it. "And now?"

"District assistance, sir."

"That seems a step down." She couldn't tell if he was baiting her or not.

"I am glad to serve where I'm needed, sir. I do admit, though, I would enjoy more of a challenge than portal traffic duty."

He snorted. "Quite." He paused, as if considering something. "Appearance?" He wanted her to move along, then, and answer his questions promptly.

"I'm five foot six, sir. I have dark red hair with a curl. For duty, I wear it pinned back tightly in a bun. I'm wearing the usual guard uniform for city duty, the split skirt rather than trousers. Do you need a further description?" Deep blue wool, silver trim, pale cream tunic underneath, and black boots. What she'd worn nearly every day for the past decade and a half.

He waved a hand. "I'm familiar with the uniform. What do you think about Wilfred Douglas's approach to household warding?"

"Wilfred, sir? Most people go to Ferdinand, his brother."

Lefton grinned suddenly, a quick flash of teeth, before his expression settled back into neutrality. "Wilfred," he repeated.

"Honestly, sir, I've always rather preferred Wilfred's cantrip. There's an elegance to the flow of the working, the twist of energies not present in Ferdinand's. I've found it both degrades more slowly, and also more consistently. I wouldn't use it for delicate items, of course, but I wouldn't use Ferdinand's, either."

"What would you use?"

She frowned, flicking mentally through some of her recent reading. "It would depend on the material, sir. I read something last week that suggested a variant of Hoyle's might be much better for books than has been thought. I haven't had a chance to test it."

He said nothing else for nearly a minute, sitting there, tapping his fingers together. She waited. Finally, he asked, "Did you play bohort?"

"I still do, sir. House team for four years, sir and school team my last two. And since for the Guard." She'd almost expected the question, from Edgarton's comments earlier. "I'm selected for league teams, but not often."

"What position? And why not, do you think?" His tone was almost casual, but she could feel how he was probing.

"I don't suit the current style of play. My reflexes are quick enough, and my speed over distance, but I prefer a thoughtful solution to one requiring strength. That's not in fashion with our team captains at the moment." There was a pause, "I'm usually chosen for Puzzle or Defender, sir."

He nodded sharply. "Indeed. Call me Lefton." It was clearly a step in the right direction. He added after a moment, "My given name is Aegidius. You'll hear a few people call me Giles."

Kate murmured, "Lefton, sir." She was quite clear that she was not one of the favoured few.

Something in that amused him again, but she wasn't sure what. "What did they tell you about this problem I am supposed to solve?"

She considered for just a moment, following the fleeting whisper in her head, of making the unexpected choice, seeing where it led. "Captain Edgarton told me it would require a collaborative effort."

That earned her a snort, and a "There is that. How do you see your role?"

There were a dozen things she could say here, and most

of them felt wrong. "I only had two hours to study the brief, sir."

"You were a late addition to the list, I believe. Tell me how you would begin."

She had a number of ideas, but she had no idea how he would take them, so she would begin with the obvious. "I would like to examine the house, as closely as possible. I understand it is surrounded by thick rose bushes, but that they cannot be trimmed, plucked, or removed."

"You are correct, so far as we can tell."

"The brief was..." She paused, looking for a word that would not be insulting to the unnamed person who prepared it. "Unspecific, sir, on a number of points. Many details of the house, but even more outside. The particular type of roses, whether they occur in specific patterns. The precise size and shape of the bushes. Whether there are other plants, mixed in."

That earned her a thoughtful grunt, but more silence.

After a minute, she ventured, "Have you been there, sir?"

"Not yet. Our lords and masters in their infinite wisdom felt it was better to find me a colleague, first." His voice was a smooth drawl that affected not to care about anything.

Kate was quick to respond. "I suspect they've told you more than they told me, Lefton."

He waved a hand. "They've not told me as much as I'd like."

"They can't be expecting to keep the whole thing secret, surely? It will be one of the prime topics in every pub for a day's walk. At least the magical ones." She wasn't sure what any of them were thinking, and the question she'd been thinking about burst out of her before she could quite stop it.

"Can you work with the limitations? Are you the kind who goes where you're told and does what you're ordered?"

The words sprung out of her before she could think better. "That'd make a poor Guard, wouldn't it now, someone who couldn't make choices on the fly? I'll be having none of that." She could hear the lilt of her childhood in there, the surge of something that wasn't temper so much as passion. Then she took a breath. "I follow orders, sir, but I hope I'll be permitted to offer my own ideas."

She wasn't at all sure what he made of that, but if she'd spoiled her chance at this, better to do so this way. He leaned forward, curiously enough, then gestured, a hand indicating for her to settle. "I would rather not be dragged away from my work, you see."

She blinked and didn't know what to do with that change of topic. "May I ask about your usual work, Lefton?" She tried to keep her voice polite and was glad he couldn't see how her hand clenched and relaxed several times before she made herself still.

Lefton nodded, then said, "I am a mathematician. I hold a research chair at Oxford in applied mathematics, to be specific. Magical and otherwise. I use a variety of tools, depending."

"To do what, please?" Kate was clear enough on maths for some things, but this seemed something else.

"Puzzles, in part. Cryptography, codes. A number of them rely on the relationship of numbers."

That at least made sense. "Is there much of that now? The War's over."

"Ah, but the spying never is. The Great Game, so on, so forth." He flicked his fingers. "Mind, I am less busy than I was for a while. I suppose that's why they feel they can send me off to work on this house and its roses."

THREE

TRELLECH

Giles tried not to let his rising irritation show. This woman, this Guard, wasn't the one to blame. Logically, he knew that. Edgarton must consider her competent, or he wouldn't have sent her along.

He tried to work through the problem one more time, as if that would produce a different result. This mysterious house presented an intriguing challenge. Solving it might well lead to the powers that be admitting he was useful for more than rote code-breaking, and that was no small thing. Edgarton had suggested a mathematician's logic, and his experience with puzzle-breaking might serve here. They had, mind, been firm that he needed a colleague to assist, and that his cousin was insufficient.

Truthfully, by whatever measurement you used, Vale was not the most intelligent of his relations, nor did he have the specialised skills this matter clearly required. He'd not gone to Schola, nor shown much magical promise. Instead he'd done a clerking apprenticeship before the War gave him a chance to show some bravery and win enough honours to keep a girl hanging on his arm whenever he wanted to attend a party. Which was as often as his duties allowed.

He was not at all certain about this woman, Davies. She must be three or four years older than he was. Near enough his age, for all the polite use of sir she made. He realised, with a start, the silence was stretching too long, and coughed, before he said, "You must have questions." Now, he was baiting her, certainly.

She moved, the leather of the chair creaking softly, then she said, her voice precise. "A number, yes." There was a tiny hesitation, as if she was deciding to commit to a course of action, then she continued. "Pardon, sir, but it would be a help to know your - how things work for you. How you expect the collaboration to work."

It was awkwardly put, but it was not the nastiness he'd heard other places. A middling mark, but with the possibility of improvement if she wasn't touchy about being corrected.

He nodded, then answered the question she was clearly wanting to ask, doing his best to keep his voice light and even. "A gas attack, a trial of a new magical gas. Damage to both eyes. I can see rough shapes with my left, in good lighting, but not at all in dim or very bright light, and I can't read any kind of print. The right eye is much worse. They trained me in how to manage my personal needs, and Vale sees to bills and routine correspondence and such." He waited, to see what she made of that.

There was rather a long silence, longer than most people would be comfortable with. Then she asked, "Are there other effects I should know when considering how to approach the task?"

He liked her strategic thinking. He considered, then stood. "Would you care for tea?" He turned, moving precisely to the table along the wall that held the teapot and cups. Then he ran his fingers along the wood until he found the first cup, then the second, and set them up for pouring.

He heard, "Thank you, sir. Cream, no sugar, if it's available."

"Of course." He then busied himself with the pouring, from the keep-warm pot, holding the charmed stirrer that pulsed in his fingers when the cup was almost full. Giles then added a splash of cream to each cup, and sugar to his own. All the little tricks, for keeping things oriented. It helped, mind, that he'd always thought about space as a series of mathematical relationships, curve to angle to curve.

He paused, long enough for the tea to steep, and to see what she did with an extended period of quiet, working through mathematical counts in his head. He chose prime numbers today; counting up by primes to a thousand took him precisely two and a half minutes. When he reached nine hundred and ninety-seven, he picked up the saucers in each hand.

Turning, he checked his angle, and walking back to his usual chair, setting his own cup down. There was the moment of hesitation as he made sure it was in the proper place on the table, then held the other to her. Standing, he could just see the fuzzy shape of her chair, silhouetted by the light from the window behind.

"Thank you, Lefton." There was another of those moments of hesitation, so fleeting, before she said, "And for making your point about your competence that way."

Oh, that made him laugh, his usual sharp bark. "Few take it so well," he admitted.

She was quiet, and he wondered if there was some movement he missed here, but then she said, "Are there things I might do that would..." She stopped. "I don't mean to be clumsy, Lefton, but I'm not sure what you need help with."

He coughed, and then said, "If you're selected, we can discuss that in more detail. Obviously, I need assistance with anything requiring eyesight. Measurements and such. But I am also looking for someone who could collaborate. The initial attempts to resolve the puzzle have not been successful, which suggests it is not a simple solution. Enough of the people they sent are competent, after all."

Giles couldn't help feeling irritated. The question was not unreasonable, but he disliked being made responsible for the answer. He had not much more information than she had, and he had already protested about it to the powers above with absolutely no result.

"Do you know about the other people who've tried?" She said it quickly, as if she weren't sure what he'd think about her asking.

"Only the summary, and a few names Edgarton mentioned." He'd been kept from the full briefs and profiles - no one with sufficient authority could be spared to read them to him. From the names he'd heard so far, at least three had been given the chance due to patronage and nepotism. He was not at all sure he knew how to explain any of it to her, and decided not to try.

Realising he had been silent too long, he said, "How did you prepare for this?"

"As I said, Lefton, I only had about two hours, and I needed to change and come here. I read the brief, and a profile of you. I'd not come across your work before, not that I had reason to." She paused and said, "Your list of publications is quite technical."

He couldn't tell how she meant that and grunted. "Expand on that, would you?"

Davies took a breath, and said "I'm - pardon, sir, but I'm usually more about the application than the theory. I'm afraid a lot of the theory would go right over my head, and I'm not sure I'd be able to assist as this project involves."

Giles nodded, falling quiet and thinking about it. He didn't need to coddle someone who wasn't confident; he didn't have time for that.

"Do you want this assignment?" he asked, finally.

"Only if you think I will be helpful, sir. I mean, it seems like a fascinating problem. And much better than portal traffic duty. But it is ..." He could hear her stop, fiddle with her tea cup, then she murmured, "Pardon, Lefton, if I might gather my thoughts before continuing?"

He nodded at her. "As you wish."

She took a good two minutes, maybe three. Despite himself, he found that intriguing. Most would rush to fill the silence. He could hear her lift her cup, tasting the tea, and he sipped at his own. When she finally spoke, she said, "I believe in doing things well. I know that the other people who you've interviewed are both well-respected by officers in the Guard, and will have been recommended to you for a particular reason."

Giles had no idea if that careful phrasing indicated her full awareness of the politics and familial choices that would recommend Byles, or what. "And where does that leave you?"

"I have no patron, sir. Two uncles in the Guard, but they - they've had no desire beyond being one of the village Guard, seeing to keeping things running smoothly. I can do that, and when I do, I see it's done well."

He leaned forward. "But?"

There was a long pause, then he could hear the awkwardness. "I'd like the opportunity to try more. I had a little during the War, but -" Her voice trailed off. If she kept doing that, it would be exceedingly annoying.

Then she cleared her throat. "Sir, this seems like a fascinating project, and I would like the chance to be part of it, and lend my skills, if you think I would be of use." And then, as if she were straightening up. "Do you have other questions about my qualifications?"

Giles shook his head. "I'll need to think it over. You'll hear from me or Edgarton one way or another in the next day or two." He pauses for a moment, then added, "When could you be ready if you were selected, to stay in Oxfordshire?" He kept his voice even.

"A few hours, sir. What would I need to pack?"

"You need only one or two changes of uniform. Comfortable clothing for investigating and walking, and you'll likely want a canvas smock and leather guards for your arms, for investigating the roses, that sort of thing. Bohort gear would be fine. Whatever clothes you prefer to wear when working on notes and research in the evenings."

She coughed, and said, "I - yes, sir," with a tone that he couldn't interpret. She then murmured "Should I see myself out?"

"If you don't mind." He kept his voice pleasant.

She nodded, and said, "Thank you, sir, for the time. And the tea."

He nodded back, then considered and held out his hand. A moment later, he heard the shift of her chair as she stood. Then he could feel her palm press against his, and the warmth of her hand. He often didn't offer a handshake, it felt so vulnerable to have one's hand out, not sure if someone would take it. And yet, he wanted more of a sense of her than he could get from her voice alone. It was not as

helpful as he'd hoped, her handshake was brief, professional, and steady, but rather impersonal.

"Someone will be in touch."

"Have a pleasant evening, Lefton, and I hope to hear
from you." That, at least, was back to being crisp and polite.
He waited as he heard her footsteps go off into the hall, a
murmur from Vale as she went past the front parlour, and
the door opening. And then Vale's shoes coming back
toward him.

"Not sure what I think of her, Giles. Not really our
sort." The decorous sneer had a bit more of an edge to it
than usual. Perhaps a barmaid had turned him down
recently.

It was not Vale's call to make. Giles waved a hand rather
than point that out, he was not in the mood to deal with
Vale's sulking all evening. "Confirm the appointment with
Edgarton, tomorrow at ten, would you? And then if you
want to go out to supper, go ahead. I should do some
writing."

"Sandwich? Should I bring something back?"

Giles shook his head. "Sandwich later, maybe." His
appetite wasn't what it used to be.

FOUR

TRELLECH

Giles sat, waiting for Edgarton with increasing impatience, in one of the private meeting rooms of the Den. It was convenient to his townhome.

The day had been sunny enough he could walk along with Vale at his side, not needing to hold his arm for guidance. He could trust to knowing the walk well and the bit of uncertain sight from one eye to avoid running into people. It had given him five minutes of a glorious feeling almost like he had before, but once he got to the club, reality came crashing back.

Once, he'd have spent the time waiting on catching up on a newspaper, or correspondence, or have brought a small pocket book along, and worked through mathematics. But now, all his reading, all his tools, were not at all portable. The books were cumbersome, the abacus even more so, and the typewriter and braillewriter were downright heavy.

All in all, by the time Edgarton showed up, just past the quarter hour chime, Giles was quite grumpy again. Not that that was unusual, these days.

"Sir, your guest." That was one of the staff, followed

promptly by another voice, this one Edgarton's bright tenor. "Lefton. I do beg your pardon, two separate people stopped me on my way out the door, and I couldn't put them off."

Giles snorted and said, "You never can. They outranked you?"

Edgarton sounded apologetic at least. "Both of them. And I pick my battles."

"You always have." The apology made him feel somewhat better, as he could hear Edgarton was sincere.

There was a little rustle, Edgarton settling in, then murmuring an order to a staff member who must have been hovering. Giles ordered his usual morning tea and scone. Once that was dealt with, he settled back to wait.

Edgarton let the silence draw on. That was a thing Giles liked most about him, that Edgarton never rushed. More to the point, he never rushed any of his experts. Didn't jog their elbows, didn't demand ridiculous reports just to show work was being done. He had absurdly high standards, but he understood that insight and inspiration did not appear on demand.

Eventually, though, he murmured, "Your thoughts, Lefton?"

Giles waved his hand. "Byles won't do at all. I suppose you had to send him but he's a dilettante. Fine enough for escort duty. Tell me, though, does he tend to his boots properly? I suspect one of his heels needs seeing to."

He heard Edgarton laugh, followed by, "I will see about an inspection, then. Which one?"

Giles considered, thinking back. "Left, I believe. He's right handed, isn't he? Trailing foot. That might trip him up some day."

Edgarton chortled at that. "Goodness. Not much slips by you, does it? What else did you think?"

"Arrogant puppy. Thinks he's better than standard duties, wants something that'd let him take it easy, perhaps. Not lazy, precisely, but - not attentive to work?"

Edgarton made a non-committal noise.

Giles carried on, they both knew the necessary steps of this dance. "He mentioned he married last year. I vaguely remember the announcement, I think. Some flower of another of the First Families, yes? But he had no concern about being away from her for a length of time, didn't even ask about it."

Edgarton grunted at that. "Not surprised. Arranged match, like you'd expect. They get on well enough, but not - fondly."

Giles frowned, then said, "Even if he'd like the excuse, I'm not choosing him. Too -" He searched for the word. "Too careless. And that's not what we need at all." Also, entirely too likely to run roughshod over the way Giles wanted to do things, but that was not something Giles could say out loud, even to Edgarton.

"The women, then."

Their food came, and there was a bit of fussing, setting the plates out. Giles liked scones since he could spread the cream himself, and once he knew where the plate was, it was easy to manage the rest.

He took his time sorting things out. Slicing the scone, cream, jam, then taking a bite once it was ready, two sips of tea. "The women." he agreed. "Why did you send Davies? Not at all your sort."

"I have a sort?" Edgarton sounded amused, even teasing.

"You do." Giles considered. "I expected someone like Peck, and someone - no-nonsense, a young man of mathematical promise, perhaps. Young man, young woman, the gender is not essential. To go with the necessary familial offering."

"Is that why you asked for three?"

"Indeed. I knew you were obliged to include someone like Byles. Blast him. Is there a particular patron putting him forward?"

Edgarton coughed. "No particular patron in this case, no." Which was annoyingly uninformative. "And Peck is not mathematical enough for you?"

Giles considered that, tapping his fingers in an absent-minded pattern on the table. "Not the kind I expected. Oh, she's well-read and clearly familiar with the primary and secondary theories. More than sharp enough to keep up with me." Which was no small thing.

Edgarton laughed, and said, "Those are not easy to find, you know."

It earned him a smile, before Giles said, "Can you tell me anything about her current assignment or past ones? She made it clear she didn't have clearance to share anything."

Giles mentally filled in the wave of a hand he couldn't see. He knew how Edgarton would be sitting from long friendship, the false relaxation, covered with easy gestures, that hid whatever layers of plotting he was working on.

"Oh, she's quite competent. Jones would be sorry to lose her." Head of Wards and Protections.

"And what, precisely, does he say about her?" There was more there, Giles knew it.

Edgarton laughed and said, "Always on point. He'd say her memory is priceless, if not always prompt in finding what you half-remembered."

Giles grunted. "What's she like to work with, do you know?"

"Sure she has good ideas, which she often does. A bit

rigid in technique, but we're shorthanded on people who were more creative. A lot of - well, you know the numbers as well as I do." People who could solve problems creatively died more often in the War, one way and another.

Giles frowned again. "And Davies? She's not like the others."

Edgarton settled back, Giles could hear the chair shifting. "And why do you say that?" His voice was entirely pleasant. Suspiciously so.

"Accent. Mode. House. Background. Half a dozen other things." Where did one even start, was more the question. "Not a mathematician, at all."

"You are quite sufficient mathematician for the both of you. Do you want to go first, then? Your thoughts? I'm curious. Though, mind, some of the best Guards come from the Bear's den." Edgarton was making a point of something, Giles could tell.

Giles frowned. "I suppose." He considered. "She's very sincere. I'm used to people holding back, more. Because they're Fox, and used to it, or Owl and they forget to mention emotions. Not ..." He frowned. "She was not very contained. Controlled might be a better word. In the ways I'm more used to."

Edgarton laughed. "Oh, she's got discipline, if that's what you worry about. But - speaking, no, I expect she'd be honest."

"Not an expert in the field. Is there a reason for that?"

"No room at the inn, and no one to apply a familial elbow. And she's..." Edgarton paused, searching for words apparently. "I get the sense she reads more than she lets on, but not what."

Curious, quite curious. Giles frowned and made a show

of eating the last of his scone to give himself time to think. "What are her reviews like?"

"Steady, reliable. She doesn't overestimate her skills. If anything, she underestimates. She doesn't put herself forward, that's part of why she's not been promoted. But she has also not been in some of the situations that might have attracted the relevant attention her way. I've not been able to tell if that is deliberate or chance."

"She mentioned two uncles?"

"Solid men, both, married, Guards in villages near each other. Reasonable men of solid reputation, apprenticed at thirteen. Not a drop of ambition in their bodies. They were good to her, getting started, and she's got a way with the apprentices, even now. Doesn't talk down to them, like a lot of the Schola folk do."

"That gives me a better idea, thank you." Giles tapped his fingers again, then asked, "Has she done any notable work for you?"

"A few times in the War. She was one of my preferences for reinforcing existing spaces. You know how it can be tricky when people won't evacuate an old home. Hers held particularly well."

"I don't suppose you have theories why?"

"My wife makes noises about having the land-touch, listening to what the building needs. Folklore, the researchers say, but Alysoun is quite insistent. She's met Davies, originally when she was doing escort duty for women on diplomatic trips. After the first, she requested her specifically several times."

"Huh." Giles shook his head after a moment. "Your recommendation?"

"You're not getting me that easily." Edgarton was laughing now. "Tell me what you think of her, first."

He took his time answering. "Logic says I should take Peck." he said, finally.

"And yet?"

"And yet, I wonder what Davies might offer. You included her for a reason."

"I did. You didn't ask about her bohort."

"I asked her." Giles was mildly indignant.

"Ah, but she wouldn't tell you this. She's one of those players who improves the other people on her team. She won't make stunning saves herself, not most of the time. But she'll get everyone working together, doing more than they'd done in the past. It's a shame she gets passed over for the Guard league, but I can't actually say that to anyone." He paused, and then said, "You'd have seen her play, at Schola, of course," in that damnable way he had of dropping a crumb and expecting one to play at being a pigeon.

Giles frowned, then reached to rub his nose, before he said, finally. "If I give her a trial, and it doesn't work, can I have Peck?"

"You may." Edgarton's voice had turned broad and delighted. "You won't regret trying Davies."

FIVE

TRELLECH

"Good morning, Guardswoman." The woman behind the desk seemed very polite. Older, greying hair pinned back in a loose bun, wearing deep lavender robes. The whole effect was unlike anything Kate was used to. There was a large desk in an anteroom, and Kate could see past the desk into a large reading room, with bays for small tables, and tall shelves of books, then stairs to a narrow balcony that held still more on a second level.

The quality of the light made her realise the windows in the bays must be some form of stained glass - she couldn't see the patterns but could see flashes of brilliant blue and red and green and yellow scattering across the floor in places.

Kate ducked her head, doing her best to focus. "Pardon, ma'am. I have a research question, and I'm not sure where to start?"

The woman looked her up and down for a moment. "If you think we can help, I'm glad to try."

Now that Kate was here, she wasn't sure what to do. She'd used the library at school, of course, and the Guard library. But that was less a place with staff to help, and more a place where the man in charge grunted at you and wanted you out of his sight, not touching his books. Adria had been dubious when Kate mentioned her plans for the day. She'd made the quite reasonable point that Kate hadn't even been selected yet, and asked quite sensibly what Kate thought the main library could help with.

And yet, Kate had been certain she needed to do this, and she couldn't ignore that small nudging voice in the back of her head.

"I may have a new assignment," she began. "I'm not sure yet. But I wanted to do some background reading. It has to do with the history of Oxfordshire, and possibly roses, and possibly an unknown form of magic?" She wasn't sure how to explain any of it.

The woman considered, then said, "Let me get someone to take over the desk, and you can come back to my office. Would that be a help?"

It would. If only because it gave her more time to gather her thoughts. This had seemed like a good idea. Kate followed the quiet flurry of exchanges by sight, not sound, before a younger woman, maybe Kate's age, came over and settled at the desk. The older woman swept her along. "This way, then. I'm Madam Thornton, chief librarian. You've not been in before." It was not a question.

"No, ma'am. I use the Guard library a bit, and the branch library, near the clubs." For pleasure reading, and lighter non-fiction, not serious magical texts and research works.

Madam Thornton nodded. "I'm glad that's served you. We had to make quite the case to get it built, twenty years ago." She sounded as if she remembered fighting that battle like it was yesterday, which was a touch endearing. Then she opened the door to a large wood panelled office, at the far end of the main reading room.

She gestured Kate into the guest chair, and closed the door behind them, and Kate could feel privacy and sound muffling charms settle in place like a soft blanket. "Have a seat, and let me see if I can figure out what will be a help, then we can go see what we can find."

"Ma'am?" Kate sat. That part was simple. It was the rest of it she wasn't sure about. She looked around, the several piles of books on a work table in the corner, papers on the desk. Madam Thornton settled into her desk chair, easily.

"Begin at the beginning, as the saying goes. I'll ask you questions as needed."

The clear instruction was actually a help, and Kate swallowed, then began. "There is a house, in Oxfordshire." She was careful to keep this general, as the confidential nature of the case required. "I may be working on a project relating to its history, and magical considerations."

"What is your particular area of interest?"

"It's now a Guard project, but that library wasn't as helpful as I hoped. I think the manor itself dates from about Henry II. I'm particularly interested in the history around the time of the Pact, for the area. Possibly things around any curious consequences of the formation of the Pact."

"Oxfordshire. Mmm." Madam Thornton was clearly working through something in her head. "There are various folk tales and legends, of course. There always are. Occasionally they're true. Did you go to Schola?"

"Yes, ma'am." Honesty compelled her to murmur, "Bear House, ma'am. I'm afraid history wasn't one of my better subjects. I enjoy reading it, but I don't know much about putting the pieces together."

"And yet, here you are, wanting to do just that."

Kate gestured helplessly. "I'm better with the physical things. The objects. They make more sense to me, wondering what people did with them, how things fit together. People..." Her voice trailed off, and she flushed.

Madam Thornton leaned forward. "Go on, I'm getting a sense of what might be a help."

Kate took a deep breath. "I'm not good at talking about this, ma'am. Beg pardon if I say something wrong. But I've heard lots of talk about people in the past being stupid or wrong or whatever. And they weren't, they were as clever as we are. Creative. If they did things a certain way, they had a reason. If we take the time to figure out what that reason was, we might learn a lot more."

That earned her an approving smile. "That is why I am a librarian. I like books, but I like the idea that's how the people then share what they know with us, even more."

Kate nodded and let out her breath. "So, ma'am, what I want is to understand that house better. Understand what's normal for a house like that, so I can see what's different, special, unusual, about this one."

"Ah, that's a fascinating puzzle, now, isn't it? Have you been to the house?"

"No, ma'am. Not unless I'm chosen to assist."

"And yet you're here, anyway? Without being sure?"

Kate shrugged. "It's my day off this week."

Madam Thornton laughed. "You've got all day? Do you have something to take notes with? I can set you up with some books. We can make a limited number of copies for you, using duplication charms, but you must pay for anything over five. I'd suggest going through carefully and figuring out what will be most useful to you."

"Ma'am." Kate wasn't sure what else to say. "I do have a notebook, ma'am. And spillproof ink."

"We'll set you up at a table right out here and then find you some books. Architecture, domestic spaces. Do you believe this was in a magical family?"

"It seems likely, ma'am, but we're not sure which one."

"Genealogies for Oxfordshire, then. And there's a book or three about local legends, and I'm sure I remember something curious about a house or a garden or something. You don't know about the roses, either, I suppose?"

"No, ma'am. My mother keeps them, I know about them in general, but I've not seen the roses there yet, either. And the current descriptions are dashed unspecific."

Madam Thornton snorted. "Right. You get yourself settled out here, I'll show you a table with the good light. I or the assistant will bring you things. No writing in the books, not that I need to tell you that." Apparently bringing her own spillproof ink indicated Kate had an idea of the appropriate protocol with other people's books.

In short order, Kate found herself tidied into a nook with a large table. By the time she'd set out her notebook and pens and ink. Madam Thornton had brought her books. Big books, architectural sketches. She tapped one as she set it down. "Start there. I'll have more in a few minutes."

Books upon books, enough that they brought her a wooden cart, scarred and polished with use, to stack things on because they ran out of table. She worked straight through lunch and until the angle of the light through the windows made it clear they were well into afternoon. Kate looked up with a start, at a quiet cough from the end of the nook.

"It's half an hour to closing. Do you want us to keep things for you tomorrow, or?"

Kate took a deep breath, stretched, and felt half a dozen joints pop. She considered. "I'm on duty at ten, unless I end up with a meeting about the assignment." she said. "I think - this has been tremendous. I think best to shelve things again, I mean, is that a lot of work for you, can I help?"

Madam Thornton waved a hand. "That is one of the things we're here for. And the books are here to be used, and you've made quite a nice tick mark in our statistics for the month. Anything for copying?" Kate handed over eight books, carefully flagged. "We'll do that for you, then. Do come back. And you can work right up til closing if you need to finish up notes."

Kate nodded, and spent the next twenty-five minutes wrapping up her lists of references and titles that might be worth more time later, if she needed. She was finishing stacking the last of the books neatly on the cart, sorted by call number, when Madam Thorton came back.

Her tidiness earned her a broad smile, and a "That's thoughtful of you," and then after a long glance at the cart, "And actually correct, which is more than most manage. Do come again, especially with that kind of puzzle. Copies are at the front desk, you can pay there."

The kindness made Kate flush. "I - you've been really helpful. Thank you. And you made it...." She stopped and tried again. "I was scared you'd be mad I didn't know things."

"Ah, knowing things is for after you've been to the library. Not when you walk in the door."

SIX

TRELLECH

Giles was pacing. Very precisely, in the strip of floor along the bookshelves at the side of the room. He trailed one hand an inch from the shelf, just enough to signal him if he wobbled out of the proper angle. Five paces up, turn, five paces back, turn.

He'd been at it for at least twenty minutes when he heard footsteps. "Still at it, Giles? She'll be here in five." Which meant it was coming up on two o'clock. "Why you're fussing over this, I don't know. Byles seemed a much better fit, and he's the sort of man who can share a good brandy when the work's done."

Giles grunted. "Give it up, Vale." That was the fourth time Vale had said something of the kind, and it was growing more than tiresome.

He'd asked for a second meeting with Davies, to convince himself Edgarton was wrong, and he'd be better off with Peck. Now, though, he was feeling as if that was the wrong move, that she'd be making assumptions. Or something. He wasn't sure what, precisely.

"Have a seat and stop pacing. I'm sure she'll be prompt. The Guard generally are."

He was being herded, and Giles had no patience for that at the best of times, even when Vale hadn't spent it all on treating the matter as a guest list for a club outing. Edgarton was pressing him to decide promptly. The pressure bothered him, of course the mystery needed solving, but from what Giles knew there should be no reason to rush.

Giles was still lost in thought about it when there was a knock at the front door, then footsteps, and a "Giles, Guard Davies for you. I'll be out for a bit." His tone was dismissive.

Giles ignored him and gestured at the chair. He heard her come and sit, the little creak of the wood. "Lefton, good afternoon." Very precise and crisp.

"Davies. I hope the time isn't a bother?"

"I could take it as my lunch break, so that works out well enough."

"A late lunch, surely?"

"I was up early, but my shift started at ten today. I had a little reading I wanted to finish."

Giles frowned. "I asked you to come by, because I've..." And then he realised the last part of what she'd said. "Reading?"

"I spent yesterday in the library, looking for information that might apply to the house. The main library, down at Temple Court."

"Any reason?"

Kate coughed, then said, "I wanted to know what I wasn't seeing, if you don't -" Her voice trailed off.

He waved a hand. "It's a common verb, don't be an idiot about using it." People were, and he had no time for that.

She cleared her throat, then said, her voice clipped, "I

wanted to know what I wasn't seeing. The connections. Madam Thornton was very helpful in finding material. I didn't explain the entire puzzle, but that it was a house in Oxfordshire, and there were roses, and I have some possibly interesting leads. If you hadn't already sent the note with this appointment, I would have asked to see you, just so you'd have the information for whoever you choose."

She didn't think it would be her. That was crystal clear to him. He leaned back in his chair. "Tell me what you found, then."

Kate paused, then she did something he hadn't expected, her tone shifting. "Is there a chance of a cuppa? I can go without lunch much more easily than tea."

It made him laugh, both the way she put it, and the fact she was willing to ask, and he stood. "You tell me, I'll listen."

She began with the meeting at the library, of Madam Thornton, a formidable queen of her own domain, and how she'd laid out the question. Giles listened, attentive, but he couldn't fault how she'd framed it. Nothing that would give their focus away to others. Though it had been a quiet day there, being the tail end of June, and Thornton was known to be fierce about the privacy of her patrons.

By the time he'd brought the tea back, she was ready to start on the meat of her discoveries. "They brought me the architecture books first. I think because I'd asked about what an ordinary house of the time would look like. What rooms it would have, how it would be set up."

"Do you think that matters?"

"There's something unusual about this house, but I don't know what it is. Maybe the shape, or the way it was used, that's why it could be hidden for so long. Even if it isn't, knowing how it's laid out would be a help for figuring out where we might get in, or what to expect if we do."

He had to admit that was a very practical approach. "Do you expect problems?"

"People don't usually hide houses for centuries who aren't paranoid and tricksy." It was rather baldly said, but again, he couldn't argue with it.

Giles settled down in his chair and considered. "Fair enough. What else did you find?"

"There's folklore in that area, that doesn't seem connected, and yet..." Her voice trailed off. "You'll probably think it's silly."

"One never knows what might be useful. Go ahead." Besides, he was curious now.

"There's a legend about Rosamund Clifford."

"The name is promising, isn't it?" He considered. "Mistress to Henry II, wasn't she? Supposed to be exquisitely beautiful."

"That's part of the story. The rest has her penned up in a maze made of rose bushes as some stories go. And there's one about Queen Eleanor making her way in, and offering Rosamund the choice of a dagger or a cup of poison. It's a ridiculous story, really."

"Which part?" Giles was curious, there being rather a lot of options.

"Well, a maze made of rose bushes would take ages to grow. Rosamund died when she wasn't yet thirty, and she'd only been mistress for two years, maybe three. And clearly the queen knew where she was. But if you were going to confront a rival - I mean, Eleanor was Queen of England and a lot of other places, healthy sons, all sorts of things. I can see how she might have been jealous, only that's rather petty. I always rather liked her, you know?"

It was not a well-organised argument, Giles felt, but it was well-meant.

But then Davies followed it with, "But besides all the emotional reasons, history says that Eleanor was imprisoned by that point, for standing with her sons against Henry. Which makes the story even more ridiculous. Even though they let her out for holidays, one book said, it's not like she'd be let out on her own to do something like that. Even if she wanted to."

Giles laughed. "The logic there is impregnable." He considered. "Do you think it has anything to do with the legend?"

There was a long pause, and Giles couldn't figure out what to make of it. She made no noise to give him a clue, and he couldn't see any specific movement, as fuzzy as it might be. Finally, he heard her say, "I think the legend is an illustration of what might be involved, but not the thing itself."

"The legend attaching itself to another phenomenon, or something of the kind" He could see the connection immediately.

"That. It's not Woodstock Palace. Or Blenheim, obviously. We know where the one was, and the one is. We're further north than that. By a few miles."

"Do you think it's something similar?"

"That would be the next thing to research. Houses that went missing, or were known to go missing, or something else of the kind. I did part of that. But it's a lot harder to find a thing that isn't there than a thing that is, and people don't always list the things that went missing."

Giles laughed. "True enough. And you were rather busy with other pieces."

There was a tiny pause, then a "Ta, for noticing." that was quieter than he expected before she went on. "It's complicated, isn't it? The different moving parts. If I ..."

Giles immediately murmured, "Go on."

"If I were taking this on, I'd want another two days, maybe three, to sort out what I could in a really good library. And to figure out what books would be useful to have on site."

"Do it." Giles said it before he thought it through, but it was the right thing, he could feel it, like layers of code snapping into meaning something. "Three days. Apply to Edgarton for funds for the books you need on site, put the order in if you can't get something immediately."

"Sir?" She was startled, it was clear in her voice.

"Three days. We'll go to Oxfordshire on Sunday afternoon, be ready to start work on Monday."

"Lefton." It was a sound of agreement. "May I ask the arrangements?"

"I'll have Vale prepare some notes for you. There's an old manse or something, down at the end of the road near the manor, a half mile or so. A housekeeper to do the cleaning work and make meals, mine here won't travel and she's off helping her sister as it is. That's no problem, it will be handy to have someone who knows the area right there." Davies was a professional, she wouldn't require chaperonage, but people watching them wouldn't know that.

He continued, "Should we meet anyone, magical or otherwise, the cover is that I'm researching folklore, you are my research assistant, and Vale my secretary and valet, which is close enough to the truth. How are you with horses?"

"A decent enough rider, sir."

"Good. We'll be about five miles from a town of any size, and I may need you to help take messages from time to time. There'll be a mount or two in the stables."

"Lefton." It was a sound of definite agreement. "How

much may I pack?"

"Your service trunk would be fine. If it will be much more than that, coordinate with Vale about it. Two changes of uniform, but civilian clothes most of the time, as I mentioned."

"I was thinking about the books, sir." Her voice was now decidedly amused. "Rather than clothing. I'm not one for fripperies."

"Ah, the books do not count against your personal allowance. A trunk for your personal items, and a trunk for the books, if required, or any tools or reagents or such you require."

"Lefton, yes." She made a considering sound, as if she was trying to decide whether to venture something, then she said, "I did a moderate bit of alchemy. I'm out of practice, but the things that might be a help don't take too much skill."

"Ointments for the doors, you're thinking?"

"That sort of thing, yes. Or possibly some testing for the roses. What they're sympathetic to, or against."

"That's a good thought. Put the costs on Edgarton's tab. His aide can explain how, and the limits you can spend without explicit permission."

"Thank you. I appreciate the - leeway." Her tone was inexplicably slow, uncertain. He wasn't sure what had confused her there.

"No point in having you hobbled before we start. I want to see your best work, Davies." He made a point of using the word, even if he'd be doing his seeing with his ears.

That earned him a laugh, breaking the odd tension. They settled down to specifics of what would be worth having on hand, with her making up lists before she left to make her arrangements.

SEVEN

OXFORDSHIRE, NEAR A MYSTERIOUS MANOR

By the time they arrived in Oxfordshire on Sunday, Kate was exhausted. The entire trip had been full of complexities she didn't quite understand. Some of it was the usual bustle of seeing to a lot of luggage, but some of it was simply confusing in both its unfamiliarity and total lack of explanation.

It turned out that Lefton went outside holding someone's arm, and with a short cane. The arm made some sort of sense, but they had not explained the cane, except it was clearly part of his method of moving around easily, outside a known space. Then there had been going to the portal, and using it to reach the small magical village nearest their destination. On the other side, there was a good five miles in a small carriage over rough roads in a drizzle. Kate had been expected to ride with the carriage driver up front.

They finally pulled up to the manse, which was solid enough but dingy around the edges. Kate was damp, rattled, and then left entirely alone to manage her own trunk, and the books besides. Vale immediately co-opted the carriage driver and the stableboy to bring things in, barking instructions. The military bearing was rather more obvious now, an officer making his men scurry to do his bidding. She wondered, for a moment, what rank he'd had.

There was a housekeeper, a Mrs Hitchcock, in the back kitchen. She shrugged when Kate introduced herself, and said, "Your room is under the eaves on this side, dear. That stair."

Small, over the kitchen, out of the way. Kate was quite sure there were plenty of bedrooms in the house. The room itself was cosy enough, and it was clean and had a fireplace and no leaks. But time had faded the wallpaper, and there were knickknacks all over, little china ornaments that made Kate roll her eyes. Nothing like her tidy, crisp rooms at home, with a few photographs but little clutter. And there was no room for a bookshelf here, at all.

Now she'd found the room, she went back downstairs, triggering the charm on her trunk that made it lighter to carry, feeling the energy draining from her as she did. Less than it would take to carry the thing, mind you, and much less chance of dropping it or causing an injury, which was more to the point. She couldn't afford that, not here and now.

An hour later, she'd unpacked as much as she was going to, and she was trying to decide what to do when she heard a bell from downstairs. She came down to find a rather formal setting in the dining room. There were lamps on the table and a platter with a roast chicken in the middle, with the housekeeper bustling in and out. Lefton was down at one end, and Vale irritably gestured at her. "That's your seat."

Kate swallowed, then said, "Good evening, Lefton. Good evening, Mr Vale." Someone in the room should be polite. It earned her a quirk of a smile from Lefton.

"Davies. Pardon, still getting used to the space."

Vale busied himself carving the chicken out, then filling Lefton's plate. "Chicken at three, potatoes at six, carrots at nine, roll at noon," he murmured, as he handed it over.

Lefton nodded. "Thank you, Vale." he said. "What do you want Davies to call you?"

"Vale is fine, thank you." He served himself, and then sat down, leaving Kate without food. She waited a moment, then shifted to serve herself.

"Last names are the custom in the Guard," she said, to fill the silence. "How are your rooms?" It was only as she said it she realised that it wouldn't come across well. Too personal, too intrusive.

Giles waved a hand. "Everything in the wrong places, yet." He sounded resigned about it, as if this was a problem he faced often enough to find it boring. "Vale will sort it out."

Vale looked decidedly unhappy with that. "I'll be using the office, down here, for my work, Davies," he said, and his tone made it clear both that he was not asking, and that he expected to be left undisturbed.

"Of course. I'm sure you have things to attend to."

"There's a library here, not as big as my workroom at home, but it will do, when some of the furniture's been cleared out," Lefton said, encouraging the conversation along. "You and I will work there, principally. When we're not on site."

"Of course. I have some of the alchemical materials - the trunk is out of the way, but I should set things up tonight. Is there a room I could use?" Kate timed this for the house-keeper to hear.

It earned her a lot of tisking and, "Well, I never, women fussing around with that kind of muck. Well, I suppose you're what they call one of those professional women."

Kate was familiar with this line of scolding, at least, and she said, as mildly as she could, "I've duties here, Mrs Hitchcock, and I'll do my best by them. I need a solid table, no wobbling, a stone top if you have it, wood if not. Good ventilation, by a window, is a help."

That at least got the housekeeper thinking. "There's a sort of stillroom, on the back of the kitchen. Windows look off toward the manor. Would that do?"

"If I could come look after supper?"

"Here until half-six, dear. Any time before then."

Kate glanced at the clock, it was six already. "As soon as I've eaten, then. Wouldn't do to trespass in your domain, I know."

The housekeeper gave her a warmer smile at that. "Ah, you've respect for a kitchen, then."

"I do. My parents run an inn, out near Cardiff. I'm no cook, other than the basics, but I appreciate what goes into it. I know you must have arranged your things just so."

She thought she heard Lefton make a noise, but when she glanced over at him, his face was entirely neutral. Vale's, on the other hand, was decidedly unimpressed. She fell silent, not sure what to say next, so there was a long pause.

"Your room, Davies?"

"Up under the eaves, but cosy. Though, Mrs Hitch-cock? There are a number of delicate items. Would it be all right to pack a few away? I'd hate to knock something over by accident."

The housekeeper gave her a thoughtful look. "I'll bring a crate and newspaper up. You can put it in the box room."

"Thank you. Are you - familiar with the house?"

"Oh, aye. Being leased for all of you, but it's my niece's

husband's father's and his aunt has the room you're in. They're staying elsewhere while you're here. Convenient, really. Annie had a bad fall, hurt her leg, can't manage the stairs. They're the ones noticed the manor was back."

Vale cleared his throat. "Thank you, Hitchcock," he said, quite quellingly. "We should sort a few things out."

The housekeeper sniffed, but took herself back off to the kitchen.

"Doesn't do to let the help get above themselves." Vale's voice was dry, and something in it made Kate itch. It was quite clear he considered her to be just another servant, if one in uniform. She looked to Lefton for some comment, and he said nothing.

It left her focusing on her food for several minutes, which was edible, but not skillfully made. The chicken was a bit dry, the carrots and potatoes a hair under-cooked and dense. She snuck a glance or two at Lefton, watching how he managed the food neatly enough, though the density of the potatoes was clearly something of a challenge. On the other hand, they were about as much of a challenge for her.

"I'll arrange the menu for the week and see to the household bills. Should anyone try to speak to you about such things, Davies, you are to send them directly to me." Vale clearly wished to be certain that no mere Guardswoman would trespass upon his domain.

"Of course. I know my role." She kept her voice even.

Lefton spoke, then. "I was going to suggest a walk down to the manor, to get a start tonight, but that was a long trip, getting here. You sort your alchemy out, Davies, and we'll start first thing in the morning."

Kate paused, and then said, "How do you define that, then? I'm used to Guard shifts."

It made Lefton laugh, which was something, in this

increasingly awkward meal. "Breakfast at eight, begin work at nine, lunch at noon. Tea at four, a light supper at seven, and we'll likely need to do an hour or two of note-taking and other work after supper. A long workday, but we may find we need to pause, and that gives us several segments to work with."

Kate nodded. "That is fine. I'll start two of the salves tonight that I thought might be useful." She paused and added, "And one for scratches. Given the roses."

That earned her another laugh. "Sensible."

Kate was finishing her plate, still a bit hungry, but disinclined to try for more, when Mrs Hitchcock came in to clear the table. "If you'd like a look at that room, miss?"

"Thank you. Good evening, gentlemen," she said, standing. "I'll see you in the morning."

"Davies, good evening," was all the answer she got from Lefton, and nothing at all from Vale. She could hear them begin to talk as she followed the housekeeper back into the kitchen, then back beyond that to what was clearly a little solarium.

It had a table, there, though, designed for pastry work, she thought, given the coolness of the marble top. "Oh, I'd not expected something like this. This will do very well."

"It won't damage it? Poison it, or the like?" Mrs Hitchcock was cautious.

"Oh, no. Stone is safer - no chance of something burning it, but I'm careful, I promise. And what I have with me, so far, anyway, is mild. A step up from household salves, but the same sort of thing you'd make for a burn or a scrape, or a cold."

The housekeeper was still dubious. "What're you to them, then? Making things?"

"I'm in the Guard, Mrs Hitchcock, assigned to help

Major Lefton with his work. I don't know exactly what I'll be doing until we get a good look at it. We're supposed to figure it out. I did research, already." She paused, then ventured, "I don't suppose there's anyone around here might talk to me about the local legends? Things that might not be in books?" She had been told that Mrs Hitchcock knew they were here to look at the manor - there would be no hiding that - but that details were not to be shared.

Mrs Hitchcock sniffed. "I'll think about that. You do what you need to, here." And then she went off, clucking and fussing and doing the dishes. Kate spent a good fifteen minutes clearing off surfaces, making a sketch of where things had been, and then tucking objects into the shelves. About the time she had enough space cleared, she heard an "Off for the night, dearie, back for breakfast."

"Good night, Mrs Hitchcock!" she called out. There was no point making an enemy of the housekeeper; she had enough challenges to deal with. She put the newly packed items in the box room before going off to find the trunk and set into the fussy and tiring task of setting everything up. Getting the first two salves she wanted started had her up until well past ten, leaving her worn out and fit only to fall into the narrow bed in her tiny room.

EIGHT

OUTSIDE THE MANOR

"What do I do?" Davies was doing her best to hide it, but she was audibly uncertain. Again. Or perhaps still.

"Best begin as we mean to go on," Giles said, keeping his voice even. He hoped she wasn't going to be difficult about this. "You walk beside me, and half a step ahead. I'll take your arm, here, just above your elbow. You tell me if the ground drops or get rough, though I have my walking cane here, to be a help."

"Left arm or right?"

"Let me take your right, if you don't mind. I'm better with the cane in my right."

He could hear her take a breath, and he expected an objection of some kind. What she said in the end was "Of course."

Giles lifted his voice. "Vale, we'll be back for lunch."

He waited just long enough for the answering, "Yes, Giles." The sulkiness in the tone made him suspect Vale was hoping they'd be out for the day without any need to interrupt whatever Vale was doing with his time. Lounging around in idleness, likely.

"Come along then. You brought the equipment out?" He couldn't make Vale industrious, but they could get along with their work.

Davies replied, "Yes, they've put together a small shed out near the entrance, so it can stay there. It's about a quarter of a mile. They mowed down a path, but the ground's uneven. No mud, though." He rather thought she was babbling, but it was harmless enough and she had some reason for nerves.

They walked along for a couple of minutes, with her murmuring a few times when the ground rose or fell. Once she got the hang of it, he began letting her know what worked best, offering a "That helped, thank you," to a comment about the ground getting rocky for a short stretch. Very civil, very polite.

Finally, he felt the earth change under his feet, and murmured, "Stop here. How close are we?"

"To the manor? The open ground around it starts here. We just crossed over into a meadow."

"I will need you to explain exactly what you see. Is there a chair?"

"Yes, sir. Lefton. About another fifteen feet."

"That will do. I'll want to explore the ground later."

She led him to the chair, then said, "Um. The chair's right here," before she realised that didn't help. "In front of you."

"If you'd put my hand on the back, I can manage from there."

"Oh. Yes. Rather." She sounded startled and unsettled again. Then she took his hand in hers for a moment, the angle awkward, before resting it on the back of a canvas chair. "Do you need a table?"

"Not at the moment, thank you. Tell me about what you see." He worked his way around to the front of the chair, then tucked his walking cane against the arm.

"Are you sure Vale wouldn't be better for this? More practice?"

"No, he wouldn't." His voice was sharp. "Vale is good at his duties, but we have long since determined that accurate description is not one of his better skills." He did not understand why the woman seemed to be trying to convince him she had nothing to offer.

He heard her inhale, then she was brave enough to ask, "How did he describe me, then?"

It broke the tension, and he laughed, more easily now. "He got your height right. But he said you had too many curves for my previous taste, your hair was unfashionable, and he didn't understand why women in the Guard didn't show off their legs, since the variant uniform allows."

"Oh, goodness." He could hear her move a step or two away, giving him a little space. "He's not wrong about my hair but skirts get me tutted over less by the elder generation. I don't know about your tastes, so I can't speak to that." She hesitated for a moment, then said, "Thank you for your honesty. I don't think he likes me much."

"No, he doesn't. There are plenty of days I'm not sure he likes me much at all either." Certainly he had been taking every opportunity he could manage to be about his own affairs, of late, regardless of the inconvenience.

"Well. Good company, maybe." She offered it hesitantly, then changed the subject. "Do you want to get a sense of the space before I tell you details about things? You might pick something up I don't."

"That's a properly logical idea. Tell me which way I'm facing, would you? Direction, and what's in front of me, in general terms, then more specific. The light's not as useful as I'd hoped."

"We're facing north, toward the manor, on the left side of the drive leading into the main space, about twenty feet back from the wall of roses. The roses extend over to the left of where we are, a fair bit, forty or fifty feet, and the same on the other side. The shed is back by the path."

"So we came up at an angle, from the maps they gave me?"

She must have nodded and caught herself, because there was an awkward pause, then a "Um. Yes. The raised one, in the library?"

"Pins in a cushion. Ridiculous, but effective for something like this. Right. Let me get a sense, first. Can you take a few steps off, ten feet or so, maybe by the shed?"

"Of course. Give a shout when you're ready." He could hear her retreating, a slight shift of grass and wind. One of his teachers at St Dunstan's - a sighted man - had sworn that blind folk developed other senses. The other instructors, and most of the other residents had laughed at the idea. Giles did feel he had a better sense for presence and absence than many people. But he'd had it for years, he'd first noticed it quite early in the War.

His remaining vision was no help to him today. The angle of the sun meant that he couldn't use the shadows to get a sense of the outline of the building, even a fuzzy one. Instead, he closed his eyes, and tried to feel out a sense of things. The ground under his feet had been softer, different.

This manor had disappeared before crop rotation, and he contemplated how that changed the soil. He was diverted, for just a moment, by wondering how he might even figure it out, what it was like all those centuries ago.

The wind had smells. Roses, as he'd expected, but the fragrance was more overwhelming than he'd anticipated. Mingled with that was the smell of cut grass, from the path, and clover. Also the path, he thought.

Then, he smelled something more like the kitchen at the hall where he'd grown up, or the kitchen garden at the townhouse. He couldn't pick out the specific scents, other than the mint, but there was something there, behind the roses. But why could he smell it here?

His other senses didn't bring him much. The wind seemed like wind. There were no unusual noises from the direction of the manor, or even from Davies. Other than the feel of the ground, nothing to touch, at least not yet. No other sense of presence, not that he'd trust that. He sat, just in case there was some small sound, but after another minute or two, called out, "Davies, ready."

He heard her walk back, and murmur, "Next to you."

"Right. Tell me what you see, in detail, this time."

Davis took a breath, perhaps marshalling her thoughts, and began, her voice crisp. "The main thing I can see is a wall covered with roses. Some are white, some are red, some are striped, I believe, but I'd need to examine it at close range to be sure. There's no clear pattern of the flowers, though it's possible there's a pattern of the bushes them-selves, once I make a closer examination. The wall is about six feet high, leading to large iron gates at the front, where the roses have overgrown. They will need to be cleared, somehow, to open the gates."

"Good, that gives me an idea. What about behind the wall?" He kept his voice even, but she was doing a decent job of telling him what he needed, if not in quite the order he'd prefer. He found it easier when people started with the closest thing, working their way out. The gates, in this case.

"I can see the top of the house. As in the pictures I was shown, it seems to date to the era of around Henry II. Long tall windows, quite a lot for the time, not at all defensible, but they'd make it a pleasant space inside. Are you familiar with any of the places he built?"

"I saw pictures of Stourton Castle, the hunting lodge, once," Giles said. "In some detail."

"Smaller than that, sir. Lefton," was the immediate reply. "But that's the right idea on the design. It's difficult to tell much about the layout from this distance, the house is set back from the wall." She paused. "Trying to estimate how far, sir. Perhaps thirty or forty more feet. But the angle is bad."

Giles considered. "Anything else? Weather vanes, or flags, or anything like that?"

"No flags, but there's something that looks like a pole. No signs of habitatio. I can't see any sign of people moving, or any smoke from the chimneys, and a big house like this would have had a fire going for cooking nearly all the time."

Giles considered. "What do you smell? Anything of note?"

"Roses, of course. Very strongly. More than a modern garden." And then she paused, and said "May I go closer, sir?"

"Certainly."

"Back in a couple." He could hear her walking away, a slight jingle of something in her pockets, before it faded. She was gone for several minutes, maybe five, before she returned. "Lefton..." She sounded puzzled.

"Go on?"

"I can smell what smells maybe like a kitchen garden.

Mint. Chives, I think, or something in that family. Behind the roses. But I couldn't see anything like that. I went to peer through the gate, see if I could see anything."

"Could you?"

"Nothing useful." Now she was more frustrated than perplexed. "A long drive, covered in loose stone. Grass and other plantings to each side, I think, but I couldn't get a good enough look at them. Maybe with a ladder. Do we have a ladder?"

"You can get Vale to arrange one."

"Of course." She did not sound like she had any particular enthusiasm for talking to Vale. Not, he supposed, that he could blame her. "What do we do now?"

"Now, we take some measurements, as many as we can, and we see if they tell us anything. I'd like to make a model, so I can understand it better, as we learn more."

"That makes sense. So we'll need me to go measure things."

"And I will keep note."

NINE

OXFORDSHIRE

"You must have measured wrong."

Kate flinched, though as she could scarcely step away from Lefton, it only went as far as her shoulders. "I measured five times. Different numbers every time. We're in the library, here's your chair." She set his hand on the back and stepped to the side.

It was too sharp a way to address someone who was technically her superior officer, but she couldn't help it. He'd been sniping at her technique for at least half an hour now. She had followed his directions to the letter. The last two times, step by step, her confirming each piece before she did it. It hadn't helped at all.

"Tell me again what you did." It was command voice, the tone that made Kate immediately want to obey, despite her growing annoyance.

She took a breath, and then another, and then said. "Sir, it has been a long day. I will go wash and change. Supper is in half an hour. If you wish to discuss this again after supper, we can do so then."

With the dark glasses, she couldn't see enough of his

expression, but after a moment, he waved a hand. "Dismissed." It was brief, and rather brutal for all the theoretical civility in his voice.

She went. She did her best not to flee back through the back of the house, up the servant's stairs, into her little room. But she went quickly, not bothering to listen to see if Vale or Mrs Hitchcock were there. Only when she was alone, with the door closed, did she bury her face in her hands.

"Bloody stubborn git." The language made her feel a bit better. Not enough.

"Sir, had it perhaps slipped your notice, sir, that the puzzling house might be magically protected in ways that complicate measurements by mere mortals, sir? Sir, had you not considered that five distinct sets of measurements, no two the same, suggest something more complex than my idiocy? Sir, you are being a bloody stubborn git, and don't you take your issues out on me, sir."

She made as if to kick the footboard of her bed and thought better of it only a moment before her foot connected. It unbalanced her and she went thudding down in a pile on the floor.

Ten seconds later, Mrs Hitchcock called "All right, dearie?" up the stairs.

She couldn't do anything right. And Mrs Hitchcock calling her dearie, making her being a woman more of a thing, would not help. "Fine. Just slipped. Fine," she called back. "Down in thirty or so."

Kate stood, rubbing where she'd landed, before she went to wash up in the little bathing room off her bedroom. That, at least, was private. She had time to settle herself, to rearmour herself. By the time she came down, she was sure Lefton would have told Vale how right he was, and how wrong she was. There'd be no living with either of them.

She took a full twenty minutes to get ready, to put on a clean tweed skirt, a shirt, and vest. Her version of a man's country suit, easy to move in. She wrangled her hair in a looser bun than when she was working, but tight enough to contain her curls. She settled the cuff with her house stone around her wrist, perched on the bed, and settled in to do her breathing practice.

Dinner itself was awkward. The food was marginally better: a roast chicken that was reasonably cooked, and with some summer vegetables to go with it. Vale and Lefton talked between themselves of people she had no idea about. They left her alone beyond one or two gestures to pass something or set a serving bowl out of the way. She was paying such close attention to them both that they didn't need to ask.

When the table was cleared, Lefton said, "Davies. Library." It was sharp again, and it wasn't until he continued, "Vale, I'll be an hour or two. If you could transcribe for me."

"Of course, Giles." Vale sounded terribly amused by something, not that he was explaining anything at all. Not that either of them were. "Let me show you to the library."

It left Kate trailing along, uncertain. Once Lefton settled in the chair he'd chosen as his, she came and took the one facing, without him saying anything. "Sir." Enough to tell him where she was.

He sat in silence for at least a minute. Elegant silence, in a smoking jacket of deep green silk, looking like he had no cares in the world.

When he spoke, it was clipped, as if he were speaking to an errant child. "What happened today?"

She grimaced, then settled on providing an accurate report. "I did the measurements five times, as you had suggested and I agreed. Each time, they came out with different measurements."

"Yes. Vale is transcribing the notes for me. Why do you think that was?"

"Sir, mis-measuring is a possibility. But we used several different approaches, including the rope. Even if one of them was wrong, they should not all be wrong, by that much, in different directions."

He was silent again, this time for much longer. She crossed her ankles one way, the other, then gave up and tucked a foot under her. It wasn't like he could see it to disapprove of it.

"What do we do tomorrow?"

"Something else, sir." She couldn't keep the dry irritation out of her voice, and she knew it.

Rather than blame, she was startled by the tiniest quirk of a smile. "Doing the same thing over and over again when it does not work does not lead to better results, no."

"Sir..." She paused. She didn't want to offer him something, only to have him dismiss it immediately.

"Go on."

"I am wondering if there are any ... patterns in the errors. If one was much larger, one much smaller, or if there's any mathematical relationship."

This made him stop, consider something, and then say, "I will run the numbers and see if I find anything." It was a little grudging, but he sounded less upset. He went quiet then, for several minutes, and she just waited. Nothing good came from rushing officers in this mood.

Finally, he said, "What are your thoughts?"

She kept her tongue, pausing to find better words than

the first three versions that sprang to mind. "I think we need to return to first principles, sir. Thorough observation, including whatever patterns present themselves."

"You still think the order of the bushes is relevant."

"It seems likely, sir. And they are very - prevalent. Enthusiastic."

"That will be a problem to investigate."

"The Guard has falconers, so we have falconry gloves in Stores."

That brought him up short, mouth open. It gave her a certain guilty pleasure. "What else did you bring with you?"

"Clippers, though I do not intend to try those without more research. Yarn and ribbon, to mark specific bushes more clearly. Pots of paint and brushes, ditto. Some wire netting, to create shapes or baskets around specific areas. Various reagents for ointments and salves. A few sizes and shapes of trowels. I wasn't able to pack larger items, sir."

"What sort of larger items did you have in mind?"

"I wonder about ladders, sir, as I mentioned this morning. But surely they must have tried that, the first people they sent?"

Lefton frowned. "I would have thought so, too. They just provided the brief, not details. I can inquire."

"If you would. Sir. Lefton. I'm sure the request would be taken more seriously if you made it."

That earned her another pause, and a considering noise. "You're very attentive to rank."

She was tired enough and frustrated enough that her response was a flat, "I'm in the Guard, sir. I know my role." It came out harsher than she'd meant, and she immediately murmured, "Pardon." Even if Vale had been having some private joke at her expense with him earlier, that was no excuse for her to step out of line.

Lefton waved a hand. "How does that work for you?"

"I would have thought Lord Edgarton explained? I am on assignment. I am to assist you, however that is needed. I am expected to follow all Guard regulations, except where appropriate in the case of uniform."

"And that means?"

"Exercises to maintain magical abilities. Enough activity to maintain my physical abilities. Three times a week, more involved exercise, to push my limits and ideally increase them. Study of works related to my current assignment, or a list of general interest. Moderation in food and drink, and in other personal indulgences." She paused for an instant, and offered, "I do not find the last one a challenge, sir."

"Not inclined to drink?"

"No, sir. I don't mind a beer after a long day, or cider. But I've seen too many people mess their lives up by falling into a bottle or some other such thing."

Lefton nodded. "I'm sure you have things to do. I'll see what comes of those patterns. You may just be on to something."

TEN

OXFORDSHIRE

"She gone up to bed?" Giles looked up, out of force of habit, not that it did much good. He could barely see Vale silhouetted against the hallway light.

"To do some other work."

"What on earth possessed you to pick her?" Vale strolled over, settling in the other chair. He set a glass of something down, brandy, most likely. He tended toward brandy.

"You'd have liked the other two options even less."

"Oh, I don't know. Byles is grand for a lark."

"You know him?"

Vale sounded amused. "You didn't ask, old man. Not well directly, but we move in similar enough circles."

"Young men about town."

"Exactly." That was a broad drawl. Vale had had more than one brandy already. He must also have a snifter in his office.

After a moment, Giles offered, "Sorry to drag you out to the back of beyond."

Vale didn't make the expected demurral. Instead, he

said, "Not my choice, no." There was something with an edge of harshness there, before it smoothed out into a tone suited to asking a favour. "Look, if I've got to be marooned out here while you're off gallivanting with your Guard, could I at least have visitors? Afternoons, while you're busy, it wouldn't interfere."

"This is a confidential mission, Vale." For whatever bloody reason that might be, which no one had explained. He could not shake the memory of her pointing out the house would be a point of gossip for miles around, nor construct a system of equations that solved for the hints Edgarton occasionally, grudgingly, had dropped for him.

"Oh, I wouldn't bring them anywhere near your work. Just the house, here. There's a pleasant enough terrace, and the other parlour. Plenty of space."

"Give me a list to pre-approve. We can't have any of your loose-lipped drinking friends traipsing through."

"Oh, gentlemen of utmost discretion, only. We'd not get in your way at all." Vale's tone had a note to it Giles did not like, but there was the question of how far to push back.

"No women." Giving Vale the opportunity for a dalliance out here seemed likely to go entirely pear-shaped.

"I say, old man!" he protested. "Fine thing for you to say when you're going about with that dish."

"Vale," he said, in his most quelling tone.

Vale laughed. "Well, anyway, not like Miss High and Mighty can do for you. Pretty sure she has more idea what to do with a sword than with a man."

"That's unkind, Vale." It came out of his mouth without thinking about it.

"You know it's true."

"She's here to work, and more to the point to assist me. She pointed it out tonight, that she has obligations, being in the Guard, beyond the direct she's work doing for me. Keeping fit, keeping her skills up."

"Oh, she's quite fit. Lovely legs, wish we could talk her into breeches as a matter of course. I mean, you'd not get the benefit, but."

"Vale." Giles tried to put a bit more warning into his tone. "She's here for work."

"Plenty of girls like a tumble with a workmate." Vale paused. "Mind, I suppose she wouldn't be one to me." Giles did not like the direction that was taking.

"Not your usual sort, though, is she?"

"Well, she is in that difficult place. No family, but a professional woman, that's trickier. And not one of our sort, who knows how the dance goes."

"And that matters to you?"

"Well. Girls of no family, you tumble and leave. Fun for everyone, no commitment." Vale's voice was matter-of-fact. "Someone from one of the better families, they might object. Or their relatives might. But they'd know the score, going in."

"Is that why you had trouble, a few years ago?" Giles had only heard about it, in a roundabout manner, alluded to in letters. Or the bare half a sentence here or there when his mother visited him at St Dunstan's or the Refuge.

"Thought you'd have got all the gossip, old man." Vale sounded a bit more defensive now.

Giles shrugged. "I was a trifle busy. Occupied."

"Oh, I suppose. It would have been - oh, yes. You were at that place."

"St Dunstan's. Mother wouldn't talk about it, you know how she is. Especially with the impoverished around." His mother's term, for people who had no magic, and not enough money to make up for the lack.

"Your mother's topics of conversation are flower varieties, tomb rubbings, and obscure 18th century chamber operas." Vale had Mother to rights, but Giles had difficulty admitting it.

"I believe the opera gives her a better grasp of human nature than the flowers or the rubbings."

Vale laughed, then said, "You're right enough there." There was a long pause before he said anything else. "I was caught up with one of the Warrington girls. Smashing bit, legs up to the sky, rest of her body to match. Piercing laugh, and she had such a taste for pink wine, but you can't have everything."

Giles wanted a drink of his own, but interrupting Vale would lose him the story. "What happened?"

"She thought we were more serious than we were. That she'd swept the dashing war-hero off his feet. She couldn't understand I was home on leave and a brief assignment, and that was it."

Giles wasn't sure he liked where this story was going. "And?"

Vale did something, probably waved his hand. He kept forgetting that kind of thing. And, worse, kept forgetting how annoying it was to Giles. "Threw the most Gods-awful fit in the middle of the Crystal Cave, you know, the after-dinner place, in London, for our sort?"

"Never went, but I know the name."

"Screeching all over everything, upset everyone dreadfully. Had no sense of proportion. Some foolishness about promises and expectations."

Giles considered. He was so very tempted to point out that taking up with Vale's class of women hadn't done him any good. Saying so, of course, would not do any good. Instead he murmured, "Oh, that sort of thing." Then he coughed. "Pardon, I should ask before we end up too deep in our cups... How are the practicalities, here?"

"The food's abysmal, the wine is only tolerable because we bought it. I have half a dozen errands already that need a town of more than a few hundred people. I intend to take the carriage to the portal tomorrow unless Miss High and Mighty isn't enough for you."

That was decidedly more challenge. Giles considered. She was unpractised, even clumsy, with his needs. "When do you expect to be back?"

He could hear Vale thinking. Not a fast-brained man, at the best of times, and Giles rather suspected that he was trying to get as much time as he could. "Ideally?"

"Minimum required and your preference."

"Hour to the portal, two hours in Trellech if all the errands run smoothly, an hour back and half an hour or so to put everything away."

"And your preferred?"

"Oh, lunch and supper in town, come back with a lantern. The road seems easy enough."

"Lunch and tea. Back before dark." Giles offered. "We're still near enough midsummer the days are long."

"You worry about my safety?" That was teasing.

"I worry more about the horse. Even a well-maintained road can have an unexpected hole. And we don't know the countryside well, or what's around that might cause trouble."

Vale snorted. "Not much that would trouble me."

Giles grimaced. "We needn't court trouble. Unhappy farmer, unhappy cow. Misplaced hole." he said.

"You're too cautious." Vale's voice got harder, flat. Giles wondered again exactly how Vale's wartime commendations had come to pass. Heroism was one thing, but he suspected Vale tended more towards reckless, far too often.

Giles shrugged. "I've some reason." He tried to keep his voice light. "What do you need in Trellech, anyway?"

"The paper didn't get packed, the special heavy stuff you use. We have some, but not enough. A few preparations for photographs."

"I didn't know you'd tried shots of the place?" Giles thought they had plenty of paper for the braille writer or the slate, but Vale might have a point about the photographs.

"I tried this morning, before you went out. The prints didn't come out at all."

"A technical error, or something else?" Some magics resisted being fixed in any way. Perhaps the problem with measurements had the same cause. If so, he might owe Davies an apology.

"I'm not sure, that's why I want a fresh set of chemicals. Sometimes travel affects things if the solutions are older. I can go after breakfast, then?"

"Yes, yes. Davies is capable enough of managing lunch for me if we make sure it's simple. Sandwiches or something of the kind."

"I'll tell the housekeeper." There was a pause. "She doesn't enjoy having someone blind in the house."

Giles frowned. "Not her call, is it?"

"No, but I suspect she's the sort to do the things you hate. Move furniture, not tell you where things are."

"I'll manage." It wasn't like Giles had a choice. He could manage, or he could sit in a tiny room with no furniture except one chair and maybe a desk, and a bed, and not do anything. He was having none of that.

Vale nodded. "So. Back after tea and before dark. Let me know at breakfast if you need anything, right?"

Giles nodded, then frowned. "I'll be up for a bit. Or, no. Can you bring the abacus and my notes upstairs?"

"Need an arm?"

Giles frowned. He hated being dependent on it, but this was still a new house he'd not learned "Better if I do."

"Upstairs, then, and I'll bring the rest up after."

It took a good fifteen minutes before Giles was settled at the desk in the master bedroom with his abacus, the stylus, and a braille slate. Vale had taken forever to bring things up. It rather made Giles wonder whether Vale had taken the opportunity to get another drink and left him waiting on purpose.

The notes had at least been transcribed. Vale had left the little stack of sheets on the bedroom desk. Giles worked on each, attentive, forming the abacus into patterns, forming the shapes of the measurements in his mind, and yet nothing lined up. He went through it twice, recognising that it must be getting later and later, with no useful result. Usually the patterns came to life under his fingers, even if that were more literal these days than it used to be. Tonight, though, nothing made sense. At all.

Finally, grumpy, he undressed, leaving his clothes over the chair, and rummaged for his pyjamas, laid out on the bed. It must have been later than he realised, because as soon as he was between the sheets, he was asleep.

ELEVEN

OXFORDSHIRE

Kate was up early, well before breakfast. She pulled her hair back, put on the breast binder, trousers suitable for running, and a tunic over all of it. Respectable enough if someone stopped her. Probably. She wasn't sure about English country manners. Or how close non-magical folk could get to the house here.

She made her way downstairs as quietly as she could. No one else was stirring yet, the house was dark. She released the wards on the kitchen door, then reset them behind her, and took off at a steady pace. The ground was a bit uneven under her feet as she went up the path toward the manor. It smoothed out as she hit the manicured lawn near the wall. She wondered, for a moment, if the grass stayed that short, or if it was how it had been trimmed by the earlier investigators.

Kate needed to think. And if she was going to think and run, she might as well circle the manor, and see if she noticed anything about their puzzle and problem. The first time around was a respectable lap, enough to make her breathe hard.

The second felt decidedly shorter, and she didn't think it was just because her mind was settling out. Running, activity, always had that effect. Once her world narrowed down to one foot in front of the other, to her breathing, of planting her feet one after the other and pushing off, things got easier.

Generally. This time was less successful than she wanted. By the third lap, she was working harder to keep her chosen pace, and it felt like the house was a lot larger, in all dimensions. Nearly double her second lap. And the problem of Lefton and Vale was still front and centre in her mind, hanging there, like a red cape, impossible to ignore.

The fourth lap, she ignored her other thoughts, and counted steps. And then her fifth got an entirely different count. She was now certain that the manor was changing size. Each time she passed the gates, she thought. She still couldn't figure out a pattern in the changes, as the fifth was smaller than the fourth, not larger.

Finally, she had to stop for a breather, pausing to the west of the gates, and then wondered if it made a difference which direction she circled. She'd been instinctively circling clockwise. All the Guard were trained to move clockwise by default. It made for more systematic investigations, everyone working the same direction, nobody getting underfoot going the wrong way. But sitting there in the dew-soaked grass, with the sun coming up to the east, she suddenly wondered if that made a difference here.

Once she'd rested, she put it to the test. Kate stood, then turned right and picked up a steady pace, the kind of even stride that let her count easily. She went around the building once, crossing the gates then turning left again. She counted as she ran, then did another circuit, to exactly the same count.

The discovery left her giddy, so much so she stopped, and sprawled out in the grass to one side of the gates. Her pocket watch chimed as she lay there. She levered herself to her feet, and made her way back to the house, grinning broadly.

"You're late." Vale was standing on the porch.

"Beg pardon?"

"You're late. And you're a mess, Davies. Grass in your hair. Do you not have any self-respect?"

Kate drew herself up. "I was out for a run," she said, trying not to feel like she had to justify herself.

"I'm off to Trellech for the day. Giles isn't down for breakfast yet. Go wash up." He didn't quite say the next sentence, some sort of insult, but she could see it on his face.

Twenty minutes later, she had just sat down at the table when she heard footsteps on the stairs. "Lefton? I'm at the table. Do you need a hand?"

She heard the grumbling in his voice before the words made sense to her, something that ended with, "Fine, thank you."

He took several minutes to arrange himself at the table, and Mrs Hitchcock bustled out with a plate. "Eggs, sausage, potatoes."

Lefton sat there, not eating for a moment, then let out a long sigh, and picked up his fork, asking "Did Vale go already?"

Kate had been watching his hands, and his question startled her. "About fifteen minutes ago, I think. I went out for a run first thing, and he was heading out when I got back."

Lefton winced, and then moved his left hand to feel for the plate, then poked at the surface with the fork.

"Sir, um." She had to think, and her head was still full

from her morning. "Eggs at six o'clock. Sausage at ten, pota-toes at two."

He looked up sharply, and she could feel something shift in his attention to her. Then he nodded, and went to work on his meal, with a ferocious concentration that forbade any comment or conversation.

The silence grew and grew until he put his fork down. "Is there tea?" He folded his fingers under, resting his hand on the table.

Kate nodded, then said, "Down by me. I'll pour, the teapot's quite hot. You like one sugar and cream?"

He nodded, and she spent the next few moments pouring and adding the cream and sugar, attending to the precise proportions. Once she had it ready, she murmured, "Here, Lefton."

He reached for it, and she was struck again by his fingers. They were elegant, as one might expect for someone of his family and House, but also very, the word she wanted to use was 'decisive'. It was quiet again, except for the sound of him sipping the tea and the rattle when he set the cup down. "I had no luck with the patterns."

"Sir." She wasn't sure how to begin with this.

"There was nothing there, Davies. I was up quite late, making sure." He was upset with her again.

She paused, and then said, "I found out something new this morning, sir. Lefton." She kept wanting to be formal with him as if the formality would protect her from some-thing. His temper, perhaps. She noted the tendency, marked it, even as she kept going.

Giles leaned back in his chair. "Oh?" He sounded unin-terested.

"I went for a run, sir. Before breakfast. Around the manor."

That earned her a raised eyebrow, but no comment.

"When I ran clockwise, as we did the measurements, they changed every time. I didn't measure fully, but I counted paces. I wrote them down, the rough counts, but they were quite different."

"Your first clause suggests some experimentation?" It was in a dry tone, suddenly distant, and she wasn't at all sure what to do with that, what he meant by it. But she pressed on. On was the only way through. "When I went counter-clockwise, Lefton, it stayed the same size."

"Huh." It came out of him in a puff of breath, and she could see he'd closed his eyes behind the dark of the glasses. He was thinking hard, fingers tapping in some pattern that made sense to him. "How big?"

"I'd have to measure properly. About one hundred strides by two hundred. For the walled space."

"That's a fair size. Four acres." He must have done the maths automatically in his head. "Enough for some significant gardens." He frowned. "Where does the ... shifting start?"

"I think crossing the gates. I wasn't sure how to test it."

Giles nodded, then said, "Go do whatever you need for the moment. I want to think about this. Back in half an hour, ready to go out."

Kate nodded, then said, "I have an idea for a salve. It will take longer than that, so tonight."

Giles waved his hand, and Kate acknowledged it with "Half an hour" rather than a gesture before taking herself to her room and writing her notes, in as much detail as she could. Twenty-eight minutes later, she came down the stairs, with her own notebook handy, sharpened pencils, and a sizeable ball of yarn from her trunk.

"She's making sandwiches. Grab them?"

Kate blinked. The comment had come from Giles, sitting on a chair in the hall. "Of course," she replied.

Mrs Hitchcock was tidying the kitchen after the food preparations. "He says you'll be out there for lunch, here's sandwiches, meat paste, hope that's all right, and egg. Lovely chives in the egg, grand things, chives. Bottles of squash, and there's a thermos of tea."

Kate took the picnic basket and said, "Back when we're back." When she came back out to the hall, Giles was waiting for her, leaning lightly on his cane.

"Take me out there, and set us up in the right quadrant in front of the house."

"Sir." Kate did as she was told, quietly leading the way, and then getting him settled in a chair.

TWELVE

OXFORDSHIRE

Giles was feeling irritated with the world. It felt like he'd got out of bed on the wrong side, and everything was cascading downhill. He couldn't tell if it was his native pessimism, a premonition, or not enough sleep in a strange bed. Whichever it was, he'd felt chilled and on edge since he woke up.

Then Vale had been gone, without warning. Giles had said lunch and tea, not earlier. He'd expected Vale to be there to manage breakfast. Instead, there was a brief note in braille he'd almost missed on the dressing table, and then Davies at the table.

To her credit, she hadn't fussed, hadn't tried to cut up his bacon for him or spoon feed him. He wouldn't put that past the housekeeper if someone left her unsupervised. And Davies had been paying attention, about describing food based on the clock face. It was something.

There was still the matter of the size. Now he was settled here, he was trying to figure out what to do next. First, he drew out the notes Vale had transcribed for him, and then, reluctantly, rummaged for the braille stylus.

Giles could hear the shift behind him, then he heard, "May I ask about that, sir?" The question was very polite, at least.

"It's a stylus and slate, they let me write braille on the go. That's the raised dots." He kept the explanation short and crisp. Other people did not care about the varieties of braille, or Moon type. All of which he was forced to have opinions about whether he wanted to or not. "Vale transcribed yesterday's notes, that's what I'm reading."

"Would it help for me to go pace off the space and bring you today's numbers?"

"Not yet." His voice was crisp. "Let me review, first."

He let his fingers slip across the rows. Numbers were straightforward. Even without his abacus here, he could more or less keep the patterns in mind, or rather the places where the patterns broke. He let his fingers brush across a row, then he said, "Do you still have your notes from yesterday, Davies?"

"Um. Yes, sir, in my notebook. Just a moment?"

He could hear the flicking of pages, then a "Ready, sir?"

"Read out the numbers for me, one last time."

She read out the numbers, series of threes, because each side was several hundred feet. He let his fingers drift over the braille, feeling the raised dots he'd learned so painstakingly. She read out a series of numbers, then another.

"Stop." He could hear the paper rustling. "Read that again. The full sequence."

She read it, starting from the beginning of the sequence.

"Are you certain that says two hundred seventy?"

"Yes, sir. Quite sure."

He frowned, felt the paper again. "Keep reading." He would not explain. Not yet. He could hear her shift on her canvas chair, but she kept reading, naming each new sequence as she got to it, her voice precise. Rather pleasant to listen to, he realised, with the hint of the Welsh lilt, before he dragged his attention back to what she was saying.

Three times more, he had to stop and review a number. Each time she was certain that hers was correct. She reached the end of the last set they'd done yesterday, and she waited, quiet.

He reached to feel for the little work table next to his chair, and said, "I need to walk for a moment, think. Tell me if I get too close to the thorns."

"Sir." Her voice was very quiet.

Giles stood, felt for his cane, and made his way twelve steps closer to the wall. He could feel how the breeze was different, as he got closer, and the way the ground was a little softer. He stood there for perhaps five minutes, clearing his mind in half a dozen different ways, before he gave up, pivoted precisely, and called out, "Davies?"

"Here, sir." He aligned himself on her voice, and when he got closer, she said, "Chair three steps in front of you, sir."

Giles nodded, took the last few steps, and settled himself again. "There was an error in the transcription."

She said nothing. He supposed that asking her to comment on Vale's competence - or lack - was unfair. It was irritating, even when it was the sensible response.

After a long pause, he said, "So we will do the measurements again, after I revise my notes. If you could read them from the beginning again, more slowly, this time, as I repeat each number?"

"Sir."

That whole tedious process took far longer than he wanted, and then there was the traipsing about with measurement tools. It felt both wrong and right to be circling counter-clockwise. He'd always been taught that that drew the Fatae, and they did not need that complication at all.

He was trying not to comment on it, when he heard her say, "It's about lunch time, sir. Perhaps we could take a break?"

Giles nodded, and she offered her arm to lead him back to their little base camp.

"Mrs Hitchcock gave me a blanket to sit on, sir. If you'd prefer that to the chair?"

That took him aback, but after a moment, he nodded. "No one to see my lost dignity, mm?" He thought he heard her laugh, but if she did she covered it well.

"Here's meat paste, or egg salad with chives. Do you have a preference, sir?"

"How many?"

"Two of each? And scones, and some jam, and bottles of black currant squash or there's a flask of tea with plenty in it."

"If you've no preference, how about we split the bounty? You've been earning your keep. And since it's a picnic, the squash, please."

Not a drink he had often, but something about being in the open air, sitting on the ground in the summer sun made him feel like he could indulge himself in the childhood memories.

They ate quietly for several minutes, then he heard her making all the small sounds people did when they were working up to ask something. He didn't know what to expect from her, if it would be the awkward questions about blindness, or about his War, or what.

"Lefton, I feel like we got off on the wrong foot, somehow."

Not what he expected at all. "Oh?" It sounded foolish, but it was all he could think of to say in the moment, without letting the pause draw out too long.

"I'm finding the work here very interesting, but I'm not clear, if you don't mind the question, how you got roped into it."

"I mentioned, I hold a chair in mathematical studies, yes?"

"You did, sir. I'm not - um. I am not sure exactly what that means? Some in the Guard did academic work after leaving school, but I went straight into apprenticeship in the Guard itself."

"It means I'm affiliated with a college, at Oxford, and I research and sometimes teach undergraduates. Term is out for the summer now, of course."

"Do you live..." She paused, and she sounded embarrassed. This, though, he was glad enough to answer.

"I prefer living in Trellech; I can use various magical tools to help, and my club knows my preferences. I go up to Oxford regularly in term time, of course, as needed, but just for the day. Most of my students come to me for tutorials."

"You're quite near Portal Square," she agreed.

"Beyond that, I spend my time writing and doing research on various topics. Largely the intersection of maths and magical ritual, but some pure maths as well." He knew that part bored just about everyone.

He expected her to ask about that, but she said, "And the - writing you use? That's not the right word."

"There are a number of systems of writing used by people who can't read print." Who were blind. He still didn't like saying it outright, it felt crude. "This one is braille. Developed by a Frenchman, about a century ago. There's a number of different versions. The Americans have half a dozen variants floating around. I mostly read what's called English braille, or there's another called Moon Type, that is shapes, not dots."

"Thank you." Her voice was very quiet. "I appreciate the explanation." There was a pause, then she said, "It would be handy, when print isn't an option. Like during the War."

"That's where it came from, originally. Another Frenchman, looking to pass messages at night on the battlefield."

"Oh, sonography! Barbier, for Napoleon."

Giles was startled, but nodded. "Just so. Barbier gave a lecture at the Paris school for the blind, and Louis Braille developed the idea for writing from there." It startled him she knew that piece of the history, though he supposed it would be a useful skill for some kinds of Guard tasks, after all.

"May I ask where you're from, sir?" Now, she was not quite so tentative, but searching for an acceptable topic.

Giles nodded, then considered, willing to venture that much to make things less awkward between them. "I grew up not too far from here, actually. A county or three over."

"Oh?" It was still quiet, but very attentive, somehow, even in that short syllable.

"My parents are very proper. Hands off, a series of nannies I spent much more time with, then tutors. One rather older brother; he made it through the War much better off than I."

He could hear her almost say something, get as far as the inhale of breath before she stopped, and said instead. "Then Schola?"

"Then Schola," he agreed. "That is what they expected, at least."

"Not what my parents expected, but we made do."

He almost asked what it was like for her, to go to Schola without knowing at least some of what to expect. All the things he'd learned from his parents and brother and extended family through a lifetime of conversations, with the knowledge then refined by his tutor in all its integrals and derivatives. But they did not know each other nearly well enough for that kind of intrusion, and he could not think how to ask it, anyway.

There was a pause long enough for her to finish her meal and tidy up the wax paper and whatever other items came with it. That done, she said, "What is our next step?"

"More measuring. And then some research, this evening."

"Of course." She sounded amiably resigned to the necessities, at least. He had noticed that about her, no grumbling about the grunt work, even when it was tedious. It made quite a change from Vale's usual griping.

THIRTEEN

OXFORDSHIRE

F ive days later, they had not made measurable progress. They had determined they could get fixed measurements of the space. She had made map after map of the variation in the rose bushes. Lefton was in spasms of delight over them, moving little markers around on a checkers board in the library, showing how they formed a complex fugue of interwoven number sequences.

It at least made it clear what he was brilliant at. Watching him make the patterns near dance was enough to convince her that he was the right person for this project. He spotted connections she couldn't begin to grasp until he pointed them out. And how he pointed them out, that kept her on her toes, but she was learning a great deal.

Not all of it was about the project at hand. A chance comment led to her being made to listen to an evening of recordings by a Viennese composer whose name she could never quite pronounce correctly. Welsh was easy on her tongue, the proper Viennese umlaut was not.

She had allowed as how the music was mathematically

intriguing, especially when Lefton unbent enough to actually explain it to her, but it was not simple to listen to.

None of this got them any closer to finding a way in. Or what to do next, for that matter. They were in the midst of another afternoon, wondering if there was some secret level or stone or incantation that would show an entrance. They'd worked well down into the list of folk tales and legendary words, when Vale came bustling up the path.

"Look sharp, Davies. Your superior officer's here to see you. I'll see Giles back." He then immediately turned away from her.

Kate blinked. She'd not expected anyone, and certainly not Lord Edgarton. She had sent back her reports every three days through her issued journal, and no one had even asked her questions so far. Just marked it as read with the formal stamp used for such things.

She tugged her vest down and smoothed her hair, jamming hair pins back in place. "Thank you, Vale," she said, determined to be polite. "Lefton, I'll see what he wants, and we can talk about the next steps this evening."

Lefton waved a hand in dismissal, turning toward the path for a moment as she murmured her goodbye. Kate looked back over her shoulder to see Vale standing beside him, both of them pointed toward the manor and the rose-covered walls, their backs to her. Apparently Lefton wanted to stay out there a few more minutes. There was something in the way they stood, wearing properly tailored clothes of fine fabrics, like they had all the time in the world, that suddenly made her feel completely irrelevant to the realities of their universe.

She hurried back along the path, keeping herself at a pace that would be prompt but not leave her out of breath.

Mrs Hitchcock met her on the porch. "The gentleman from the Guard is in the library, ma'am. I brought some tea."

"Thank you," Kate said. "I'll go right in."

She knocked on the door and got a deep bass in reply. "Enter." It was all the warning she had that it was not Lord Edgarton.

Opening the door, she said, "Guard Davies, sir." She closed the door behind her, settling into the rest position. Feet evenly spaced, hands behind her back. It felt wrong to do this not in uniform, but she had no choice.

"You are not in uniform." His voice was curt, sharp.

How to reply without sounding defensive. "Major Lefton expressed his preference for civilian clothes, sir."

"The man doesn't have to look at you." The officer snorted, stepping away from the window that gave the best view of the manor in the distance. With the tall summer grass, one could only see the top of the wall and the buildings and banner behind that. Once he moved, she could see him better. Tall, in his early fifties perhaps, with grey at the temples he surely considered distinguished.

"If you'd prefer, I could go change, sir. I'd only be a few minutes."

"Stay." That was flat and cold, the way you'd command a dog you didn't like.

She nodded and waited. That was the only thing she could do in a situation like this.

"I am Temenos Sibley."

Kate straightened. "Lord Sibley." That had been a test, and she was fast enough to see it coming. Lord Edgarton had made her memorise all the titles. He'd drilled her in particular on which noble lords were so insecure about their status they would destroy the career of someone who got it wrong. Not that he'd put it like that, but he hadn't needed to.

It earned her a very slight nod. "Tell me why you have failed in your task."

She paused for the smallest of pauses, enough for a breath. Keep your feet beneath you, keep your air even, keep your claws dug into the ground. All the reminders they had taught her, her teachers who she trusted.

"It is a complex problem, sir. As Major Lefton and Lord Edgarton expected, given that the earlier attempts were not successful." She didn't expect an appeal to authority would do any good, but there was no reason not to make the attempt here.

That earned her a flick of his fingers, and he settled in the easy chair, the one Lefton preferred, and reached into his pocket to light a cigarette. "Explain."

She only had her small notebook here. The others were with Lefton or on the table behind Lord Sibley and utterly unavailable. "May I refer to my notes, sir?"

It earned her a small nod, and she withdrew the notebook, flipping the pages. "Our investigations so far have determined that one part of the enchantment is directional. When one travels clockwise around the walls, the manor changes size. In proportion, but we have not fully delineated the patterns, since it did not seem relevant to the solution." Also, there were only so many times she was willing to run around the building if it wasn't doing any good.

"And the other direction?"

"A stable measurement. Based on the Golden Ratio, sir, though we are uncertain whether that is architectural preference or inherent to the magical systems in place."

"And the roses?"

"Planted in a series of numerical sequences, sir. Major

Lefton has the notes on that, and can better explain the specifics. They overlap at certain points. There are three varieties of roses, all Gallicas. We believe."

"Gallicas?" He asked it with a little sneer. "Explain."

"That is an ancient variety, sir, that dates back to the Greeks and Romans. They grow profusely, but with notable thorns and suckers." She hesitated for a moment, then decided that not saying this would be worse than saying it. "There is a curiosity, sir, though."

"Curiosity?"

"The roses are blooming. It is now some weeks after the manor appeared, and gallicas normally bloom only once. Some of the blooms should have faded by now, but there is no sign of that. We are not sure why."

"How have you investigated that?"

"I brought a portable alchemical lab with me, sir, and prepared some field tests. I was able to gather a petal from each variety, and test for chronological magical influence. Also grass from the field, and a small sample of dirt at various distances from the wall."

He grunted, as if he'd not expected that.

Kate went on. "I have samples ready to go next someone returns to Trellech, and it is possible more advanced equipment or testing would find something I did not. But there is no sign of the usual chronological influences. Some of them, as I am sure you know, sir, rely on trace elements difficult to remove once applied." The powders and dusts should have fluoresced in her testing, unmistakeably.

Lord Sibley waved a hand. "And what are your next plans?"

At that moment, she heard footsteps in the hall, and Kate could not tell from here if it was the housekeeper or Vale and Lefton returning.

Kate paused, considering her options, then shifted into the Guard's Tongue. The others would not be able to make sense of it. That was the point of lost languages. She began with the formal phrase for such a shift, the "From my tongue to your ears," and waited for his acknowledgement.

For just an instant, she was sure he was grimacing, then it passed, and he made the proper acknowledgement. "I am listening."

She straightened. Something about speaking in the Guard's Tongue felt so comfortable to her. Reassuring. That there was something shared, there. "Sir, I would like to find out what was tried by those before us, so we do not duplicate effort."

"No." It came out flat, and it was the hard no, the word in the Tongue that indicated any further question would be insubordination.

Kate couldn't keep from flinching, though she controlled herself as quickly as she could. Now she had to think what to say instead. The grammar, the implications of the grammar, meant she had to find a new door, a new way of talking about this thing.

"Sir, may I ask what concerns brought you to this station?" Again, a set phrase, and he seemed more comfortable with that.

"Resources are limited. We can not allow waste."

Curt, but more of a response, if again only set phrases. She nodded. "We are working hard, but it is a complex problem." She lingered for a moment on the word that implied the degree of the problem. It was precise, and elegant, the one that meant it was not a thing that posed risk. The word that meant something held a great mystery, and mysteries brought their own concerns, and that it was largely a magical concern, not physical or social.

He waved his hand, and said a syllable, then cut off. He paused, inhaled from his cigarette, and only after he'd taken his time at that, did he respond. "English."

She nodded. She could scarcely do anything else. "I am listening, sir."

"I want a report on my desk tomorrow morning by ten am. I do not care how it gets there. With all the details of your work so far."

"Of course, sir. Is there anything else?" She could scarcely say no to a direct order, and they both knew it.

"Dismissed."

"Yes, sir."

FOURTEEN

OXFORDSHIRE

G iles could hear them talking, when he came back in, but though he could hear they were saying something, he couldn't make out the words at all. He wondered, for a moment, if his hearing was going, but then suddenly the words became clear again, and he heard the demand for a formal report.

It was unconscionable, bossing Davies around like that, for all she was not arguing. They had no formal written report ready beyond the working notes she'd been submitting. The idea that one was needed was ridiculous.

It wasn't at all like Edgarton to insist on something like that, not without a great deal of external pressure. To get it there by ten the next morning, someone, Davies, would need to set off at dawn. Likely after being up all night writing it.

Mrs Hitchcock had brought him tea in the little parlour. The room smelled musty, of lavender and dried flowers, and made his nose itch. When he heard the final exchange, he came to the door of the parlour, and caught the footsteps on the stairs.

"Davies?"

"Sir, pardon, sir."

"Would Edgarton like to speak with me?" It had not been Edgarton's voice, but the error would get him more information than asking who it had actually been.

It wasn't the question she expected, he could hear that from the sharp inhale. "It's Lord Sibley, sir. I don't know if you are acquainted? He didn't say if he wished to speak to you." Her voice was higher pitched than usual, tense and rushed.

He nodded. "I'll knock. You see to what you need. We can discuss later."

"Sir. I'll be in my room, sir. Washing up."

"Take the time you need." With that, he shifted, running his hand along the wall between the parlour door and the library, and then knocked.

"Who is it?"

"Major Lefton, Lord Sibley."

"Come." It was brusque.

Giles opened the door, and the light was all wrong to help him. Too bright from the window still, all he had was the silhouette of the chair, and enough of a guess that that was where Sibley was.

"Can I be of help?" Giles could smell the cigarette smoke. That would take some airing out. He much preferred to be able to smell the cues from the room, the fresh air from a window or the soot from a fire. All the little things that helped him keep the arrangement of the space fixed in his mind. Cigarette smoke got everywhere.

"Your progress is inadequate, Lefton."

"It's rather a complex problem. If it had been simpler, it would be solved by now. Quite a unique form of magic." The house was not going to go anywhere if they did not solve it immediately, which left the puzzle of why someone like Sibley would think it was worth making trouble over.

He'd had more than enough experience with men like Sibley, he was sure there was the little dismissive sweep of the hand, the scowl. "I told the girl to make sure there's a full report on my desk by ten."

"Ah, that's a thing. I have some additional mathematical modelling to finish. Essential to the next report, but it will take time to do. Quite helpful, Guard Davies, but her expertise is not in the mathematics. The equations take quite a lot of proofreading to make sure everything's ticketyboo."

He was laying it on thick, but it was the proper mode with overbearing idiots who had rank because of their aristocratic blood, not because of their competence.

The other man made the sort of undistinguishable noise that drove Giles up a wall. He could not tell if the man was nodding or shaking his head or thinking.

"I can give her until five tomorrow. She must be prompt, mind. I have evening plans."

"Garden party at the Healing Temple, isn't it? I'll be sorry to miss it." Giles kept his voice even. "Always quite the select event, and I understand the Four O'Clocks are particularly colourful this year. And the lotuses are always stunning, I don't know how they do it."

It earned him a grunt. "Tell her, then. Blasted long way out here you are."

"It is where the manor showed up, sir. Do you need a flask of tea for the drive back? I'm sure the housekeeper could put something together." All very civilised, easy, good-natured.

There was another grunt. Sibley was not very articulate at all. Then he said. "No, I've got a car and driver, it won't take terribly long." Giles could hear him stand up. "Tell

Davies to have that report to me no later than five, or she'll regret it. See to your models or whatever they are."

Giles nodded, and triggered the charm that hung from his watch-chain, that would ring a bell in the kitchen. He could hear Mrs Hitchcock thumping through the house, then her "Sir?"

"If you'd show Lord Sibley out and check his driver has everything he needs?"

"Of course, sir. Lord Sibley, this way, when you're ready?" Giles could hear her deference to his lordship, but he kept a pleasant smile on his face.

Once Sibley was gone, once Giles heard the motor take off down the lane, there was a knock on the door, and a "Sir?"

Mrs Hitchcock had come back again. "Thank you, Mrs Hitchcock. If you'd tell Vale I'd like to see him. And if you'd go up and let Davies know that Lord Sibley is gone. When convenient, I'd like to talk to her about the next steps when she's ready. No need for her to hurry. If it's not a bother, perhaps something nice for tea? Oh. And I suspect one or more of us will be gone much of tomorrow, possibly overnight. We'll let you know at supper."

"I've some clotted cream just ready, sir, thank you sir." He could hear her go off, first upstairs, then down the hall to the back.

"Giles?" There was Vale.

"Could you make sure the room's arranged properly? And air it out, Sibley was smoking, you know what that does." Giles could hear Vale move, slowly, but at least without too much argument.

"Any reason for his visit?" The man had even put Vale on edge, turning up unexpected and making a racket.

"Demanding a report on his desk tomorrow morning. I

got him to delay it for the afternoon. I'd like to go back to town, and likely stay overnight. Make the arrangements, if you would, and see if Edgarton's free for a drink or supper. It's the Healing Temple garden party, I don't know what his plans are, but as late as he needs if it's after."

"Davies?"

"I'll ask her if she wants to come back, or would rather stay here. I assume you'd rather come with, but I won't need you once I've dropped off the file. I thought the club, rather than open the house, and that would leave you free to come and go as you prefer."

"Appreciated, Giles." That was warmer, Vale was clearly pleased. "I'll see to the arrangements. Here, do you want your usual chair? I've rearranged as needed, and there's a good breeze from the window."

Giles shook his head. "The worktable, if we can manage the breeze." Vale helped him over, and they spent a minute figuring out where he could set which items without them blowing away. "There, I'll be fine until tea."

Vale said, "I'll be upstairs, then," and took himself off. He was in a grand mood with the prospect of the city and parties in his near future.

It was a good hour before he heard a quieter knock on the door, and a cautious, "Lefton." He pivoted in the chair, and gestured. "Come, bring a chair or a stool if you want."

He heard her walk over, then a rather tentative "Sir?"

"Let me lay things out for you, Davies. Lord Sibley has agreed we have until five tomorrow to deliver the report. I made up some muck about needing to do some modelling, so I will need to do some modelling to go with it. I hope you don't mind helping with that after supper?"

There was an audible inhale, then she murmured, "No, of course not. I..." She broke off.

"Speak freely. I don't care for him one bit." The latter encouragement seemed particularly necessary.

"Sir." He could hear the relief there. Then, after a moment, as if considering what to say, she said, "He didn't care for me being out of uniform. I think he was very annoyed we'd not made more progress. He said nothing of why he was here."

"I overheard something I didn't understand, when I came in."

"That was the Guard's Tongue, I'd be rather surprised if you did."

Giles laughed. "Well, no. You seemed fluent, though."

"I pride myself on it, sir." She seemed like she was going to say something else, then changed her mind. "May I think about the rest, sir, and discuss after dinner? I am..." She paused, searching for a word that she didn't manage to find.

He rescued her from the awkwardness. "Quite understandable if you're flustered. Go out for a ride or a walk if you want. Though Mrs Hitchcock promises clotted cream for tea."

There was a momentary pause, before she said, "It's just about three now, sir. How about I help her get the tea ready, and go out for a bit between tea and supper, clear my head?"

"Excellent plan. I'll be thinking about what sort of modelling we can work up that will look impressive and not be much work to pull together."

FIFTEEN

OXFORDSHIRE

That evening, Kate presented herself at the library as requested, twenty minutes after dinner was over. She'd taken just enough time to wash her hands and organise her notes. She knocked on the door, and Lefton called out, "Enter."

"It's Davies, sir."

He was sitting at the desk, a lamp lit for her benefit. There was a chair waiting at the open edge of the long table, the one that wasn't too close to bookshelves for comfort. "Have a seat. Is that comfortable for you?"

She peered at the chair, then settled herself on it. "It is a rather odd colour, sir, but a perfectly reasonable chair."

Her try to lighten the mood made him smile for a moment. "Ah, is it chartreuse? Mauve? Something else?"

Kate contemplated how much was the lamplight and how much was the chair itself. "A mangey puce?" she offered. "But the legs are sound."

Lefton nodded. "Here. First, about tomorrow. Do you want to come into town? I thought I would deliver the report. And I want to have a drink with one or two people, see if I can find out why Sibley turned up here without so much as a by-your-leave."

"Sir." She wasn't sure what to say to this.

"First question first. Town?"

Simplifying it made it easier. "I'd like to consult the library again, if it's not a bother."

"Do you need a place to stay?"

"No, I can stay in my rooms at barracks."

"Of course. I'll be at the Fox's Den. My club. Not worth opening the house up for a night. If you'd like the library, we should set off in the morning so we're there by luncheon."

"And Vale?"

"His club, or elsewhere, depending on what company he finds. He'll likely have a hangover in the morning, mind. So you're forewarned against making loud noises."

Kate inhaled, thinking of what she'd glimpsed earlier, then she ventured, "He doesn't... seem very happy being out here, sir?"

"He enjoys being in town. With plenty to do, and people to drink with. And I need a little help, but not so much as to keep anyone busy as a full-time thing."

"May I ask, sir, why... him?" There were ways in which they seemed so similar, but there was something about Vale that did not seem to fit right. And she did not like the company he kept. She'd run into one of his guests the other day, who set every hair on her neck upright for all he'd been smoothly pleasant.

"He's a distant cousin, he needed a position that would offer room and board and at least a modest salary. I needed someone who wouldn't fuss too much. And he was willing to learn to transcribe into braille, which turned out to be a sticking point for rather a lot of people. Mostly he does it with a device like a typewriter, not the stylus, it's not hard."

Kate almost said something, then caught her breath. It was not her place to tell this man that his assistant was lazy. Or had been rummaging on his dresser like she'd seen on the way downstairs. And he was already clear Vale drank more than he should. Clearly, Lefton did not require overwhelming hard work out of his man.

"And the other options weren't appealing?"

"The other options ran to older widows who'd lost sons in the War, who would spend all the time fussing over me. The sort to bring me a cup of tea every five minutes and rearrange things without telling me and fill the place with frippery. That would get in the way of my work."

Kate risked, "You do not seem one for frippery, no. Even I can tell that on short acquaintance."

It made him laugh and changed his whole face. "Ah, but you are an intelligent and observant sort. Far more so than most. And I suspect you appreciate a clean workspace."

She smiled, then said, "I do, yes. So, this report?"

He paused, the kind of pause where he was analysing the options, making some sort of decision. "Before that." He paused. "You are not the sort of person who deals well with complications to your chain of command."

It startled her. She shook her head, and only seconds later remembered to respond with words. "No, sir."

"So if I asked you what you thought of Lord Sibley, you would say something polite and non-committal, and avoid trouble."

"Yes, sir."

"Giles. If you prefer."

That made her start, and this time he must have realised she'd be speechless, because he went on.

"I heard enough with him to know he treated you poorly. I am very pleased with your work so far. Your attention to detail, your willingness to learn. Starting with the fact you thought to go to the library when no one else apparently did."

Kate ducked her chin, then ventured "Sir? Um. Giles." And then, "If you'd prefer, people call me Kate, informally."

"Not many, I suspect. Katherine, your full name?"

"With a K, yes," she agreed, choosing to be pleasant rather than remind him she had told him before, at that first interview. He had no particular reason to have remembered, after all.

Then she straightened her shoulders. "I had the impression from the original brief that we were to take our time to investigate thoroughly, and make sure there was no unexpected danger. That the Guard's role was to make sure things were safe for people in the area. Lord Edgarton didn't imply any particular rush, he has always been careful to mention deadlines and expectations. Do you have any idea why Lord Sibley is so insistent?"

He shooks his head. "He did not share much with me either. Less, I think, than with you."

That encouraged her to press a bit more. "There were several things odd in the conversation. And I think, I was thinking, when you gave me time to, that I should tell you."

"The part I couldn't understand?"

"Yes, and before that."

Giles settled back in his chair. "Tell me what you think it would help me to know. Even if it seems silly. You've a fine head on you, but I know more of the politics, I suspect, even in the Guard."

That made Kate snort. "Probably, sir. Um. Giles. I try to

avoid that. It's dangerous to a career, at my level. Politics are for officers."

He made a considering noise, drawing it out. "Do you intend to stay a Guard all your life? Not advance? No, that's a distraction, we have a deadline. We can talk about that some other time. Begin at the beginning, whatever that means."

"He called me in and scolded me for being out of uniform. I said you'd expressed a preference for civilian clothes. I hope that wasn't overstepping."

"Since I said it, not at all. You have my full permission to use what I've said in such situations if they come up. Let's see. I explicitly request and desire you, as part of this work, to answer questions from other parties using your informed judgement and discretion. And when necessary, I expect you to use what I have said to defuse the situation."

Kate shivered; she couldn't help it. At least it wouldn't show. "That's - Giles, that's a very broad defence. At your cost."

"That's how it should be. That's an officer's role. Even if I'm not one, anymore." He lingered for a moment. "Nor your commanding officer, precisely."

"It helps, though. To know how you see it." She coughed and returned to the story. "Lord Sibley was... I think he was testing me, about identifying his preference for the title. He asked bluntly why we'd failed, and I said it was a complex problem."

"Which it is, and which any fool could tell. We've only been here a week." He seemed faintly disgusted, as best she could tell through the decorous precision of his manner.

"I asked to refer to my notes, explained what we'd found - all the things that were in my reports. About the roses, that's part of what I'd like to check at the library, magical properties. That I had done some initial tests, but haven't found influence of chronological magics, but I had samples for testing. I've already packed them, for tomorrow."

"Nicely done." Giles agreed.

"Then, I - we're all supposed to know the Guard's Tongue, it's how, it's how we do certain orders. I'm not permitted to teach it, but I can explain some of how it works."

"I will not ask you to break your oaths, Kate. That would... I suspect that would break you, and we can't be having that." There was a tone there that seemed to surprise him as much as it surprised her, something warm.

"I asked, in the Tongue, about what people tried before us, so we didn't duplicate effort. And... there're different ways to say no. A smooth no, a flat no, a sharp no."

"And this was - sharp? Is that the worst of them?"

"There's a word that means no, and that any further question, any comment at all, is automatic insubordination."

"That's not on. It's a reasonable question."

"And then I asked what brought him here, and he..." She stopped and gathered her thoughts. "I don't think he's nearly as fluent at the Tongue as he should be, as any officer should be."

She'd thought through the consequences of this, all the time she was out walking and changing and eating. She couldn't unsnarl it herself, she had to tell someone. And Giles, at least, seemed to understand the challenges.

"What made you think that?" The question was calm, looking for data.

"There are stock phrases, things that are used regularly. Formulas. And what he said was one of those, about resources being limited, and not being able to afford waste." She paused, then said "Sir, Giles. Are they worried about safety, somehow? Or something else like that? What he said had so many edges, and I don't know how to sort them out."

Giles considered. "Safety? I wish they would tell us more about the earlier attempts. If they cared about our well-being, you would think they would at least tell us what not to do in more detail."

Kate frowned. "They may, pardon, consider us more disposable. One way and another."

He could not argue with that, as unpleasant as the idea was. Not even just what it meant about his value, but he found himself wanting to defend Kate's skills and expertise to anyone who could be made to listen.

"And yet they are not. I will see if I can get something more out of someone tomorrow." He considered. "Let us go through this in order. On the question of waste, I know what my rates are, and I know what the Guard rates are. I can guess at what Mrs Hitchcock and our food runs. As projects go, we're quite frugal. At least for a month or two. So that's an excuse, then, and something that he could say without embarrassing himself. And then?"

"There are also many words to describe problems. I used the one that means there isn't a great risk, but there's some mystery or magic, and those have their own concerns. If you see the implications?"

"Oh, yes. And my, that's elegant. Nearly an equation in letters." It was high praise from him, she could tell. "It does rather imply that our safety is not the thing he's thinking about. Did he answer it at all?"

"He forced a switch back to English, said he wanted the report by ten the next morning, and dismissed me. No answer."

"That part." His voice was dry. "That part, I heard. It was uncalled for."

Kate paused then decided the risk was worth it. "May I ask why?"

"If I am unhappy with your progress, I should be the one to tell you. If our superiors are unhappy, they should come to me. I dislike this."

"Which is why you want to go to Trellech?"

"Precisely. And speak to a few people who will probably be more usefully forthcoming."

Kate smiled, she had to. "They could scarcely be less and say anything at all?"

"Rather. So. Let's turn our considerable talents to coming up with a report that will look good and make it clear we need more time, mmm?"

SIXTEEN

TRELLECH

The morning was an utter mess of finishing the report, then waiting while Davies copied it. There was fuss about getting the carriage ready and fuss about whether to bring sandwiches. Once they were moving, Giles found things rubbing at his mind. He could have sworn the road had more bumps and potholes than when they'd arrived. He found it exhausting to not be able to predict when he might be jolted. Or when they'd need to slow for a flock of sheep or cows in the road.

There was not much conversation either. Vale had a newspaper, and was rattling it, and he thought Kate had a book. She certainly wasn't saying anything. He had insisted she ride inside, not with the driver, at least.

Giles had noticed she got quieter when Vale had come in to the library a few times while they were working. He couldn't tell if it was awkwardness, or something between them he couldn't see. All he knew was that they were being civil by being silent. It was most annoying. And uninformative.

He'd noticed a contrast, too. Yesterday, Kate had been

chewed out, through no fault of her own, by an unexpected intruder into their project. She had every right to complain, and she had not done so. Even when they had been more relaxed, late in the evening, she hadn't even murmured anything about the injustice or the rudeness.

Vale would have whinged for a good twenty minutes, going on and on about how unfair it was, how demanding Sibley was. Probably another half-dozen minor injustices like the state of the wine cellar, the cheese plate, and the comfort of the beds. On one hand, it often provided Giles with useful information that Vale would not otherwise manage to mention. On the other, it got tiresome.

He wondered whether Kate did not indulge because of concerns about repercussions, or some other cause. She was naturally cautious and thorough. From the first day they'd worked together, that had been obvious. She had been formal with Sibley, and hearing how carefully she answered Sibley had made Giles realise she had been very formal with him, as well. That attention to saying things the proper way, it carried through.

He did not like the thought that she was treating him the way she treated Vale, never mind Sibley. It suggested that she also found him threatening, for all they were using first names now.

Finally, they arrived at the village portal. Going through it into the bustle of Trellech shook him. He took a deep breath, as soon as they'd made it to a quieter spot. "Enjoy the library, Kate. I'll have someone write or take a message round if we need to meet before the portal back at ten tomorrow."

"Of course." She paused for a moment, then said, "My rooms are in Prudentia, and there's a porter on duty all night if you need something."

Giles startled then said, "Ah, right, the residences are named for virtues, aren't they? Good hunting."

"Tomorrow."

He could hear her boots, going away from him on the stones, and then coughed, and said "Vale, I've the file to drop off. What time is it?"

"Just after three."

"Let us do that, then. After, you can take me to the Den, and I'll manage from there."

They walked in silence. Well, between themselves. There was more than one muttering, half-heard comment. Giles could never tell whether the ones about it being two men arm in arm bothered him more than the ones about being blind. Both seemed to have a nasty edge to them.

One of his tutors, a specialist in sympathetic magic, had been prone to opining when drunk that people tsked about the things they most feared. A way to control them, limit them, fence them in. Or away, as the case may be.

The older Giles got, the more he thought there was something to that.

Getting through into the Guard offices was easy enough, he had all the proper permits. At the third stage, as he expected, someone detached Vale and told him to sit in a waiting room. Here, at least, there was a murmur of "This way, sir, if you'll take my arm."

They walked through the halls, surrounded by the little sounds of people stepping out the way, or the business of the day, until there was a "Lord Sibley, Major Lefton." His guide stopped in front of a chair, and said, "I'll wait outside, sir."

Giles heard the door close.

"I thought you'd send the girl."

The tone rather suggested that the man had been

hoping to continue the previous day's dressing down, entirely on his own territory with nothing to interrupt them. Giles carefully suppressed any sign he was bristling at the idea. "Davies has research planned, I am the one at loose ends. Here is the report, and our current models." He withdrew the sole file in his satchel.

"Will you be at the Healing Temple party?" The question sounded casual, but it had an edge to it.

"Likely not, no." He considered, then said "I'm afraid crowded events aren't my thing, these days. I'll be at the Den for the night if anyone has notes for me before we head back."

"Your models?"

"In the report. Davies had a thought about next steps, but it required additional research."

There was something then that might have been a gesture, and of course, Giles couldn't make sense of it.

A moment later, Sibley snapped an irritated, "Well. Go on, then. I'll write if there's something else." He raised his voice. "Matthews!" and Giles heard the door open.

Matthews, at least, was both quiet and competent. Giles wanted to ask if Sibley was always in that kind of mood. But he was quite sure someone who worked with him day in and day out would not risk truth on that topic.

They made their way through the winding halls, leaving Giles turned around. Matthews paused and said, "Your assistant, sir?" and he heard Vale say, "Giles."

"All set." he kept his tone light. "The Den, and then you can go off on your own errands."

Twenty minutes later, he was settled in a chair in the conversation room. He'd detailed one of the staff to look out for a list of ten people he'd like to talk to especially. While he was waiting, he at least had a brandy in hand and a comfortable chair.

"Giles, old man. Thought you were out of town." That voice belonged to the older brother to one of his school friends.

"Bramble, goodness, it's been a while. Just back for the night for the staff to run some errands. Look, I wanted to ask about the current state of the Guard. Projects and all."

He immediately got the brush-off. "Not my territory, old man, sorry. Goodness, see someone needs me. Have a good night, won't you?"

There were two more rounds of that, with different people. The same pleasantries, the same dodging any meaningful answer. More to the point, that brush-off even before he'd asked about anything specific. None of them made with much grace, which just added insult to injury.

Eventually, he could hear the place emptying, and one of the staff came by, with a soft, "Would you prefer a sandwich here, sir, or the dining room?

"Oh, a sandwich would be fine. I expect they're all gone to the party."

"Yes, sir. Very quiet. Can we bring you anything else?" The staff were well-enough trained to remember not to offer a paper or a book from the library.

Giles frowned and then said, "I suppose the music room's free. A sandwich, then if someone would take me there, for an hour or so. I'm meeting Edgarton for drinks after he's done with the party, but he wasn't sure how long he'd be."

"Oh, of course, sir."

That occupied a good ninety minutes or so, until someone who'd reserved the piano turned up, hoping to practise. The conversation room had filled up, leaving Giles to be placed in a table much closer to the door than he preferred, right by the foyer.

The marble and wood made sounds echoed, making it much harder for him to sort out if someone was coming to him, or somewhere else. The constant small noises kept him on edge, unable to relax, enough that he startled when he heard a voice address him from right in front of him.

"Giles, old man. I thought you were rusticated."

"Back in town for the night; staff working on some issues."

"I heard you had a girl working for you?"

"Guard Davies, yes. Do you know her?"

"Oh, heard a fair bit of gossip. There's quite a few people who wouldn't mind being alone in the country with her."

Giles tried to figure out how to answer that. One answer would make him seem even more damaged than people thought him and come with a dose of pity. Another would demean her. A third would imply horrible things about her professionalism.

In the end, he said, with a casual ease he did not entirely feel, "She's doing excellent work. It's a complex problem."

"I suppose they don't drag you out of your cave for the easy ones."

"Generally, no. And at least it's the long hols, so no tutoring assignments to juggle."

"Not from the best sort of family, of course, but that just means she might be ripe for the right sort of opportunity to make good."

Giles, again, wasn't sure what to say, then said mildly, "I'm not the sort to press. Not while we're working together." And then a more cheerful poke. "Besides, Norman, didn't you have that horrendous matter with that young woman with five brothers who all came after you?"

He couldn't see Norman's face, but the spluttering and the tone in his voice as he made his excuses told Giles everything he needed to know.

SEVENTEEN

TRELLECH

"Good afternoon, is Madam Thornton available?"

The young woman at the library information desk looked up, over her glasses, then blinked. "Guard Davies. She's in her office, do you remember where that is? She'll be pleased to see you."

Kate blinked. She hadn't expected that kind of reception. She assumed that a head librarian would be a busy sort of person. Or that the staff would be more formal about sending someone back. Not treating her like she belonged there.

Nevertheless, Kate been given specific instructions, and she would follow them. She walked back through the reading room, noticing scholars tucked into about half the nooks, bent over books at long tables. The office door at the back was open, a light on in the room, and Kate knocked carefully on the door frame.

Madam Thornton looked up, then did a double-take. "Guard Davies, come in. We've found a source that might be handy. Or do you have a specific question?"

Kate ducked her head, not quite sure where to start,

then she settled herself on the edge of the indicated chair, nudging the door closed behind her. "I have a specific question or two, yes, ma'am. We've not made as much headway as we were hoping."

"Ah, we may have a reason for that. There are some indications in our research that the house disappeared from the written record at the time of the Pact."

Kate frowned. "I - suppose that makes some sense, ma'am. Only I don't quite see the specific connection?" She tried to figure out how to talk around the parts of the assignment she'd been told to keep private. "I'd be interested in what you found, of course."

"We made some copies, you can take them away with you, if you like."

"The fee?"

"We know where to find the Guard, but if you've coin on you, I believe it came to three and twenty, all told."

Which Kate had, if she got supper in the mess hall instead of somewhere with more variety. She nodded. "Of course, ma'am."

"You said you had a question?"

"I'm interested in, in the integration of chronological magics and plants. Using plants, a pattern of varieties, to anchor the magics. It seems a very fragile sort of system."

"It does rather. We're not talking about yew trees, I suppose? I could see it with yew."

"No, ma'am. Roses. Three varieties, we think. Not all of them were blooming evenly. An interwoven mathematical chain."

The librarian tapped her fingers on the desk. "How long do you have?"

"This afternoon and evening, ma'am. Maybe a little first thing tomorrow morning."

"We close at six tonight, and we're closed Wednesday mornings. Let's see what we can find you, and perhaps we can send copies of other things along."

Kate nodded, feeling blown along by the planning. "Whatever works, ma'am."

"Your other question?"

"Magical applications of the Golden Mean in architecture. Um, in a form someone who's not an architect might understand. I understand the very basic principles, I think, but not how the magic fits."

"Ah, I know just the book or two for that. That's an easy one, actually. Here, let's find you a study room. More privacy, yes? Madam Aldebarana isn't in today." Madam Thornton gestured, then lead the way briskly to a little room in the other back corner of the reading room. "You sit right there, take your things out, and we'll bring you books. We've a list, so we'll give you the order they're most likely useful."

An hour later, and Kate's neck was aching. Two hours later, as they were closing up, her eyes were aching too. She carefully shut the book, making a list of copies she'd like if they were available, and a future list of questions and resources. As she was finishing, one of the younger librarians came up to ask, "This your list, Guard?"

Kate nodded.

"Beg pardon, but is your sister Gwen Davies?"

Kate blinked and then nodded. "She was. Gwen Morgan, now."

"I knew her at school. You look alike. Except where you don't, if you see what I mean?"

Kate did. Her sister was all the things Kate wasn't. Slim, ladylike. Near enough the same shade of auburn hair, but Gwen's was tame and well-behaved. Much like Gwen herself. "I don't get to see my family much - duty schedules and all. But I'd be glad to mention you in a note?"

The librarian shook her head. "I doubt she'd remember me." She considered, then said, "I'm glad I got to meet you." And then she snagged the cart, and pushed it away, back to the counter.

Kate was still looking after her when Madam Thornton came by, closing everything up. "You look puzzled? Asenath's very competent, but sometimes puzzles people."

"Puzzle's the word. She said she knew my sister, but - not the kind of knowing where she wanted to be mentioned?"

"Oh, she had a hard time in school. Not the classes, but everything else. Your sister didn't go to Schola, then?"

"No, ma'am. Alethorpe. She's got more than a touch of skill at healing magics. It's handy in a harbour inn, turns out."

Madam Thornton pursed her lips. "Oh, I imagine. Asenath's interest is what's in people's heads, trying to understand. She started with an apprenticeship at the Healing Temple, but they found she has an amazing knack with the indexing and practical charms, and sent her to me." Madam Thornton then smiled. "Also, she wasn't very good with actual patients. Quite effective, but blunt enough many of them found distressing. Saying things someone else would soften or dance around."

The librarian's affection for her assistant was obvious, warm and approving. Kate had a sudden rush of wishing someone would talk like that about her, and knowing it was unlikely they ever would.

She frowned, a sudden thought occuring to her, then said, "Has she done much with... would she mind if I asked her a question, ma'am?"

"She is a librarian. We are fond of questions, on the whole."

"Beg pardon, ma'am, then, if I can catch her up?"

"I'll bring the last things over. You go ask what you've thought of."

Kate hurried through the long reading room, and then came to a stop where Asenath was clearing the cart, before coughing. "Pardon?"

"Are you going to ask something that will make you feel awkward?"

Kate had to laugh at this. "Yes, I think so. About your speciality, though."

"Oh?" Asenath turned her head and said, "That's different." She shifted, turning to face Kate fully.

"Do you - are there books, or articles, or things, about the effects of people hurt in the War? Hurt in ways they won't fully recover from? The kind of thing that changes a life?"

Asenath's expression lit up. "Oh, there's not nearly as much as there ought to be, it's quite a big problem, and people don't talk about any of it. It's all parades for the war heroes, and stiff upper lip and people not talking about it, and how is it ever going to change if no one talks about it, that's what I want to know."

Kate blinked at the long sentence, but then she had to smile. "Like that. Exactly like that. Are there books or articles or anything at all?"

"I could write up a bibliography for you. If you liked. I mean. Most people don't like to talk about it. Or read about it. Or think about it. Like not thinking about it will make it go away."

Kate paused, considering. "But the people living with it, they never get a break. Least I can do is read about it."

It earned her a broad smile from Asenath. "Should I keep it here, or send it somewhere?"

Kate gave the address. "Seal it to me, would you? There's someone who might try opening mail, and I don't want him to." She handed over one of her cards, meant for the process. "You know how to use this?"

Asenath peered over her glasses, and then said, amused, "I am a properly trained librarian, thank you."

Scolded, Kate nodded. "And I owe you, for the copies?"

Asenath named a figure, and Kate counted it out. That was all but a few pennies of what she had in her purse, she'd have to at least tell Giles. Maybe he'd see about feeding her. She didn't think he wanted her to go without on the project expenses, even if the copies would be pocket change to someone like him. But she still hadn't got the reimbursement for the things she'd bought before they left.

Once all of that was taken care of, Kate waved to the two librarians, and set off from the library down to the clubs, walking along slowly. It was a beautiful night out, she kept passing people in the street in summer dresses and straw hats with beautiful ribbons. All the things she'd set aside, and yet still wondered about.

Her feet brought her to the Fox's Den, and she hesitated for a moment on the step, before murmuring to the attendant. "I'd like a word with Major Giles Lefton, if he's available. He knows I might stop in."

The attendant left her waiting in the foyer for several minutes, and as she stood there, she could hear voices, nearby. One she didn't recognise, talking about someone who wasn't quite the right sort of family. It was the kind of conversation she'd heard hundreds of times before, men trying to arrange a tumble.

It shocked her when she heard Giles, his voice echoing

much more clearly. "I'm not the sort to press. Not while we're working together." His voice turned lighter, teasing. There was something she couldn't hear as before there was another murmured interruption.

Did he think of her like that? Did he assume she thought of him like that? That she'd spread her legs for a tumble, once they were done. She actually didn't know much about Giles, not gossip. Some men, you heard a lot, their tendencies. Or that you shouldn't be in the room alone with this one or that one. That this one came up too close in training, that one liked to cop a feel.

On the other hand, she had been closer to him than to any other man in ages. She'd had to be, with him taking her arm, or her guiding his hand to a chair. She had thought the touch was routine, practical, and he'd certainly not taken advantage of it, even when he might have had an excuse to brush against her. But did he feel differently about it?

She heard a cough, then, behind her. "Guardswoman? This way."

The attendant led her straight in, and it was obvious why she'd heard Giles so clearly, he was tucked into a chair right by the door. "Sir, the Guardswoman."

The man Giles had been talking to had lingered. Tall, broad-shouldered, handsome enough. The sort who assumed women would fling themselves at his feet.

Giles turned his face to her, and Kate said, using the more formal name. "It's Davies, Lefton. I had some luck with the research, but made quite a few copies." She paused, trying to figure out how to say this so Giles might notice. "How did you want to handle the expenses?"

"Oh, Vale will do that in the morning. Why don't we meet for breakfast? Around nine, I know that's late for you, but I expect I'll be up talking here and there. If you want to take yourself off for the night."

Kate swallowed, but nodded. "Of course. Nine tomorrow. I'll work in getting the notes in order." Food in the mess for her, and all the noise and commotion to go with it, and people asking her about her assignment. A sandwich or pasty from the keep-fresh box was even less palatable, but would at least be less exhausting.

All of that was far less wearisome than the merest concept of explaining the question of funds to a man like Giles. Especially with other people close enough to hear.

EIGHTEEN

TRELLECH

The club got quiet for several hours, people filtering out for the evening's social gatherings. Giles amused himself with a conversation with one of the older members, arthritic enough these days to prefer a comfortable chair to standing around and being social.

The problem, of course, was that Giles got a series of digressions on this person's great grandfather, and that person's uncle, and this other one's third cousin twice removed. Punctuated, apparently at random, by comments on politics. Not the politics of today, that might actually be useful, but the politics of thirty years ago. Less relevant to his life, Giles thought. Everything had changed with the War.

Around half-nine, people trickled back in. Giles could hear them come in, small groups continuing the party, with ones and twos breaking off into conversations. Just as the clocks chimed ten, he heard, "Giles. A late-night snack?"

"Edgarton." Giles stood, and felt one of the staff appear, hearing the murmured "Sir," that was barely an interruption.

They made small talk while they got settled, while someone took their orders. The garden party had been good, the flowers had been brilliant and well-behaved, the Temple was doing well, the omens were promising for the coming year.

Edgarton settled into talking about who was there to be seen. The Healing Temple was neutral ground, in the best senses of that word, a place where people from different backgrounds could mingle, collaborate, and do a little good.

Giles appreciated the temple, but stayed far away these days unless he had an appointment. No one liked the reminder that his injuries couldn't be healed. Not him. Not the healers. Not the other people at the party. More to the point, large gatherings still baffled him. The people at St Dunstan's and at the training hall, they'd helped him figure out so many things, but no one had covered parties.

He remembered the days when he could track the room in glances and positioning. When he could follow the patterns of who was there, which ones he wished to talk to, and how to chain it all together. Now he couldn't do that. He had to rely on people coming to him, and whatever order they wanted to present themselves in.

He caught his mind drifting, murmured something to Edgarton, and at that point their food came. Finger foods, easy to manage.

"You had something specific in mind?"

"Davies." This part, at least, was easy enough to lay out.

"Not asking for an exchange, I hope?"

"No, she's more than satisfactory." He paused, trying to figure out how to put this. "Lord Sibley came out, yesterday. He demanded a report from her. I left it with him earlier today, and I have a copy for you with me. I thought that safer than leaving it in your office."

He heard the snort. "Oh, rather. Sibley's getting in on it, then?" It was a non-committal sort of answer.

"Anything you can tell me?"

"What did he try?" The fact Edgarton was asking him was suggestive, that Edgarton was more than a little at sea in the dynamics. Or alternately, protecting someone else.

"Sibley showed up, called her in from where we were working. He scolded her for being out of uniform, demanded she account for herself. When I came in, they were speaking in the Guard's Tongue."

"Ah." Edgarton's single syllable told Giles a lot. It was the tone that aimed to avoid trouble. Sibley was clearly an unsolveable variable in a gratuitously complex system of equations for more than Giles, then.

"Whatever I think of her, she did not deserve that..." He rummaged for words. "Discourtesy. Disrespect."

"You know I can't comment on other officers."

"No, but you can comment on Davies."

"If she was out of uniform, I feel sure it was your expressed preference. As I am also sure she has been working attentively in collaboration with you, according to her assignment."

"She's very sharp. Mentally. More than I expected."

"She is. Detailed, thoughtful." Edgarton paused for a bite of his food. "She notices gaps. I think that's at the heart of her defensive magics. It's a knack few people have."

Giles nodded, considering that explanation. "That fits. I know she's frustrated we haven't made more progress. I am too." He then ventured, "What can you tell us about the earlier attempts?"

"Did she ask Sibley?"

"She said he gave her a no that indicated any further question would be insubordination."

"Ah." There was a long pause, a minute or maybe two. Eventually, Edgarton said, "The early attempts were not at all successful. Destructive. Attempting to harm the roses is contraindicated." So someone had got hurt, and badly, in classified ways. Possibly ways that stirred up a hornet's nest, in either 'who' or 'how'.

"That is not much help." It was dashedly unspecific, for one.

"If there is a solution, it will be unconventional," Edgarton said. "That's all I can suggest. And of course, if we can provide resources." He let his voice trail off.

"Thus far, it appears to be reagents for potion applications and copies from the library. A ladder?"

Edgarton made a sound, like he was going to say something, then said, "The reagents are easy enough. Have Vale give me the expense reports." He did not comment about the ladder. After a moment, he added, "He made an appearance tonight. A well-dressed woman on each arm, in that gaggle of bright young things he goes about with."

Giles snorted. "He was rather pleased we'd be back tonight and not tomorrow. I expect he'll have a head and a half. He never remembers a palliative for hangovers."

"And you don't remind him where to get one."

"I'm not his keeper." Giles shook his head. "Davies."

"You keep coming back to her." Edgarton was definitely amused now.

"What do you know about her background? She told me a little, but I'm not clear on how she got where she is."

"Ah, that part she might not think to mention, no. What did she tell you?"

"Mostly what I got from her in the interview. Her parents have an inn, her sister's there now too, there's a handful of brothers in trade. Two uncles in the Guard, who she thought well of, in village postings."

"Davies is the only one to go to Schola. Her sister was at Alethorpe. Not top of her class, or she'd be at the Healing Temple or something like, but solidly good, and honestly, very useful where she is. One brother was at Forvie, one at Dunwich, one apprenticed to a shipbuilder directly out of grammar school."

Giles frowned. "I assume the shipping line of work, then? If they're on the seacoast? That's a very mixed family, mind."

"Shipping and navigation, yes. And fishing for the other. They make an interesting trio, actually, the kind that would lead to half a dozen broadside ballads if we were living in a time before radio and recordings."

Giles nodded, then said, "Not necessarily comfortable to grow up with, though. Especially as Kate's the youngest."

"Kate, is it?" Oh, that was a slip.

"She indicated as how I might. When I suggested she call me Giles."

"Alysoun will be fascinated. She's not seen Davies unbend that far."

"She was formal with Sibley. And generally with me. I don't think I'm that intimidating?"

Edgarton laughed outright. "Giles, you are everything she has been told to be wary of, in a particular way. Money, privilege, everything from your accent to your clothes to the fact you have a man." He paused for an instant. "And the fact you are one."

"Is that a problem?"

Edgarton waved a hand. "She's generally been more at ease with women. Whether she's friendly, I don't know. It's not a thing I'd be permitted to see. But agreeable. Laughing, smiling, bending a little. With men, she's very aware of the need to be a step ahead of them."

"Trouble from that quarter in the past?"

There was a long pause, and Giles was sure that Edgarton was weighing several dozen pieces of information. "I don't believe so. But I suspect someone she knew or was close to."

"And she didn't go overseas as a nurse or a driver, to be nearer the fighting?"

"She wanted to, I think, but she let us talk her out of it. She was more use here. Many people can drive, if they're brave enough, not so many could work through how to solve puzzles without easy answers." He added, lightly, "Did you look into her bohort record at Schola, then?"

"You did not mention she led Bear to the championships." Someone else from the Refuge had had the bohort records brailled in their entirety, and Giles had never been so glad for someone else's obsession. Once he'd thought to ask, he'd got a long chatty letter back from Atherton with as much detail as he'd hoped for.

"Mmm." He sounded entirely too amused.

Giles could not let that go unchallenged. "And when did you take an interest?" Edgarton made a small sound, and Giles went on. "Don't you deny you have, it's as plain on the nose on your face."

It earned him a long laugh. "Oh, I suppose. I like how she thinks. We need more people who think first, do after. She's good with the apprentices, I told you that. If she'd had family connections behind her, we'd have put her through officer training long since. Or, well, she'd have been an officer from the start."

"What did Master Trenton say about her? I know she worked with him."

"Surprisingly little. That way he has, of making you sort it out yourself. He was clear he'd recommend her for whatever she wanted, mind you."

Giles nodded. "So, given the overall situation and the available resources, how do you suggest we proceed?

"I'll copy out some notes from the earlier attempts. Entirely informally, of course, you haven't seen them."

"I'll not be seeing anything, no, so that's convenient."

Edgarton laughed. "Precisely. Other than that, I'd encourage Davies to explore her inclinations. Give her her head. I'll see if I can divert Sibley and his pack of ne'er-do-wells a bit."

"You really can't tell me about the earlier attempts?"

"My instructions have been very clear, Giles."

"It is a damnably annoying way to conduct an investigation, and you know it as well as I do." Giles was getting more and more frustrated at the lack of key information.

"That does not mean I can disobey orders. But I'll give you what I can. Redacted, but you can read between the lines sufficiently, I think."

"And the ladder?"

"No ladder." There was a long pause, and then Edgarton said, "They tried a ladder. It ended particularly badly. No ladder. Please don't have Davies liberate one from a nearby farm."

Giles frowned, but then nodded, and decided he had got as much as he was going to tonight. "Much appreciated. Every bit helps, as the saying goes. Am I going to owe you a favour?"

"Oh, a dinner party or two when you're back in town. Alysoun appreciates that she can pair you up with anyone from a glowing maiden to a frail old aunt and rely on you to make conversation. Though she hopes you'll think about someone of your own some day."

"Do not let her start matchmaking again. But I will gladly come to dinner when I'm back. You know that."

He heard Edgarton stand. "I'll make sure you get those notes tomorrow before breakfast. Shall I send one of the staff along?"

"Please. And ta, for the time and the drink." He leaned down to withdraw the file he'd brought with him. "Here's your copy."

"Always a pleasure. And always productive, to boot."

NINETEEN

TRELLECH, GUARD QUARTERS

"You're here?"

Kate startled, feeling the knock on the door, the intrusion of someone near her, before she consciously heard it. She took a breath, trying to calm her reflexes. Flipping the sign on her door was habit, but maybe it had been a mistake.

"Adria. Come in?" The younger woman stuck her head in, then the rest of her followed. Adria was in what passed for an off-duty uniform: a plain tunic top, split skirts, her hair back from her face but not pinned and charmed tightly into place.

The desk was a mess. Kate had brought her pasty back with her and demolished it, and an orange as well. That had been an unexpected treat. The peels were scattered on her plate, the napkin askew.

"I thought you were on assignment? In the country?" Adria sounded very uncertain.

"Just back for the night. I had research and Major Lefton had something to do."

"Oh." Adria slumped. "Only tonight?"

"Have a seat? Something's up." It wasn't a question. Adria wasn't subtle. Everything was high or low with her, very little middle ground. Kate thought it was an exhausting way to live, mind you, but Adria seemed not to care.

"Mm-hmm."

Kate sighed. "Adria. C'mon. I've got to be up early, and you do too. And I don't know when I'll be back."

That got a nod, then a "Same thing. Drills." Adria closed the door behind her and perched on the end of the neatly made bed.

"They're not taking you seriously."

"No. They take you seriously. Why?"

Kate shrugged. "The same reasons we've always talked about. They respect the Schola training, even if they sort of don't want to. I made it clear what my skills are. And I rubbed the right noses in both those facts a few times."

"And I can't do that." Adria sounded dejected.

"You can't change your life so you went to Schola. But you can do the other two. Do your drills, work with the masters, get yourself into the extra trainings, a few. It will help."

"It takes so long." Adria drew the last word, sounding for all the world like a six-year-old told she had to wait for her birthday.

"Everything has a rhythm." Kate paused, then said, "None of them have - hurt you, more than in drilling? Tried to get you alone?"

"No, I've been watching out for what you told me."

Kate settled back in her chair, tucking a foot up under her other leg. "Good. You tell your captain if there's any trouble like that. Or another officer. Or the staff healers."

"That's part of what they're there for, yes, I remember

the lecture from last time." But it made Adria smile a little, shyly. "I wish you were a captain."

Kate snorted. "It seems unlikely. I don't have the connections, or the training, or..." She shrugged. "I'm decent at some things, but being in charge of other people, that's a whole different set of skills. I have enough trouble taking care of myself."

Adria gestured at the room. "Your quarters are always clean and ready. Well, unless you haven't cleaned up yet? I can take that down for you." She nodded at the plate.

"You want the orange peel for your salves."

"Well, yes, but that's just proper. Using all the parts. Such a treat to have them for supper." Adria paused. "Was your Major Lefton at the garden party, then?"

"I don't think so, no." Kate paused. "I don't know if he goes to social things?"

"I thought officers did. That was part of why they had the shiny uniforms?"

"Someone's been pulling your leg again, love." Adria was a dear, but she could be very gullible and she'd had a more sheltered apprenticeship than some. She was just out of it now, and trying to figure out the larger Guard.

Adria blushed, then flinched, her head retreating into her tunic collar.

Kate sighed, and offered, "Officers are complicated, you know that." She considered, then said, "Major Lefton is one of the war-blinded. He has a house, here in Trellech, he does maths, but he will not serve as an officer again, the same way. I think he's classed as a consultant, not an analyst, but I'm not sure? He doesn't know the Guard Tongue, he's not one of us." Which made her realise that while she reported to him on this project, it was not the formal chain of command she was used to.

"I've never known - I mean, not to talk to - any of the consultants. Not many of the analysts, even."

"Aren't you due to rotate into Continuing Magics?"

"Two months from now. Escort duty is so boring."

"It lets you meet people, though, and sometimes that's interesting. And it shows you're reliable. If you pay attention and do things right even when it's boring and there's no reason you needed to be there, then it's easier to trust you when things might go wrong."

"I suppose. But it's still boring."

"Patience. There's a reason it's one of our virtues."

"We live in Prudentia, not Patientia. I'd rather be prudent than patient."

Kate laughed at that. "Well, perhaps. But that doesn't mean we can ignore patience. Even if prudence suggests there are things we have to be careful in handling, doesn't it?"

"That doesn't explain officers, though."

"No, it doesn't." She frowned. Master Trenton had talked to her about it when she was at school. And then people since. But a lot of the time, it was people hinting. One thing she'd decided about officers is that most all of them were incapable of saying a thing plainly. Unless, of course, it was an order they wanted obeyed, in which case they could be most clear.

"Officers are responsible for other people. Seeing the bigger picture. Not just what we're doing right now, but moves and moves ahead."

"Like bohort."

Kate nodded. "The matches about puzzles and sequences, more than the ones about who's strongest or fastest or whatever, yes."

Adria swung her foot, thinking hard. "What's Major

Lefton like?"

"He played bohort. Quite well. Not quite my standard, I think, but close."

"That's not convincing me you couldn't be an officer."

Kate grinned. Adria teasing was a good sign. "No, but it's mostly me bragging about my skills. Just a little." It gave her enough time to think of what else she wanted to say. "He thinks things through. He goes away and thinks about them. Even if he thinks I'm wrong." She considered. "Maybe especially if he thinks I'm wrong. To see if I'm right."

"So he's one of the good ones."

"Mmm. Yes. He is. He can be stubborn, but people get to be stubborn. He listens. He lets me try things. Some of it's working, at least a little." Saying it out loud, she began to realise how rare that had been. Edgarton approved of her, but he rarely said as much. Giles was generous with his praise, and clear in his correction. She was beginning to wonder how she'd go back to something else.

"Not so much as you want?" Adria's question yanked her back to the present.

"Well, if it was as much as we wanted, I'd be there, not here, sorting it out, so not yet. But we have hope."

"What'll you do after?"

"Wherever they send me. You know that. It's the only way to get enough experience to maybe get a say. Do what I'm told, as well as I can."

Adria frowned, chewing on her lip. "It's not fair."

Kate said, "Fair's not the issue. Working with what we've got is. Think that one through, let me clean up." She turned to tidy up the tray and plates, wrapping the orange peel up in a spare clean handkerchief in a tidy make-shift pouch. She set the tray on the table by the door then washed her hands in the bathing room sink.

Coming back to the desk, she poured two mugs of tea from the keep-warm pot and passed one over to Adria. The younger woman immediately cupped her hands around it. Kate frowned.

"Are you feeling cold, then? Still?"

Adria looked at her hands, then back up. Quietly, she said, "Maybe?"

"How bad is it?" Kate's voice got firmer.

"Like." She stopped, then started again. "I was thinking what you said, how to describe it, and it's like being out in November. Not December or January, and not up on the moors proper, where the wind's bad, but a good breeze. That's okay, isn't it, that's not too bad?" Only then she ran out of breath, and there was a catch in her inhale that Kate didn't like at all. Especially since this was July.

Kate frowned. "It's not good, is the thing. Come on. We're going to the healers."

"We? I don't want to be a bother, and you said you had to be up early."

"Won't be the first time I've gone short on sleep."

TWENTY

TRELLECH

By three in the morning, Giles had given up on getting to sleep.

It took him like this, sometimes. At St Dunstan's, they'd said it could happen with people whose eyes no longer told them when it was night or day. They said the mind got confused, not sure whether to sleep or rest. He'd had less trouble with it recently, being outside examining the manor, but he'd been under cover most of the last day.

He kept turning conversations over in his mind, snatches of sentences coming back to him. He had not had a great memory for conversations before. Now, when words on paper were harder to come by, and fewer people came to talk to him, he found sentences would circle in his head.

Take the conversation with Edgarton, for example. The man had taken an interest in Kate, one that sounded avuncular or mentoring, rather than something more distasteful. Mind, Edgarton adored his wife, and she him, a degree of mutual affection considered quite unusual in their social circles. That Alysoun approved of Kate said a lot by itself.

She suffered no fools and definitely did not tolerate incompetence.

Edgarton's comment about the family intrigued him. A very mixed family to go to four of the five schools and an apprenticeship. Giles knew that who went to which school was often a matter of family focus and preparation. Unsurprisingly, those familiar with the Schola exams, who had gone to tutoring houses, did much better than those from families who had no idea what to expect.

That variety, though, suggested a family of strong but individual magic. Native intelligence, an ability to learn quickly, or they'd not have passed the exams. More so, though, a calling to the magic each school specialised in.

Giles had a sudden desire to meet the sister, to figure out what the differences were between them.

Some women in the Guard were hard-edged, like their swords or knives or the magic from a wand. Kate had not come across that way to him, not in her first interview and not in their work since. She was scarcely soft, but it was more like the refined flexibility of a bow.

Giles gave up, and got up, pulling on a dressing gown. He found his way to an easy chair near the window where he could let the moonlight touch his skin, some hint of the outside. Settling, he thought about the different approaches.

Some of his friends liked to sort people by house - even those who had not gone to Schola. Two preferred to sort by Platonic element. Air, fire, water, earth. He'd thought Kate a creature of Earth, like the Bear of her house at Schola. Her public persona came across as solid, sturdy, even grounded.

The more he thought it over, though, the more he thought that was wrong. Edgarton had been clear that her siblings were all drawn to water. Healing arts, that was soundly there. Shipping and navigation, of course. No trade, no craft, was solely one thing or another, but he could almost see the shape of the water running through the family, shifting and slowly wearing away. Edgarton had said that she noticed gaps, and water certainly did that, flowing to where the space was.

He laughed, then, realising. She'd done it to him, Kate had. She'd begun as formally as anyone might ask or expect, and yet there had been that slow unbending, a gentle thaw. Not even of her, so much as of him. That he had been shaped to find it easier to speak with her, to treat her as a partner.

Giles suspected she was doing it almost entirely unconsciously. Oh, she might know the effect she wanted, lean toward it. But the way she did it, that was instinct, not artifice. Only a gift for that particular approach could lead her to say the right thing. The moment where she might encourage a fleeting vulnerability, a shift in the wave, enough to change things. And only a gift, a talent, might wield it as gently and deftly as she did.

He knew what it was like, to see someone use those skills deliberately. Alysoun did it, for that matter. Edgarton was a man of rational thought and reason, all the intellectual skills of air, if he could keep himself focused. Though he had the Fox's sharp regard for his own station and his own benefit, as a flavour.

Giles let his mind drift, then, thinking through how those different combinations might suggest answers to their problems. Kate had been thorough in her investigation, he knew that. She had talked through each step with him, reported the results, organised her notes to provide summaries on demand.

That, though. He paused, trying to take a step back from his assumptions.

The conversation with Edgarton had made it clear she had an instinct, if it could be applied. So far, they had been rational, logical, scientific. Her whim, circling the manor counter-clockwise, was the biggest advance they'd had yet. Logically, he knew there were magics where direction mattered. His Ritual classes in school had been full of them. But many of them were impractical for daily work. Who wanted a home you could only approach from the left?

Giles stopped, letting his mind drift backward. He wished they'd had a full accounting of what those earlier efforts had tried. Since they did not, perhaps they should go back and try anything that they knew was not strictly contraindicated. No cutting the flowers or the brambles, for example.

More than that, though, he should give Kate her head, encourage her instincts. He wanted to discover where that water would flow, given an opportunity. It might take him by surprise, or both of them, but it could scarcely be a worse idea than their current approach. And something in him wondered what she could do if she were fully given her head.

Giles mulled it over more. The other thing, the thing he'd not really taken seriously, perhaps, was figuring out why the manor had disappeared. Kate had described it as dating to Henry II, but they had discovered records of the manor up through the reign of the last Plantagenet, Richard III. The time of the Pact.

He considered. History had never been his strong suit in school. But he knew enough, and he'd had plenty of time to read more in the early days of being bogged down in the trenches in France. The disappearance of the manor must be related to the Pact somehow, but how, that was the question.

He hoped Kate had found something in her research. Giles rummaged through his memories. The Pact was between the people with magic, and the magical races of the British Isles. There had been something about preserving the family lines of magic, and avoiding undue interference by non-magical sorts. It wasn't, as some thought, cold iron that was the problem, but something else, more complex and difficult to label.

That didn't explain the manor, though. Did it hold something of one of the Fatae? Not the Belin, they were in Wales, more than Oxfordshire, and of the deep earth. Not the shape-shifting races, the selkies or wulvers or kelpies. Not the hidden people of the air. This was more shaped by hands than anything he'd ever heard about any of them.

Perhaps it was the Pact itself, when Richard III, desperate to protect magic in the land, had made that agreement with them. It had been an agreement as sharp-edged and shattering to the way things were as the Magna Carta of his ancestor had been, or the invasion of the Conqueror, or the Romans, further back in the past.

None of that explained why the manor had reappeared now, in what seemed to be an ordinary summer. If it had appeared in 1914, he might have believed it some omen for the coming war. If it had been in 1919, it might have marked the era after the War.

Even those, personally and globally shattering though they might be, seemed too small. Since it had disappeared, there had been wars and fire and battles and death, all over the country. For all the death and destruction of the Great War, it differed in scale, and was further away, to boot. Not on English soil.

It made him wonder again what Sibley was up to. Giles had heard the rumours of people who thought about a next war, already. Surely Sibley wasn't one of them, that would require a more farreaching mind than Sibley had demonstrated thus far. Nothing he could think of answered the question at all well.

Giles shook his head, and then moved to settle in bed again, since sitting up was doing no one any good. Perhaps Kate would have a better idea in the morning.

TWENTY-ONE

TRELLECH

"Here, Guardswoman. Sir, do you need more coffee?" Kate followed the waiter into the breakfast room, where Giles was seated at a table by himself. He waved a hand. "When you come back for her order. Kate, good morning." There was a slight edge to his voice.

She did her best not to yawn, and settled in the chair, letting the waiter push it in for her. "Good morning, Giles." She wasn't sure what to say next, after overhearing him yesterday evening, and then a long night of making sure Adria was seen by the Healers and taken seriously.

They ended up sitting in silence for several minutes. It gave Kate a chance to glance at the menu, then the waiter returned. Giles ordered more coffee, and did not comment on her request for black tea, or for rather a lot of food. He seemed to be waiting for her, but finally he asked, "How was your evening?"

"The research went well." She paused, trying to figure out whether to say anything. "I'm sorry, I was up much later than I expected, helping someone in quarters."

"Oh?" She got the sense it was more polite than anything, then his voice sharpened. "Why?"

"I convinced a friend - a junior, just out of apprentice-ship - to see the Healers."

"You had reason, I assume?" Still sharp.

"She had a nasty cough." Whether to tell the truth, or fudge, that was the question. Truth seemed the better road. "Certain people have a taste in unpleasant magical jokes."

"In this case?"

"A vile curse sewn into the back of the laundry label on her uniform jacket. She was well on the way to pneumonia."

Giles frowned. "Isn't that a matter for the officers to act on?"

Kate nodded, then remembered to say something. "It is, yes. That would be why I was up early. To make a proper report as soon as the officer of the day arrived."

She could see Giles doing the math in his head. Easy sums for him. "How late were you up?"

"Past two."

"And you were up before six, to be there when the day shift started."

"Yes." Kate didn't expand on it.

"And not enough time between that and meeting me to nap. You could have sent a note along." He paused for a moment, then went on. "Clearly, you should be permitted a pause. I don't expect we'll see Vale much before noon. If you'd like a room here, I'm sure they can arrange something."

"Wouldn't you rather have someone handy? To talk to, if nothing else?" Maybe if they talked more, she could figure out what he'd meant last night, or how she felt about it.

"I can entertain myself. We need you in good shape for the next phase, whatever we decide that is."

Kate paused, then nodded. "As you wish." The dismissal smarted, but she couldn't argue with it.

"Do you want to discuss your research now?"

"I'd rather save it, for being back there, if you don't mind. Though I do..." She cut off, and he caught it.

"Out with it."

"Do you have - I'm sorry to ask? But I spent my last coins on copies at the library, and there's a few items the research suggested. Gardening supplies, nothing very expensive?"

"No gold-touched roses, then?"

"No, just bone meal and blood meal."

Giles startled. "Now I do feel we've wandered into a fairy tale."

"They're what you feed roses. Sparingly, but they found me a recipe from the period, for magical roses, a potion of sympathetic magic. It links the liquid you apply in small amounts to the roots to a store of the meal in some stable location - the shed we have, for example."

"Goodness. That seems thorough. Within your alchemical abilities?"

"First year, really. Nothing at all difficult. Easier than baking."

Giles laughed at that, and said, "I've never baked, so that's not helpful."

"Baking requires more precision, then. This is - oh, rounding to the next five. Baking wants the precision of some decimal places, comparatively. Slightly more complex than tea."

He half-saluted her, a little flip gesture of his hand. "That puts it in better array, yes." Then, more seriously. "I didn't realise the money would be quite that much of a concern. Let me hand you my purse, take what you need. Keep your receipts, make a note it was from my purse."

"Are you sure?"

Giles waved a hand. "Should be a variety in there, a few larger coins, save those. Vale's due to do another run to the bank. But there should be plenty for gardening."

Kate opened the purse, rummaging in it, then she said, "There's enough for what I need, sir, but there's only a five in here, nothing bigger."

Giles blinked. "Goodness. Well, take that, we'll sort the rest out later."

Kate nodded, extracting the coin, then pocketing it. She had finished writing out a receipt, one for him and one for her records, when the food arrived and she tucked in.

"We used to say that sleep could substitute for food, or food for sleep, and I think that's true. Is that why you were hungry?"

"That, sir, and I allowed the Healer to use some of my energy. Not all of it, of course, I'm quite aware I'm on duty. About what I'd have used if I'd done my proper exercise this morning instead."

She wasn't sure what he'd make of it, and what it got her was a broad laugh. "Oh, so there is a fracture in your insistence on following all the rules you're given?"

Kate smiled back. "Well, that, and the Healer gave me a pass for the day. She said I was doing more good as I was."

He was quiet for a moment, then he said, "You have been busy. And we've not even got to the research."

"Was your evening pleasant?"

"Oh, well enough. Several conversations. A few people curious about you."

She stiffened, then said, cautious now, "Any particular reason? I hope I've not offended anyone."

"Well, some puzzlement why I'd pick you, and not one of the others they presented me with." There was no way for her to ask. Not at all. He let the silence draw out. Then, he laughed. "You will not ask, will you?"

"It's not my place." She hesitated for a moment, then added "Sir."

That made him frown. "Did I offend?"

She shook her head, forgetting he'd not get that. He hadn't, not exactly.

"Kate?" She looked up, and then his voice was stern. "You have to tell me things, I can't see them."

She shivered, and said, "Pardon, sir. I'm not fit company. May I be excused?"

He frowned again, then nodded, waving a hand. "Go see to the purchases. We'll aim to leave at noon. If you're done early I'll leave word they should find you a space to rest."

She nodded, then murmured. "I'll be back before noon, thank you sir." Then she fled. It wasn't brave, it wasn't polite, it wasn't at all proper. But it was the only thing she could think of, because she'd got tangled in something she didn't understand.

There were things she knew she didn't understand, would never understand, because they weren't things anyone explained, or in books. They were the things you learned by being born in the right family, in the right way. By having someone reach out a hand to guide you, whether that was a parent or an aunt or uncle.

Kate was well out on the street, halfway to the centre of the city before she realised where she had wound up. She ducked into one of the small pocket parks, found a bench. This was Albion, there was usually a bench. Enough for her to pretend everything was all right hard enough to make it true. Or at least seem true to everyone else.

She took fifteen minutes, but then she could gather herself and make the walk to the garden supplies store someone had told her about. It turned out to be a narrow building in the crafter's district, crammed between a carpenter and a potter. There was a line, which left her wedged between a fussy older woman with a list of particular demands and a pair of younger society ladies who were chattering away about the gossip from the Healing Temple party. One was dark haired and sharp-boned, the other with auburn hair in an unusually short bob.

"And did you see Phil? Turning up with Alcmene and Delen Gordon of all people, one on each arm? I'm surprised he doesn't cause more scandal."

"He doesn't get out like he ought to, hero like him, poor thing," sighed the other. "That dreadful clerking job he has for his shut-in cousin. It's a shame, he could take me to Flanders anytime."

It had the tone of a euphemism, but Kate could not make either head or tail of it, particularly not while she was getting over the shock of realising they must be talking about Vale. It sounded salaciously like something sexual, but hearing it in the garden shop meant she could only think of the line of poetry about poppies.

She had to wait another twenty minutes to explain what she needed, and that she needed specific things, but in small amounts. It took longer yet to get out of the place without explaining the entire layout of the roses and the garden they sat in.

Gardeners were remarkably persistent, if this was any sample of the type. On the other hand, she left the shop with half a dozen further resources. She also had the names of two rose experts who, the owner said, would be delighted to consult on matters of old roses.

W hen they finally got back to the house, Giles was in a foul mood. Like the other two, apparently.

Vale had a hangover. A particularly nasty one, by the way he had snapped at the portal staff. He'd insisted on stopping at the inn at the other end for a drink, and then he'd made no friends yelling at the innkeeper about the noise.

Mercifully, Vale been obliged to drive home, and it at least kept him up front of the carriage. Giles was sure the sun wasn't doing him any favours.

Kate had been terse when she arrived back at the club after her errands. One might reasonably describe it as prickly. Giles had tried to start a conversation several times and only got the briefest of replies. He gave up after his "Did you get what you needed?" got only "Yes" in response.

When they pulled up to the house, Vale stomped off to see to the horse, and Giles said, "This evening, we'll talk more."

"If you wish."

It was on the verge of uncivil. Giles made his way up to

his room. He changed into country clothes: comfortable slacks, a tunic. Nothing fancy or formal. That done, he settled down at the desk. He spent the next hour making sure everything was in order.

It was. Even the money. He was just finishing up when Vale knocked. "Come."

"Me, Giles. The horse is put away, your papers are in the library."

"Did you manage to get to the bank?"

"Here's the petty cash for your wallet." Vale came over and handed over a small pouch. "Coins, as you said."

"I must have miscounted." Giles said it easily. "Kate mentioned I had less than I'd thought."

"Does she have expenses?"

"Copying, and some things to try with the roses. Nothing extravagant."

He could hear Vale's snort. "What, she can't cover them?"

"Guard's salary doesn't stretch that far without help, Vale." He frowned. Kate had had other expenses; surely Vale had seen to those.

"Well, that's for her to manage, isn't it?"

Vale didn't do a good job of managing his own money, mind you. Giles said, more firmly, "It's a consulting expense, it shouldn't come out of her pocket."

"I'll see to her receipts." It was grudging. "Anything else tonight?"

"No, thank you. I'll be down for dinner, but you can take yours how you want."

"My room, then. Don't care for being fussed at by a housekeeper. I can make my own bloody pot of tea."

"As you wish."

He heard Vale go off without a by your leave, and the

door closing. Giles settled in to taking a few notes, thinking through what he wanted to discuss.

Supper was made of equal parts silence and Mrs Hitchcock fussing, both of which were more tiring than he wanted. When she'd cleared the table, he said, "Kate, the library? We should talk through the next steps, and I've something for you to review."

"That's what we're here for." It was less grudging than Vale, but still rather terse.

Giles waited until they were both settled in the library, and then said, "I had an interesting chat with Edgarton last night. Unofficially."

He felt, more than heard, a stiffening of her body. Some slight inhale, a rustle of clothing, a shift of a slipper on the floor. "Oh?"

"He was complimentary about your skills, but I knew that. He passed along some new information. Informal notes on what they tried before they put me on the case. Would you have a read and tell me about it?"

"Vale didn't transcribe it?"

"Fewest eyes best, don't you think? If you don't mind reading it out?"

She paused, then stood, and he held out the case. "It's in here." She took the case, but didn't return to her seat, he could hear her breathing near him, close enough to touch. "Is there a problem?"

She retreated to her seat, and he heard her open the case before she said, "I had a difficult time last night. And beyond that, it's not my place. I was reminded of that, last night."

Giles frowned. "Is something wrong? Can I be of help?"

"Thank you, no." It was politely said, but as firm and unyielding as the manor walls with all their roses. She turned pages, the rustling suggesting she was skimming to get a sense of the pages before going back.

He waited, willing himself to be patient.

After a couple of minutes, she said, "I'm not sure what to make of this." Her voice was not warm, but it was curious, intrigued, and that was promising. It was at least not "sir" and prickliness.

"Start at the beginning of the file?"

"Can you tell me, more precisely, where this came from? What Lord Edgarton said about it?"

"He said it was informal notes from the early attempts. He did not mention the precise source, unless there's something in there. It is redacted in places, I gather."

She rummaged through the paper again, flipping pages, back and forth a couple of times, then "May I rearrange them?"

Giles gestured in the direction of the table. "Whatever makes sense to you."

She was several minutes more, and then rustled them, putting them into some sequence. "All right. I am ..." She paused. "I am honestly rather dismayed."

"That sounds like a problem. Sit? Tell me about it?"

"The notes are very scattered. In three sets of handwriting. And they are just ... not at all logical about the problem."

"They tried to force the gates, I assume?"

"They did. That's the attempt that ended very badly. Three people still in the Healing Temple, one may not recover at all. That's all sketched out in the margins." She paused. "I almost get the impression they were expecting some sort of active defence mechanism. Only I wonder why they assumed that."

"What else?" There was more.

"They didn't try some obvious things. I'd wondered about a ladder, over the wall. Or dropping something on the other side. I'd assumed they tried it."

"Edgarton was very clear we should not try a ladder. The specific order was to avoid having you go liberate one from a nearby farm." Giles frowned. "Were you thinking of dropping something over the side?"

"I'm not sure if the manor would like it? Think it was an invasion?"

"Have we tried pushing something through the metal gates with a stick?"

There was a long pause. "No?" Then, she murmured. "I wondered why they hadn't tried that either."

"What do we offer a manor?" This was not an area he'd studied.

"I have the bone and blood meal, but that's for the roses, not for the manor. Something with a little magic? Something non-threatening, a stone set to glow, something like that?"

"Just enough of the personal, you mean?"

"I think that's the way to go. We're not..." Then she stopped. "Do you have a seal, a signet ring? And some sealing wax?"

"I do, yes."

"You come from the right sort of family. Would it be a name the manor might have known, the people who created the gates."

"We're thinking it was closed off around the time of the Pact?"

"Mm-hmm."

Giles tapped his fingers on the arm of the chair. "I think we packed my writing box without taking anything out. In which case I've a seal that comes down my mother's side of the family that dates to the right period." .

"Then - if I might write some sort of message, and we use your seal, and a small amount of magic from both of us?"

Giles nodded. "That is as logical and practical a solution as anything suggested so far. Rather better than pitching things over the walls and hoping they aren't pitched back out at us."

Kate snorted, and Giles was glad to hear her unbending a little. "Then the roses."

"What did you find in your research? Besides the bone and blood meal?"

"More of a history of the building. Nothing we didn't suspect, but I found conclusive evidence that it was no longer being included in census documents after the Pact went into place."

"And the owner at that point?"

"That's where it gets curious. There are a lot of legends attached. There's the one I mentioned, about Rosamund Clifford being poisoned by Eleanor of Aquitaine in a labyrinth made of roses. I think that might be part of why there are roses? That legend, or something like it. But the manor itself was here then, but much smaller, and the later growth seems to be under a Master Florey, an alchemist and astrologer of some significant reputation."

"Cryptography?"

"They didn't use that word, but people talked about his fondness for patterns and puzzles. Does that mean something?"

"You've thought for quite a while that someone planted the rosebushes in particular patterns for a reason, not just the mathematical pleasure of it."

"It seems so ridiculous when I try to talk about it. I couldn't even really explain it to the librarians, and they were very kind."

"Some magics protect themselves, had you considered that? There's the rumours about the Fatae and their ways, though those aren't the only option. I did wonder, when going counter-clockwise." Giles waved a hand. "How detailed are those notes?"

There was a long pause again. "Scattered." Her voice had got softer, less certain. "You think that's why?"

"It's possible. I found - even with Edgarton, who knows about the problem - I found myself disinclined to go into details about most of it." Edgarton had been unwilling to speak up about a number of things, and Giles wondered how much that was related.

"What does that mean, then?"

"It means we go carefully, we think through what we're doing, and we take good notes for our own purposes. But we don't - likely can't - rely on them being useful to other people."

"Fair enough. Should I read through all of this for you, then?"

"You had better. I might spot something you don't, or you might spot something in reading them aloud. Any clue might help. Would typing bother you? I could take notes while we go."

"No?" She sounded cautious.

"And take whatever notes make sense to you. Pause if you need to."

The resulting process kept them up quite late, nearly to midnight, but it had a satisfying feel of progress about it.

"You think this will work?"

Kate rubbed her hands dry on the kitchen cloth tucked into her pocket. "There's only one way to find out."

"Walk me through the steps one more time, please?"

Giles was nervous; she could tell. It didn't show so much in his body, or even his voice. But her eyes kept flicking to the small movements of his hands, as if he wanted to read the world laid out in front of him.

"I made an oil for the gateposts, and I've made an extract for the roses. I walked around, in the proper direction, feeding a little of the extract to the base of each bush. We have the stones - one for you, one for me, that we've placed energy in, using Foxstone's Principal Method."

"And I agree, Foxstone is more than venerable enough, it should be recognisable, if anything is."

"And there's cream and honey and oatcakes on the tray."

"Because?"

"Because the Good Folk, the Fatae, they like cream and honey. And it never hurts to sweeten an offer."

"Is that something you learned at home? The folk charms?"

"It's..." Kate stopped. "It's getting your hands dirty. An offering that means something."

"But this came from a store?"

"It did not!" Kate couldn't keep the outrage out of her voice. "I was up this morning. There's a farmer, Mrs Hitchcock arranged for me to meet him, when I asked about the local lore. He keeps cows, and I was down there at dawn, for the milking. The honey's from a jar I keep for this kind of magic. I made the oatcake after that. I'll not be insulting Them."

"From?" He paused, sounding embarrassed. "The honey, I mean. Where's it from?"

"From the family hives, back home. I help out, when I can, when I get a weekend off-duty."

Giles put his hands up. "Pax, Kate, pax."

She shook her head, and then took a deep breath, letting it out slowly. "I have thought this through." Other people might think her tone insubordinate, but she hoped Giles would not. Even if she wasn't sure what he thought of other things.

"I know you have. Just, you think differently than I do. Even when we're talking about the same subject, and we've read the same things."

"That's the point of collaborating, Giles. If we thought the same way, there would be no reason to."

"A veritable touch. So. Do we need to do anything else?"

"I have the tray, the stones, the cream, the honey, the cakes. Your sealed letter of introduction. I think we're as ready as we're getting."

"Do the roses seem any different? Since you went around with the extract?"

"It's hard to tell. The light keeps changing, as the sun moves."

"Go on, then."

Kate took a breath. "Come up closer with me? Here, let me get you in the right place, and then I'll bring the tray, and push it in."

She let him slip his arm into her elbow, bringing him about ten feet back from the gates. Space for them to open toward them, if they were going to. "Right, and now the tray. I'll be back here in a minute."

She set the tray on the ground, in front of the gates. Taking a breath, she carefully pushed it across the gravel of the road, into the arch at the bottom of the gates. She'd noticed it from the beginning. It wasn't much, four or five inches, but she'd found shallow bowls in the kitchen, things that would fit under the gate.

She half-felt a slight shift, like the reverberation of a drum without the sound. Once she'd pushed it fully into the grounds of the manor, she stepped back, beside Giles.

"Tell me what you see." It was an order, but a gentle one, the insistent need of someone wanting to learn a new thing.

Kate took a long breath, and then said "I just pushed it under the gate, and there's a sort of shimmer. Like the heat over a stove. I can't see anything different in the tray, but the dishes are all low."

They both heard the creak that followed, it sounded almost like a clap of thunder, age-old metal whining against metal. She couldn't see the roses moving, but they were parting, somehow, making a space that hadn't been there.

"The gate?" Giles spoke quickly and quietly.

"It's opening. Slowly, but it's opening." There were more creaks and groans, then she murmured, "It's open about halfway. Are we going through?"

"Oh, I think so, yes. Don't you?" He made it sound like he was asking her for an afternoon garden walk followed by a decorous tea.

"Let me grab a few things, first. Be right back." She turned, moving to gather up the things she had in mind, if this had worked.

Notebooks and pencils. Plant guidebook. Measuring device. Plumb line. A variety of small stones and a handful of copper pennies, to test for magical effects. A little bag of powder, to show engraved lines more clearly. Oh, yes, and the flasks of tea. She considered, then added a loop of rope to the clip on the outside of her bag, and said "All right."

"What did you bring?"

"This and that. Things that might be useful." He settled his arm into hers, and she took a breath. "Shall we?"

"If you feel ready, lead on."

They made their way slowly toward the gate. Kate wasn't sure if she expected something to arc and hurt them, or something to glow and enchant them, or something else. The gate remained resolutely a gate. Nothing odd seeming about it except that it was open now, and had not been before, and the roses that had seemed to bind it shut had unravelled their tendrils.

She paused just before the line on the driveway the gate had covered. "We're right before the gate now."

"Go slowly. And let's try not to touch the gates, shall we? For the moment."

Kate nodded and considered. The metal had opened to leave quite a large gap, a good eight feet across. Not the full width of the opening in the wall, that was big enough to allow a sizeable wagon in, twelve feet by their measurements. But the gap was more than enough for two people walking arm in arm, even stepping around to avoid the tray.

"And we're through the gate." Kate paused, just far enough inside that if the gate began to close, they'd be on this side, not the other. She paused, with a "Let me figure out how to explain it sensibly."

Giles waited, with much better grace than Kate would have managed. She looked around, taking it in, then began. "Ahead of us is the manor. Henry II or so, as we thought, a large open U, the open end facing toward us. Maybe the original entrance was on the other side? There's a large garden, extending this way, with the main road or path in the centre. The gardens on either side are in a mediaeval style, rectangular beds, or square. I'm not much of a gardener, but they look well-maintained, not overgrown with weeds."

"Roses?"

"Roses, along the walls. But there are other flowers. I'd need the guidebook to identify some of them." She kept looking. "Over by one end, there's a plot that looks like a kitchen garden. Not vegetables but herbs, maybe, or culinary flowers."

"I thought I smelled that, earlier. The first day."

"That seems very likely, sir. It's rather extensive."

"And there's no gatehouse?"

"No." She looked around. "No buildings other than the wall within a good fifty feet of us. No kitchen, either, at least not as a separate building."

"And the structure itself?"

"Stone and timber frame and mortar, isn't that the word?"

"Wood and white plaster? I know what you mean."

"I thought that was later, though. More Tudor?"

"You're thinking of the buildings in Trellech, aren't you? They're from that period, but people were using the technique quite a way before that. Are there towers or any particular features? What about the windows?"

"There are some?" Kate was very unsure. She felt stupid, clunky, completely unprepared.

She must have been obvious about it, because Giles squeezed her arm, took a breath, and then said. "That can help us date when someone last lived here. When it was built, they'd likely only have been partly glazed, just the top, with shutters or openings below. Glass was very expensive."

"Oh!" Kate peered at the windows, and then said "I see some shutters, but I think there's glass all the way down. We'd have to get closer to be sure."

"And the building?"

"The ends on this side seem more recent, somehow? I can't tell why I think that, a difference in the paint on the plaster? Or the way it fits together?"

"As if they had expanded sometime in the past?"

"Something like that. It's well done, just it's a little different."

"That might explain why there's no kitchen building. Is there a door over by what you think is the kitchen garden?"

Kate peered over at it. "I think so, but on the side, not facing the garden." She paused, then said "Did I miss something, in my reading? About the windows?"

"Oh, no. I know because one of the family homes, the one I spent winters in, it was built around the same time. There was a huge fuss about dealing with the windows. The upper glass is still original there, and the lower is much less exciting, only two hundred or so."

Kate blinked several times, and then said "Oh." What

else could one say to that kind of thing, living somewhere that old. Even Schola had been rebuilt and renovated and rearranged, just since her time there.

"Let's see if the kitchen door works."

"Why there?"

"Well, people are perhaps less likely to put the really horrible wards on the kitchen door. It's a dreadful annoyance to deal with them when your hands are full."

TWENTY-FOUR

AT THE MANOR

Giles found Kate's care both fascinating and infuriating. She escorted him forward, pausing to explain things on either side. Not the plants, she was no herbalist by training, but the general kinds of things, the layout, how many plants there were.

Once they reached the courtyard of the house, he could feel the ground shift, stone instead of a gravel drive. "By the wings, now?"

"Yes." Her voice was thoughtful. "There's a door to the left, where a kitchen might be. And there is a sizeable chimney above, that suggests a hearth."

"It does rather, doesn't it? Let's go to the door, but no touching yet."

"I know my job." It had a crispness to it, but then a laugh, and he wondered what she looked like, settling into her proper role with the task.

They turned, walked perhaps twenty feet, then she stopped again. "We're about five feet back. I'd like to run a series of tests."

"The Rigsby series, or the Elcampane?"

"I was thinking both."

"You'll muddy the readings, won't you?"

He got amused primness in reply. "I have a plumb-bob with me."

Giles had to laugh. "Oh, well. I should let you get on with it. Is there a bench or something of the kind?"

"I'm not sure I'd trust a bench. There's the stonework we're standing on."

"I will set aside my dignity and sit on the ground, then." Giles agreed. It was good to be back on good working terms, to be at ease again, even if the unresolved equations of the earlier difficulties continued to nag at a little corner of his mind. That was for later, certainly, now they were making such progress.

She set to her work with the little murmurs of enchantments and reciting of rune-poems. And, he was sure, all the proper gestures and movements and castings. He knew this would take time. Neither set of exploratory charms was fast. He could hear her pause, scribbling down notes.

He kept tapping his pocket watch, feeling for the slight vibrations that told him the time. Twenty minutes. Thirty. Forty. Finally, he heard her.

"I don't know that we're getting in this way."

"Oh?"

"You're right they didn't use a complex renewing charm here. But they used one tied to particular keys. Ogglen's suggests they were talismans in their own right."

"Phew. That's not easy to sort out. Not without more equipment. You tried the Jonlath variation?"

"And the Perpendix. No luck."

"Was there a response to the Cormac?"

"Blue." She paused, as if reflecting. "Medium sky blue, not royal."

"Ah, now that's useful. That must have been set in the late fourteen hundreds, or it'd be some shade of green. After the Pact, but not long after."

"I'd thought that." she agreed. "It gets lighter as it's older, yes?"

"Yes. My master referred to it as fading, like ink fades on parchment or paper. Sepia tone. Any odd effect to it?"

"I caught a glimpse of something - pearlescence, is that the word? But it was the kind of thing that disappears when you look at it straight on."

He grunted, thoughtfully, but didn't explain what it meant to him. "What now?"

"Let's examine the other doors, anything we can find."

"Tell me what our options are."

They consulted. One central pair of doors out into the courtyard might be just as restricted, but worth investigating.

"We should walk around the building, first." Kate said finally.

"I agree, but your reasoning?"

"I'd like to understand the layout better. The windows, I can't see through them, it's dark inside, but anything might help."

"As you wish. You are the expert here. When there are maths, I will do them."

It made Kate laugh again, and Giles liked how that sounded. "It may come to that, if we have to sort out talismans that work." She took a breath, and settled his hand on her elbow again, and then murmured, "We should go counterclockwise here, too, at least to start."

Giles nodded. "That's sensible." He wondered how she felt, his hand against her, the required closeness. She had been proper about it, polite. She turned, then led him across the courtyard, until he felt the shade of the other side of the building, and then the courtyard stone turn to gravel.

"No door on this side?"

"Not on the courtyard, no. That's a little curious."

"Such things often come in pairs, yes."

They continued, then there was another turn, a section in greater sun, that must be the east. "Tell me what there is?"

"Glass windows. Some of the courtyard had shutters. A door, it looks like, three quarters of the way down."

Giles was about to say something, and then paused, mouth open, half-listening. "Do you hear that?"

"Hear?" Kate sounded puzzled.

He waved a hand. "Listening."

It was a deep thrum, something he felt in his bones more than heard. "That. Rumbling."

To her credit, she was quiet for a few moments, breathing shallowly. "No." she said. "Nothing like that. Should I do some tests?"

He frowned. "For magic in the area?"

"That. The Leonidas variation."

"That might be useful, yes." He paused. "And the Hexley, do you have amber on you?"

"I am well prepared." This time her tone was not prim, but arch and amused. As if one day he'd get the hint.

He spread his hand. "I will stand here and let you work."

Kate murmured, then shifted to the low chant that was the most sure way of determining the magical resonances. Giles knew the theory, but he'd never been much good at that particular kind of ritual magic, the sorts that relied on rhythm and pitch. The sound of her voice rose and fell, and he let it pull him, drifting through memory.

The lecture room at the top of the keep at Schola, just under the Astronomy platform. He remembered the play of the light on the pale wood desks so clearly, inkwells tucked neatly in the top. He remembered how the sun streamed in, how you could see the beams of light because of the dust motes, and there was something pure and perfect.

As Master Lollard had said, this was why ritual was taught in those rooms.

Giles was so lost in thought he did not notice he had taken a step back, then another. Not big steps, but enough that suddenly, he felt a force pulling at him, knocking the wind out of him. He tumbled, as if down a ramp, curling to protect his glasses and his face. Bohort had taught him that, at least, how to take a fall.

He came to a stop somewhere chilly and dark. Even with his glasses off, he could see only glimmers of light, nothing he could make sense of. A small window, maybe, not something he was facing.

"Kate? Can you hear me?" It was the first thing he thought of. "Careful."

There was a long pause where the quiet was as overwhelming as the dark.

Finally, he heard "Giles? Giles?" Louder and louder, like she was coming closer to him.

"Hold!" He put all of his command voice into it, bellowing, hoping she'd hear him in time.

The sound stopped. It was above him, to one side. Then, cautiously, a "Giles?" Pitched clearly.

"Can you hear me? Say 'cats and dogs' if you do."

"Cats and dogs." It came back.

Giles let out a long breath. All right. They had some communication.

"I fell through something. Down something. Into a vault underneath."

He heard her start to say something, but couldn't make it out. Then her voice was clearer, like she'd applied an amplification enchantment. "What are your orders?"

Her voice was precise, clear, and the most beautiful thing he'd heard in a long time. She was there, she was listening, and she wasn't making things worse. He called up, "Let me think. Moment."

Where was he, precisely? It smelled like a wine cellar or some sort of storage like that. A little damp, a little musty, a lot of stone. He reached out and felt the floor underneath him. Stone, not wood. It was too chilly for wood.

"It's some kind of storage, I think. Stone. It smells like a cellar. Nothing awful, just musty."

"Can you tell anything else? What were you doing?"

"Daydreaming. And I took a step or two back."

"And you're all right? Nothing broken?"

"Shaken up. I'm fine." He was, more or less. Bruised around the edges, but that was nothing new.

"Can you tell me anything about where you are?"

Giles levered himself to his feet. "Keep talking to me, would you? Anything, just so I have where your voice is coming from."

There was a small pause, and then she launched into reciting the Epic of Schola, as they called it, one of those school traditions that began before time and would last long beyond their bones, which had hundreds of verses, or people creating more on the fly. He listened with half an ear as he explored the room. Partway through the first side, he realised she was doing a variation about hidden spaces in the school, the ones that opened to those in need.

TWENTY-FIVE

OXFORDSHIRE

K ate came pelting back up the stairs of the house, stopping only long enough to catch a breath. "Vale? Mrs Hitchcock? Vale?"

No one answered. She tried again. "Vale? Mrs Hitchcock? Anyone?"

The door to the library opened. "Why the fuss, Davies?"

She stared at him, open-mouthed, for a moment. Did he think she'd rush about for nothing?

"We opened the manor. Giles fell down a shaft. Uninjured, but I'm not sure how to get him out."

There was a long pause, then Vale said, "Weren't you keeping an eye on him?" It was flat, as if he was distracted by something else. He was watching her closely.

Kate took a deep breath. "We are not sure what caused it. He was waiting for me to check a door, and then he disappeared. He slid down into something he described as a vault, possibly a wine cellar or storage. Stone floor, stone walls, not very large, perhaps ten by ten feet. He went around the edges. There were a few shelves, but he didn't explore them thoroughly."

That earned her an arched eyebrow. "And you didn't find the way in? I thought you were supposed to have skills." It was completely dismissive.

Kate inhaled sharply. "I looked for any obvious entrance. I thought, I thought..." She stopped, shrugging her shoulders to straighten them. "We need more help."

Vale considered, then said, "Go gather what you need. It's all in the shed, yes? Bring it to the field. I'll meet you there." The note of command in his voice was almost reassuring for a second.

She frowned. Something in that didn't quite seem right, and he wasn't her commanding officer. But her heart was beating too loud for her to think. She felt dizzy with the shock and running, and a reflexive, "Sir," came out. The protective appeasing title.

Vale smiled, a slow spreading smile. "Go on."

Kate nodded, then said, "A few things from the kitchen." She turned to get that and heard the library door click behind her. She had no idea where Mrs Hitchcock was, but there was cheese and bread and mustard on the kitchen counter. Enough for sandwiches that would keep well. She wrapped up a bottle of lemonade before filling her flask with fresh water, then the backup flask in her bag. Maybe she'd be able to pass food down to him, somehow. If not, at least she wouldn't have to leave him alone. Again.

Once the food was in her bag, she paused by her alchemical equipment for a jar of salve. She wasn't sure it was safe to use, but that was a problem for later. Better to have it and not need it. She felt like part of her was floating above her head. It was the curious sense of distance she'd had a time or two before in the middle of a crisis, like a falcon seeing the battle-problem from a different perspective. This, at least, she knew what to do with.

Going back out of the house, she paused for a moment, listening for where Vale was. She heard footsteps above, but she couldn't tell what he was doing. She thought about calling up, but the way he'd treated her, she was sure she'd get nastiness back, and she didn't need that.

Back at the field, in front of the gates, she made a thorough investigation of the shed, looking for anything that might be useful. More rope, that was important. A bucket might be handy, but this one had a hole. And splinters, she discovered.

She put a shovel out, in case. But perhaps that would be seen as a threat, by the house, like the rose clippers had been. Leather straps, that might help if they had to haul Giles out without a foothold, to make a harness. There was a handcart, she could pile things in the cart, it wouldn't be too much to manage with help.

Half the things in the shed were in a horrible condition, like someone had bunged in the least useful contents of a badly maintained quartermaster's miscellaneous cabinet. She found two horse bits, and a medallion of some kind, tarnished to obscurity.

It felt like it had been forever. Checking her watch, it had been twenty-five minutes. Plenty of time for Vale to join her. She frowned, walking back down the path to the house. She made the last turn that gave her a good view of the barn, and there was dust rising off the road. Something felt suddenly wrong, and she sucked in a breath, and took off at a run again.

She found the house locked. Not with a key, but with some enchantment she couldn't unravel with the first dozen things she tried. She didn't have time for the long ones, or to figure out what variant he might have used, and she cursed. Turning, trying to get her racing thoughts to make sense, she caught sight of the barn. The doors were closed as well, though not locked. When she got them open, she realised the horse was gone, but not the carriage.

Something was wrong indeed. She was sure, deep in her heart, Vale had done something. What, she could not tell yet, but nothing good.

She cursed the fact she'd left her journal inside - she'd thought it too likely it might get damaged, as they explored, or that the very modern magic might conflict with the house. She scrabbled in her vest, pulling out a stub of pencil and a bit of scrap paper from her library visit, and wrote a note. "Mrs H. Problem at the manor. Please message following to Lord Edgarton at the Guard, Trellech at once. 'Assistance required soonest. Suggest analysts, penelopes, pulley. Vale not present. Emerald.'"

That would have to do. The code word meant a significant issue, no current aggressive threat but the possibility of harm. And at least that was a hint of what kind of help would be of use, based on the current situation. She didn't dare say she thought Vale had run off, because he might come back.

She could only hope that Mrs Hitchcock was merely out doing the shopping. And that there was some handy young person with a horse or even a car who could make the run to the nearest portal. That Lord Edgarton was in the Guard Hall today and not inspecting something in remotest Scotland, miles from a portal. That Lord Sibley wouldn't notice a message from her and make trouble and leave Giles stranded.

There were too many things she could not control. What she could do was get back to Giles. Anything might happen there, and she wouldn't know. Protecting him was her responsibility.

Kate arranged things in the handcart, to bring them into the manor grounds, and to one side of the courtyard. She then carefully laid out what she had and fitted herself out. Two lengths of rope, one in her bag and one around her waist. Leather straps. An empty lantern that would take a magical light and extend it. She unfolded the fabric case that held her various magical testing tools, the amber and lapis, quartz and jet, and all the others. The food was there, the lemonade and water.

She couldn't put it off any longer. As much as she wasn't sure what would happen next, it was time to walk around the corner. Past time to let Giles know she was back and then see what she could do. The space looked just as she had left it. There were no new lines in the ground where the colour shifted, no places where sand or gravel had poured through.

She repeated the amplification charm, then cleared her throat. "Giles? Are you there? Giles?"

It was silent for a dozen heartbeats, she could hear them thudding in her ears, and then there was an answer. "Kate?" She felt a rush of relief at hearing his voice, that he was still there, that nothing new and awful had happened.

"Here, Giles. It's Kate." It felt inane, to explain it like that, but he couldn't tell. "Anything new there?"

"Still a vault. Still stone. I have heard nothing. Is Vale there?"

That was awkward. Very awkward. "He was in the house when I ran back, but..." Her voice trailed off, she wasn't sure what to say next.

"I can't hear." Giles sounded more strained.

"Sorry." She kept her voice steady as she could. "He was in the library. He asked me what happened. I explained. He said he would meet me at the shed. I got things, and he didn't come. After twenty minutes, twenty-five, I went to look for him."

There was a long pause. "And?" The stone muffled a lot, she couldn't tell whether Giles was upset, angry, resigned, or some other emotion.

Kate took a deep breath. "There was dust coming up off the road, and the horse was gone from the barn." She kept her words short. Clipped, perhaps, but precise. "And someone locked the house. I couldn't open it, not quickly."

There was a muffled sound from below, that went on for a good half minute. When it got quieter, she said cautiously, "Giles?"

"Mrs Hitchcock?"

"Not around. I left a note, to go to Lord Edgarton as quickly as possible. I said Vale wasn't there. I'm hoping it will help."

"That is something." There was a long pause. "Good thinking, Kate."

The praise changed something for her, like water flowing in and rinsing everything clean. She let out a sigh of relief, then inhaled. "So. What's the next step? I have some equipment with me."

"Give me the list?"

"Food, drink, my testing kit, rope..." She ran through the list of everything she'd packed, ending with "A few experimental things, a salve and a couple of extracts. Do you remember what you were doing before you fell down there?"

There was a long pause. "It will sound quite odd."

"Giles, we're investigating a manor of roses and secret doors. I wasn't expecting something to be even." It was a terrible maths joke, but she heard him laugh.

Giles shook his head. If she was managing horrible jokes, things were probably not entirely dire.

He took a breath, then let it out. "I was thinking back to the ritual classroom at Schola. You know the one, with the light and the high windows."

"The wood floors, yes."

"I was listening to you sing. Thinking about the light through the windows, the little dust motes in the shafts of light, the way the sounds echoed."

He could hear Kate, above, making a noise, but he couldn't tell what it was. Then he heard, "It was the resonance chant, wasn't it? I remember, I remember..." Her voice trailed off into a murmur again.

He let her think for a minute before calling up "Kate?"

"There's a related charm, let me try that. By the same person, and I think it's the right age."

He wasn't sure it was a good idea for her to tumble down in here.

"Can you - a note or something?" he offered, uncertain now.

"Already did." That was clear and amused. "Note and explanation of what I'm about to try, in case it works. I'm tying it to a nail up here, on a bit of ribbon, a glamour to draw the eye. If they come looking for us, someone should spot it."

Giles shook his head. "Oh. Well, I'll stay out of your way, then. You are entirely on top of things." He retreated, back in the room, away from where he'd tumbled down. There was what seemed to be a mattress, on low legs, and it at least let him perch.

Above, he could hear the chant, one repetition, then another, and the third began before it stopped, turning into a gasp. He heard her land, in a jumble, and he stood, reflexively.

"Kate? Kate, are you all right?"

He heard her move, and then, "It's totally dark down here."

"I presumed." He couldn't keep the amusement out of his voice. "Can you summon light?"

She moved, he could hear her clothes rustling. It was a long pause, and she didn't explain what she was doing. Finally, she said, "Where are you?" There was an edge to her voice he didn't like, and he didn't know why.

"Go forward three feet, there's a low bed. I am sitting on the bed. Mind your knees." There was the sound of her getting up, and something large shifting. "Did you bring baggage with you, woman?"

"A few things. Might be useful." A step, then another, her boot scraping on the ground, and then he could feel her, reached out his hands to her. "Right here. Come right over here, you can sit down and get your bearings."

A moment later, she was in front of him, and one of her

hands reached out, fumbling for his. He took it, steady, and said, "Right here, sit right next to me."

He felt her sit. They had a moment before the bed moved, rocked, then dumped them both unceremoniously on the ground. She ended up on top of him, sprawled, and he reached for her shoulder and felt his thumb brush her cheek.

She shivered, and in that moment, he realised she must be terrified. There were tears, she was trembling. She couldn't hide it from him, not in this jumble, much as he supposed she would have preferred to do so.

He moved to touch her more securely, wanting to offer her a warmth in the dark. Before he could, he stopped. He wasn't sure what was right in this moment. They were colleagues. Did she want this from him? Could he even offer?

Words. Words were safer. And a hand on her shoulder. "Right here, Kate. We'll figure it out." He wasn't sure why she was like this, what she needed, but he could be a voice beside her.

Giles could feel her stop breathing, the sudden inhale followed by an "Oh. Oh." of trying to say something. She bent, and then she was bringing her mouth down to his. He had no idea what to do. He did not want to push her away, not at all.

Before he could say anything, she was kissing him, properly. She was focused, throwing herself into the kiss like she'd thrown herself into all her other work. It was a brief kiss, as kisses go, but it was the longest he'd had in years, and she was there, and glad for him to be.

He tried to shift his hand on her shoulder, make the angles better. She pulled back, sharply, shifting to scramble away from him. "Sorry. So sorry."

It was so hasty it felt like someone tearing a bandage from his skin, a physical pain that left him breathless. When he could push himself upright, he wasn't entirely sure where she was. "Kate?"

"I shouldn't. I'm sorry. I didn't..."

"Kate." He switched into command voice, he could hear her on the edge of terror. "I enjoyed that." It was true. He had. He had not expected it, it was not in his equations for the day, but it was true. Now, to get her thinking. And settle his own rather demanding physical reactions.

He could hear her suck in a breath, then take another, slower and he kept going, letting his voice smooth out. "I would enjoy it more if we were not in a hidden room in an unknown manor and not sure how we're getting out. But I am not offended. I am glad to know you have entirely human reactions to the situation we find ourselves in."

He had to think fast, finding words to keep talking, so she would hear his voice, know where he was. So he could use his voice to calm her down.

"Oh." It was a small sound, coming out of the darkness. "Sir?"

"Giles." He kept his voice low and firm. "Giles. Here, are you hurt?" Keep her talking, keep her thinking. Keep himself moving, not lingering on how it had felt for those seconds she'd been right there and kissing him, her body warm against him. No, stop, listen.

There was a longer pause, he could hear her moving. "A bit bruised. Shaken. Nothing..." She rummaged in the bag, making things clank and chime. "I think everything in the bag is all right. I'm not sure."

"Can you make a light? I think it might reassure you."

"I tried. Before I came over. And I couldn't. What if..."

That was a problem. He swallowed. No good both of

them in a panic. He'd been in worse situations. Possibly, so had she. They were professionals, well-trained to deal with emergencies. They could figure this out. No one was trying to shell them out of their trench at the moment.

"Well, all right then. I'll just have to make myself useful. I have skills, you know. Sorting out rooms I can't see in." He kept his tone light, even, even teasing. "Have a careful feel in your bag, cautious if there's glass." He could hear her pushing herself into a more useful position.

"I'm sitting. All right. I have the bag in my lap."

"Just like that, Kate. Talk through it." Telling him what she was doing was good. Talking would keep her breathing more evenly, reduce the panic, let both of them get a grip on their nerves.

She took a few minutes, then she said, "Everything seems sound. Would you like a sandwich?"

It made him laugh, how prosaic it was. "I'll save it for later, but what kind, so I know what to look forward to?" There, she was settling. His body was settling, with the time she'd taken, the less difficult conversation.

"Cheese and a bit of mustard. It'll hold up better than other sorts. Lemonade and flasks of water. The rest of the oatcakes."

"And, I'm sure, a dozen other helpful things."

That earned him a little laugh. "More like two dozen. I'm told I overpack."

He put on his best tone of mock-outrage. "Not by me. Never by me, if you show up with sandwiches and flasks of water."

She laughed louder, more freely, and he grinned at her in the dark. Then, when she caught her breath, he heard her, softly, "You meant it, about the kiss?"

"Entirely human reaction. You are an exceptional

Guard, Kate, from all I have seen from you. But I like you being an excellent human even better."

"It wasn't..." She paused, fumbling for words. "People haven't."

"Actually," he said, keeping his voice light. "People keep telling me how fit you are. If men haven't been throwing themselves at your feet, it's not because you're not fit. Now I've had a chance to examine the evidence myself."

She spluttered, incoherent for a good half minute, and then her voice came back, very different. There was amusement now, and a resonance of relaxation. "And you weren't going to say anything?"

"You did rather hurl yourself at me. Which is not the common thing on my end these days."

"The bed collapsed! Or whatever it was. Any hurling was due to poor construction, I'm sure." She shifted, moving toward him, and he reached out, felt the brush of her arm above his, and moved to take her hand.

"We should table the discussion of your fitness for later, yes. But I look forward to the discussion, and if you remain willing, further exploration of less architectural constructions."

That made her giggle, and then murmur, "You're teasing me with a purpose, aren't you?"

"Several purposes." He was blithely cheerful about this. "But yes. We should at least get ourselves somewhere you can see, and sooner rather than later. The sun will go down, eventually."

"You're right." She squeezed his hand. "How do we do this?"

"Well, moving is easier if we're standing up."

"Won't we bump into things?"

"Slide your foot along the floor, don't take big steps. You

may want one hand at head height, back of your hand away from you. One against a wall, palm cupped and facing behind you. It keeps your fingers safe, if you hit something on the wall. And here, there are likely pillars. We'll take it slowly. I know where the door is, but I didn't want to go further on my own. You follow me."

"So our plan is to move slowly, carefully, and see if we can get somewhere with sunlight?"

"Exactly. I'm not at all certain why magic isn't working here. I don't suppose you have a device for light, or something like that?"

"Just the lantern, that enhances the light charm. I was using the space for other things." She sounded a little abashed. "And, um. My last one broke. I don't use them often. I'm good with light charms."

"No worries. We'll sort it out." He hoped he sounded more confident than he felt, but they might both get along better with a little show of confidence in a solution.

TWENTY-SEVEN

INSIDE THE MANOR

Kate felt like she was spinning in circles, her thoughts making her dizzy. How could she have done that? Kissed an officer, the officer she reported to. It was entirely out of bounds. Also entirely unlike her.

She couldn't even blame the disorientation of not being able to see. With anyone else, she might have retreated to that excuse, but this was Giles, who lived like that day in and day out. Whatever else she did, she couldn't complain when he didn't.

She sucked in a breath, working on getting her feet under her. She didn't even know which way the door was.

"Right." His voice came from quite close to her. "Where are you, Kate? Say something, so we can sort ourselves out. Just keep talking for a minute."

"I seek it from Kai, and Bedwyr, and Greidawl Galldonyd, and Gwythyr the son of Greidawl, and Greid the son of Eri, and Kynddelig Kyvarwydd, and Tathal Twyll Goleu...." It was the first thing that came into her head, the long lines of descent from the stories her mother and father had told her. She let the Welsh names flow, the rhythms soothing her.

It took Giles a little to catch on, but then there was a "Kilhwch and Olwen?" His pronunciation was not, in fact, horrible. Surprisingly. "That will do, if you want to keep going with it. There's plenty of it." Had he always been that interesting, and she hadn't noticed? Now she felt like she was hanging on his every word.

She did. Translating it out of the Welsh was just enough distraction to keep her from thinking thoughts she shouldn't be. About what it had been like to kiss him.

"And Maelwys the son of Baeddan, and Crychwr the son of Nes, and Cubert the son of Daere, and Percos the son of Poch, and Lluber Beuthach, and Corvil Bervach, and Gwynn the son of Nudd." She could hear him moving, near her. Near her, then away from her, and her voice caught, but she kept going. He had told her to keep talking.

As she got to Gwynn ap Nudd, his voice came out of the dark, quite near her. "Right. I know where I am, and I know where the door is, and I know where you are. Shall we get better acquainted with the door?"

She nodded, then remembered and said, "Tell me what to do."

"You remember how I take your arm? This is a little tricky, but you tuck your left hand into my right arm, above the elbow. That's it. Stay as directly behind me as you can. Keep your other hand up, like I told you, palm behind you, out a bit to the side. I'll have my left out the same way and use my right for doors. If you need to drop my arm, put your hand on my shoulder or if you need, my waist."

"Isn't that..."

"No point in false modesty. We must be practical, Kate."

She frowned. Not that she had objections to touching him. Rather, the opposite. What he'd said, minutes before, about enjoying it. Had he been reassuring her? Making sure she wouldn't leave him alone in the dark unknown? He'd said it was a human reaction, which didn't seem encouraging, but then he'd been kind, and he did like his abstract concepts. It made her head spin again, until she resolutely focused on the practical.

Kate swallowed, then said, "If that's what we need to do."

Giles laughed. "I do have skills. You can learn them too. You won't be good at them, yet. Like any new skill. But I am quite sure you can learn."

She coughed. "If you say so."

"Look, it's like, oh, did you ever study the match at Schola, the 1870 summer tournament, when they had those visiting professors? The entire field was charms and enchantments?"

Kate frowned again, thinking back. "What I remember about that one was the puzzles. That's what I studied, anyway."

"This was the first part of the match, a device that made the field dark, until someone disabled it. And another that created a dense fog. You could blow it away, for a little, but it would swarm back."

Kate considered, then murmured. "They had to learn to solve it."

"And they did. And no one's tried that puzzle since. When you know how to solve it, it's easy."

"We know what would solve this. Light."

"That we can't use. Most puzzles do have more than one solution. This one, we'll use our skills and our knowledge, and we'll work together."

She took a deep breath, then said, "Tell me what to do. And I'll do as you said."

"If you need to drop your hand, tell me, so I can stop at once. Right. Ready? There's your hand, like that. If there's a stair or slope, you'll feel it when I go up or down. If I bend or twist."

"Oh!" She considered, as he moved slightly. "That's, that's quite practical."

"That's why the upper arm, and not the hand. Hands are terribly imprecise. Get one banged up against walls."

"That's rather more than imprecise." Her brain was running away with her, and she said, without thinking. "You must go through pints of bruise salve."

He laughed, full-throated, and said, "Enough. That charm I can do, thankfully."

Kate let him laugh, then said "Lead on, then?"

They went step by step, slowly at first. When they got to the door, Giles said, "Door has a latch. Trying it now."

She could hear it click and then heard his sigh of relief. "Were you expecting something else?"

"I wasn't sure if it they intended to lock people in here. That would have been nasty."

Kate nodded. "Where next?"

"Let's explore. Carefully. Mind your feet, there's a lintel. Stone, I think."

She followed him, sliding her feet as he'd told her, feeling the little lip at the door. She took a step through, carefully, then said, "It feels different."

"You too? Describe it, do."

"Lighter. It felt - veiled, in there. Like a Silence-veiled space. Only...." She frowned.

"Only not the Silence. Not the same..." Giles gestured

with both hands, she could feel his arm move. "Not the same chord, I want to say. Musically. Scale. Tonality."

Kate nodded. "How - how queer." It was. It made the back of her spine tingle, uncomfortably.

"You were studying the layout of manor houses. If we're in the cellars, where would the stairs be?"

"The manor was not supposed to be shaped quite like this. But if there's no physical displacement - which is rather a big if, now I come to think of it." She heard him snort. "I would assume a stair toward the main wing. Possibly one at the far end, but I am not as sure of that."

He paused, then spoke, as if he were thinking aloud. "Option the first, we each pick a direction and follow the wall, never stop touching it, until we get to a staircase or something else promising. Option the second, we go together. You are the Guard, in charge of protection."

"Splitting up is a bad idea. It always ends horribly in stories and songs."

"And we can't have that, can we? So. Left or right?"

She frowned. "We started on the outer right side of the house, if the main wing was the front centre. So if we landed in the same position we entered, roughly, then going to the right should get us closer to the front of the house."

"That is a rather big supposition, considering."

"It's all we have to go on?"

"You have a point. So, that would be this way." He turned to the right, reaching a hand for the wall, and said "You trail the wall too. You might find something I miss."

Kate nodded, then paused. "What do we think about it feeling different out here?"

"It might have been a storage room, designed to dampen magic. Can you try the light again? I'll stay right here, so you can find me."

She laughed, then dropped his arm, cupping her hands in front of her, remembering what light looked like. She felt it, a little pulse of warmth tingling her hands, then it sputtered out, like a candle that wouldn't quite catch. "Better. Not quite catching, but I had a spark."

"Oh, that is interesting." His voice was suddenly purring, and she took a step closer to him, settling her hand on his arm again. "Getting a light would be - predictable. No light would be understandable. Almost a light, now, that's an interesting liminal state."

Kate snorted. "Are we going to stand here in the unknown hallway and discuss magical theories?"

"No, we will go find a staircase and somewhere to sit down, and possibly a lantern, and then we will eat cheese sandwiches and drink lemonade. Then, and only then, will we discuss magical theory."

TWENTY-EIGHT

INSIDE THE MANOR

C aution was for the best, neither of them knew what to expect. They moved down the length of the hallway, foot after foot, step after step. Giles could feel Kate's hand on his arm, holding securely. He liked how that felt, her trusting him.

It was about twenty minutes of slow steady movement before Kate murmured, "I see light ahead. Not much."

"What do you see?" It came out brusquely, more an order than he wanted.

She tugged his arm once, to stop. "There's a faint glow from somewhere above us. Possibly the ground floor."

"How far away?"

"Ten feet, maybe fifteen? The end of the hallway is in shadow, there's an arch. It makes it hard to tell how far it is."

"Forward, then. Sing out if you see anything at all unusual."

They made it the fifteen feet, he counted the steps like he was counting his heartbeat, hoping nothing would turn into a sudden threat.

Kate's voice was clear, suddenly much more confident. "That is light. My turn to lead, I believe?"

"Tell me what there is, first?"

"A wood and stone archway, a vaulted ceiling above us, leading into another hallway, perpendicular to this one, and a wooden staircase."

"And the stairs look sound?"

"I don't see problems. We'll go slowly. Spread our weight. Ready?"

"Sure." Giles wasn't sure he was, but there was no way out but through, he knew that. He took a deep breath, then felt her shift, moving in front of him, the bobble of her bag where it balanced on her hip.

"Take my arm, would you?" He tucked his fingers around her upper arm, and she set off, slowly. "Five steps to the stairs. Railing on both sides, though I wouldn't trust the right, that's the open side."

"Built to castle standards."

"Odd, but yes. Right. Up we go. One foot on each step, you stay a step or two below me, if we can make that work."

"Slow and steady. We are the tortoise, not the hare."

"No prize for speed, no. And I do see quite a bit more light at the top. Very promising."

The stairs had no particular surprises for them, which was startling. They were stairs, leading upwards, sturdy and well-made. They were so sturdy they barely creaked.

When they arrived at the top, Giles said, cautiously. "There's no sense of decay."

"Timeless, you mean. Or as if time paused."

Giles frowned. "When you summon light. Do you know the origin of that charm?"

"Not off the top of my head, no. I remember Master

Trenton telling me something about how there are different methods, developed over time."

"I am wondering if the manor responds to magic it knows and ignores magic that came after it was..." He frowned. "Ensouled."

"Ensouled?" Her voice was curious, not mocking. "That strong a feeling of it?"

"It liked our offerings. It did not like people clipping the roses. I don't know what else to call it."

Kate's voice was dry. "Semi-sentient magical buildings were not a part of my curriculum."

He laughed. "Nor mine, precisely. What do you see now?"

"We seem to be in one corner of the main wing, as we thought we might be. There's a large room, the stairs leading down, smaller rooms leading back the way we came, though it looks like they might link together, no hallway."

"And the other way?"

"I can see through to the next room, which is, there's a long table, I can see. And then large arched doors, beyond, going into the next area. And those are closed, possibly barred."

"Right. Let's move to the next room, and see if it is time for sandwiches, lemonade, and thinking about what we do next. See if you can find somewhere safe enough to sit down. Do you have a charm or something that will do?"

"There are..." Kate was hesitant, he could hear it in her voice. "There are some things Mum taught me. Old, from her side of the family. But they're Welsh. Would that be a problem?"

"Fourth Families? Well. I suppose we can try? I would..." He paused and tried to explain his instinct. "I would rather something purely of the Fourth Families, than something of an unknown background, or possibly of an enemy of the household here. The Welsh are - well, in the period, they were mostly a settled issue."

Kate snorted. "Well, as settled as we ever are, yes. Here, this way. There's a bench." She got them both settled, moving a small table. "I'd rather not sit at that dining table. It strikes me as a place that might have more enchantments."

"You might run your tests?"

"Quick test, then sandwiches, then a more thorough version, mmm?"

"Could we spend the night here if we had to? If it seems safe?"

There was a long pause. "There're some cushions on the benches there. It wouldn't be very comfortable at all. But we could probably make do."

"Privies?"

That was a longer pause. "In the period..." She stopped. "I'd assume there was a privy somewhere. But I don't know where. On this floor, rather than underground, I'd think. We can see about a bucket."

"If your charms work up here, I know a couple that might help."

"Do I want to ask how you know that kind of thing?"

His voice came out sharper than he intended. "Time in the trenches."

"Oh."

Giles could feel her retreat into herself, and he cursed himself for doing that. "Hush. It'll be handy now. Like my other skills."

"You were very ..." Kate stopped. "I would say brave. But you go bravely into the unknown an awful lot, don't you?"

"Rather more than the average sort, yes. Keeping a proper spirit of adventure in mind doesn't hurt."

"If one is forced to be adventurous, better to embrace it?"

Giles settled more comfortably on the bench. "Something like that. There are tremendously tedious books about blindness healed out there, did you know? Very sentimental, and with awful titles, abominable puns on light and darkness. The virtuous are rewarded, the small-minded punished."

"That sounds rather tiring." He liked how she said that, how she was thinking about it.

"It is terribly exhausting being used as an object lesson for everyone you meet. Or an inspiration." He paused for a moment. "I do appreciate you not doing that."

Kate murmured something he couldn't quite catch, then said, "You deserve better than that. I mean, most people do. But you're very skilled. Besides being my superior officer, in an indirect sort of way."

She seemed likely to tangle herself in that set of thoughts, so he said, as gently as he could manage. "Why don't you see what you can get out of your exploration, and then we can have teatime."

The phrasing made her laugh, and he liked her laugh, the little bubble of sound, when she allowed herself that luxury. Something in it made him want to get her to laugh more, longer, louder. For now, he had to content himself with her comment. "Right. You'll hear me chant, so you know where I am."

It was a long exploration, a good thirty minutes by his watch. He listened to the rise and fall of her chanting move around the room. It was a series of phrases repeating over and over again, pausing in some spots for longer, going more quickly through others. It made him wonder what she was seeing, what the magics were telling her. Or for that matter, what else was in the room besides a long feasting table and some benches.

When she returned, he could hear her grinning. "That worked a treat. And I've got a lantern lit with the charm, and found another with a good store of oil, so I can see what I'm doing even if we lose the sun. There's a small room tucked on the courtyard side of this with two cots. It must have been for servants waiting on people later in the evening or something. That room's all safe, barely a dusting of magic."

"And here?"

"The feast table's glowing with it. Plates and cutlery and chairs and benches and candlesticks and all." She paused, considering. "Nothing that looks dangerous, but so much I can't get a clear idea of what's involved without a lot more work."

"That can wait." he agreed. "Any food out? Signs of people intending to eat?"

"No food, but the entire table's set, like they would be serving a meal. It looks like good plate, too, the kind of thing you'd put away if the master of the house was staying elsewhere. I'm no expert, but..."

Giles frowned. "That raises the question of why there's no one here. You've not seen signs of anyone?"

"No bodies, no skeletons, if that's what you're wondering."

"Maybe they could get out, but not back in?"

Kate was quiet again. "I don't know which set of thoughts scares me more. Not being able to get out, or once we're out, never coming back."

"There is a solution for that. Taking excellent notes."

"Sandwiches and notes." Kate was very much in agreement.

"What about the next room?"

"The handle turned when I tried it. That's for later. It's what, four o'clock? We have until around nine. If we're not sure of a way out by eight, we'll settle in for the night. How's that?"

"Sensible. And a good plan. You know the trick of not over-extending. Do you have more food?"

"Several sandwiches, the water in two large flasks. A few rations bars, but they're awful. And I'm not sure about finding more water."

"We could find a wine cellar, but that leads to rather awful consequences in every tale of magical castles I've ever heard."

"Wine cellars, libraries, locked doors." Kate pointed out. "Magician's workrooms. We may well not be able to avoid any of them."

TWENTY-NINE

INSIDE THE MANOR

Once they finished a sandwich each and split the lemonade and an oatcake, Giles said "Right. Let's have a go at the next room."

Kate frowned, trying to figure out how to manage this. "Should we move a bench over, so you can sit and I can investigate?"

"So long as I can hear, I suppose that's easier." Kate looked up. His voice sounded strange.

She paused, thinking through how to say what she needed. "It is my role to make sure you are safe. And able to do the maths on the other end." She swallowed. "Also, before. I - well. I want you safe for other reasons." She flushed, then was grateful he couldn't see, before she hurriedly added, "And I don't know what's in there. Neither of us do."

"And you want to do your job properly." His voice was quiet.

"All the parts of it."

Giles nodded, then said. "Move a bench over by the

doors, then. So you don't have to shout. That's no way to have a conversation."

She smiled. "Oh, of course. I expect to need your advice. And..." She hesitated.

"And?"

"Telling you what I'm seeing helps me think it through." She was hesitant, wondering at the end if that was insulting.

"Time-honoured tradition, that. Explaining something to someone else helps us figure it out. And you're quite good at it. Much better than other people I've tried."

Kate smiled back at him, then murmured, "Have standards."

Giles laughed. "You do. We both do. Come on, let's have a try at the door." She liked how it was both of them, the sudden rush of pleasure it gave her to be working with him, not just next to him.

She arranged the space to her satisfaction, placing a bench where she could talk to Giles while she worked on the door. She wasn't sure what to expect. The plans of similar manors suggested this would be some sort of study or library or private room, if they were in the more public room. But assuming it was anything like a standard manor seemed likely to cause problems.

"Ready?" Giles asked, when she'd been quiet for a minute.

"I think so. One final check for magical effects, and then - well. Open the door. It sounds simple."

"Let's hope it is."

She nodded, and then tried the chant, the one that would make magic glow. There was nothing she didn't expect. The handles glowed, but not in any of the shades that would suggest a problem. There was a little glow on the other side of the door, as if something in the room was casting a lot of light. She took a step or two back, and the heel of her boot came down loudly on the stone floor.

"Kate?"

"I'm fine. Just getting a better look at something. Moment." It was getting easier to remember to narrate what she was doing, and then she had enough distance to be sure the glow was coming from under the door.

"The door is fine, but it looks like there's rather a lot of magic on the other side. I believe the door's safe to open, though."

"So we open and then go ahead carefully. As we have been doing."

"I'd prefer you behind me, please." Kate said. "Just in case. Far enough to avoid an effect until I can get a good look?"

Giles went quiet for a few seconds, then said, "That's fair."

"Promise I'll give you a good description as soon as I know how things fit."

"Right. Show me where you want me." That was brisk, but friendly enough about it. Kate sorted out where to have him stand, back and around the corner from the doors. "You're about five feet back and five feet further - that's north. Around a bit of a corner."

"In case there's some sort of area effect."

"Exactly. The big bag is ten feet behind you, on the ground. It has my healing kit. I have the smaller pouches, with the working tools."

"You prefer stones, yes?"

"Mmmhmm."

"Do you have a piece of ruby?"

She frowned. "A small one. Suitable for magical work, but not - pretty."

"May I - I'd like to apply a charm to it."

"It's tiny. Moment." She rummaged in her pouch, drawing out the ruby which hung from a thin chain. "If you hold out your hands?"

She poured the chain into his hands.

"Ah, yes." He closed his eyes, focusing on it, cupping one hand above and one below, then murmuring in a language she didn't recognise. "There. Wear that around your neck, if you would?"

She was already fastening it when she asked "What does it do?" That was as tidy a sign of trust as he'd ever been given.

"An ancient charm in the family for protection."

Kate smiled. "So you'd like to keep me safe too."

"As safe as your duties permit, yes."

"It's around my neck. Right. The door. We're both putting it off, you know." He gestured at her, and she took her place in front of the door. "Turning the handle now."

What she saw was stunningly complex. She coughed, taking it in, doing the initial incantation to make sure there was no immediate danger. Then she took a deep breath, before shifting for the chant for a lurking danger that would appear in the next minutes. Then she cleared her throat.

"Giles? You can come forward, to where I'm standing, if you like." She heard him take the steps, five forward, five to her side, as she talked.

"It's a study, a library, quite large, most the entire centre of the front of the house. Twenty feet by thirty, maybe more. Books on shelves around the walls, all sorts of sizes, they hadn't standardised yet, had they? Quite a lot of books, for the time period. Quartos and octavos, mostly, but some odd sizes, and a few folios and a few that look larger. In the centre of the room, there's a large open space, and there are chalk marks or paint marks. There's something fallen across the symbols, too, but I can't see from here what it is."

He came up behind her, reaching to settle a hand on her arm, taking her left arm this time. "Go on."

"It's... It looks like something was dropped, or spilled. Some symbols are smudged, like someone moved on top of them. It looks like liquid might have spilled?"

"That implies a ritual that went wrong. Any sign of the ritualist?"

Kate shook her head, then said immediately, "No. And you can smell, no smell of one, either."

"It's been hundreds of years."

"Surely you're the sort of family who has a mausoleum or a crypt or something?"

"I rarely spend time in them." Giles was amused, which was good. Amused meant he was more relaxed.

"There's a distinct smell. To people who've been dead long enough to -- well. Dry out."

There was a long pause. "I will not ask how you know that. At least right now. So no body, but we want to be careful about that floor. Do you think you can get a good enough view to describe the markings?"

"Probably, but stay where you are." He nodded, squeezed her arm, and then dropped it. She took a careful step or two in, bringing her notebook up. "I will do my best to sketch it quickly -- not details, but a general sense. There's a large circle, it looks like a conductive design, rather than protective or talismanic."

She paused. "Do you need me to explain my reasoning? No Solomonic features, nor the compass rose alignment, at least not to my best guess."

"What's the base?"

"Division by seven. Classical planets, perhaps?"

"The Good Folk, the Fatae, maybe. Some traditions assign the number seven there." He said it quickly, as if he were uncertain about it.

"Are you serious?"

Giles coughed. "Apologise, Kate." His voice was sharp, and all order.

She blinked, not at all sure why he thought that needed an apology. But she knew what to do. She took the cream and honey and oatcake from her bag and made a little hollow with her thumb in the cake. Pouring the cream and honey in, she said "By honey, by cake, and by cream, I make an offering to thee. Let there be peace between us."

Giles murmured, "Cake and honey and cream?"

She nodded, then took a step back as she looked up. "There's a shimmer, Giles. Gold edging to purple. Like a sunset."

"Is it changing?" His voice was fast, not as sharp as before, but deliberate.

She watched it carefully for a good twenty seconds. "No, holding steady. But it wasn't there before."

"Kate, I believe we may be reasonably certain that his base intentions were not in classical astrology. Have a look, do you see anything that looks like plant material, flowers, you know the things. Don't risk crossing into the circle, but you may need to walk around the edge. Each of the points."

THIRTY

INSIDE THE MANOR

G iles did his best to wait patiently, curling his fingers into his palms to hide his tension. Something had shifted, something beyond maths and logic. It surprised him Kate hadn't avoided it.

He listened to her make her way slowly, the slight clink of her bag against her side, the tap of her shoes on the stone floors. She was going slowly. She moved about ten feet away, and said "The points seem to relate to planetary correspondences, if I have it right - I'd need more research to confirm. But not just that, no. It's a variant I'm not as familiar with."

"We have discovered more since. Neptune, Uranus."

"Ah, but we don't include them in the magical systems, do we?" Her voice was a little less stifled. She didn't seem angry at him, at least, for insisting.

"There's rather a lot of argument about Planet X," Giles said, amiably. "But now is not the time for theoretical maths. Now is the time for accurate observation of physical objects."

That earned him a small chuckle, and she made rough

measurements, counted in steps, enough to give him a sense of the space. He let her continue to the second point, the third, the fourth, then said "Quite a large room, isn't it?"

"The whole of the front of the building, I think. What would have been a great hall, originally."

"No doors in or out? Outside, I mean."

There was a long pause, and finally she said. "Not that I can see. But there're bookshelves along what should be the front wall. Maybe there was a door once? And there's another door on the far side of the room, the same place in the wall as the one we entered through."

"That," Giles said, "Suggests some further investigation. Can you get there without touching any of the sigils on the floor?"

"Give me a couple of minutes. Let me do the identification charms on the way through."

He nodded, waiting for her. It was another ten minutes, before she called out, from much further away, a good twenty feet. "Right. Behind the desk where the door should be." She stopped. "I think I need your help here.."

"What particular kind of help?"

"There are a lot of books on the shelf, and I suspect one of them is the trigger for a door, if they didn't just wall it over? It's the sort of thing someone would build, wouldn't they?"

"Right. Can you get me over there?"

"Can you follow my instructions?" She was thoughtful. Even distracted by something.

"You've got an idea, don't you?"

"There are places it's too narrow to do what we've been doing, you on my arm. Too many things in the way, tables and shelves and the lines on the floor. Do you think you could follow my guide from a few feet away?"

Giles frowned. Definitely not his preference, and especially not with fragile objects and delicate magical sigils in play. "Is it safe enough to try it for a few steps, before I get closer to something with more risk?"

"Oh, yes." Her voice was warm. "We can do this. If you trust me."

Oh, now, that was a question, wasn't it. A blunt question. He had worked with her. Kissed her. Been leader and follower with her, turn and turn about. He liked her rather better than anyone he'd met in years, for even-handedness and practicality and brains to match his own. Even if those brains were in a different field. Maybe because they were. He realised she was waiting on an answer. "I do trust you. But let's make sure I can follow your lead first, on a safer spot?"

"Starting from where you are," she replied promptly. "Look, how is this useful for you? Steps forward, or angles, or what?"

He considered. "The challenge is orienting myself in the space." he said. "Especially here, the windows are entirely the wrong angle to be any help. And I can't set up the tools I use other places."

"Tools?"

He waved a hand. "Later, miss curious cat. Later. Get us home and I'll show you." He wondered, after he said it, if she might take offence at the phrase.

She chuckled, so he suspected he had not offended. "Answer my question, and we'll see about that."

"Could you tell me angles? Based on my current? That's rather a lot of calculation."

"I think so." She was thinking. "Start with simpler ranges. Ninety, forty-five, and so on. You take small steps and we adjust."

"Set yourself up, then." He took a breath, willing himself to be as calm as he could. It worked as well and as badly as ever, but he could feel the training, the practice, the experience settle over him. If he was not calm, he could at least pretend to be with all his heart.

"Right. From where you are, two small steps forward. Pause so we can check position, then forty-five degrees to your right."

He nodded, and took one step, then another, pausing, keeping his pace slow and steady.

"One more step that size. That's a good size. And then turn."

One step, then pivoting carefully, leaving one foot on the floor, the other turning, to point him forty-five degrees. She caught it immediately. "You're using your feet as marks. Right then. Five degrees more on the right foot."

He obliged and earned an immediate further instruction, "Three steps forward. There will be a small table on your left, about the height of your fingers by your side. The sigils begin on the other side of that."

Giles nodded, then followed her instructions. They got into a rhythm, an easy one. She would tell him what was coming up and what was nearby and then let him focus on the work. He liked how she gave him the space to do that. So many people rushed one. They were short on time, but she was taking enough to do this right. They took eight exchanges, maybe ten. He was concentrating so hard on the counts and angles, he lost track.

Finally Kate said, "Almost at the back shelves. This is the tricky part."

"We seem to have the knack, if we don't become over-confident."

He heard her low chuckle again. "Point. All right. It'll

be three steps forward, then moving between two tables. I may need you to adjust as you go."

"Ready."

"Step. Step. There. Right, five degrees right. Half step. Three degrees left, can you do that?" He did his best, shuffled slightly. He was rewarded with her saying, "Oh, right there. Last part, there's a loose board. Pick up your foot carefully, move it forward, like you're going up a stair. Yes, yes..." There was a long pause, and he worked on lowering his toe. "That should do it. The bad spot is just behind your leading foot." He brought his other foot forward, and then he felt her reach out and take his arm, wrist to wrist. He stepped to her, she gave him space.

"Well, that was faster than I thought. Nicely guided, Kate. Now, tell me about these books?"

There was a pause, like she almost said something, then she was all business again. "Let me read off titles."

Some of them were classic works. Others had the kind of obscure titles that could mean anything. There was a large segment of Latin names he half-recognised. They'd got through a good fifty, before he said. "Wait, let my brain catch up."

"Need a break? I'm afraid it's a challenge to find somewhere to sit."

He waved a hand. "Mental break. I don't need to sit. Yet. Can you go fetch your bigger bag and bring it through?"

"Be a minute or two." He heard her make her way across the room, little pauses and shifts, then the sounds faded and she returned. He could hear the louder clink of her bag, the buckle against a strap.

"You think we'll be getting out of here, then?"

"I do. I have a question, though."

"Ask?" She sounded suddenly more hesitant, and he wondered what made her like that.

"You weren't going to make an apology. Before. To the Good People."

There was a long pause, and he wondered if he'd offended her. Then she reached out, put a hand on his forearm. "You and I, we have different relationships with them. Clearly."

He wasn't following, not at all, and she must have seen it without him saying it. "Oh, I agree, giving offence is rude, and a bad idea besides. But - I was having issues with the idea that one number or another is particularly theirs. All numbers are theirs, in some traditions. All colours, all flavours, all magics. Dividing things up, drawing fences between them, that's a human thing. Labelling like that. Fixing in place like that."

Giles frowned. "Very different view."

"We're very different people."

Kate wasn't sure how to explain it better. It felt to her like Giles and his magic were at a distance. Polite, cordial. More like the things in this study, using tools and devices and mathematics to keep everything at arm's reach. Her magic, her family magics, they were much more internal. All about her, and all about getting her hands dirty. Milk and honey and oatcakes.

She rubbed her hand, the spot she'd burned slightly baking the cakes that morning. "That's a longer conversation. Let me read the titles to you."

He nodded, and she read the titles. The Latin was easy enough, but there were other titles she stumbled over, several in German, three in French, one in Italian. He raised a hand after that one and said "Make a note of that." and then motioned for her to go on.

When she came to the end of the set of shelves, she took a quick drink from her flask to ease her throat.

"What do you think?"

"I didn't move any of the books. Do you think it's a magical trigger, or a physical one?"

Giles shook his head. "Something personal. Possibly two items, making a connection between them."

Kate frowned, then said. "Why did you think the Italian one was relevant?"

"It seemed the odd one out. Though technically, I suppose, it's Tuscan. Long before the unification of Italy, this house."

Kate tapped her fingers on her leg, thinking. "Anything else stand out as strange? Do you know what that one's about?"

His face lit up. "That's it. You're brilliant, Kate."

He didn't explain himself. She loved what that did to him, the giddy, almost boyish delight. Kate gave him thirty seconds, then said, "Do explain, Giles?" She hoped she sounded more patient than she felt.

"The title, it doesn't translate well - and my Italian's not fabulous. But I think it's about the properties of boundaries, doors, lintels."

She blinked, then said "Oh! And there's the one here, Limen, isn't it?"

"Exactly. So, try each of them. If that doesn't work, try touching them both at the same time."

She took a deep breath. "Right." She paused, cleaning her hand off on a handkerchief, and then reached to touch the first book, in Italian. She had to reach a little for it, which made her frown. "It's a bit high up. Weren't people then shorter, on average?"

"Not too much so. But a good point. Try the other."

She reached for the other, and nothing happened. There was something, though. She wiggled her fingers. "Something feels curious."

"Describe the sensation." He'd settled back into teaching mode. Socratic teaching mode, even.

She grimaced, but obliged. "A tingling or vibrating sensation. Less than a mild electric charge. More than a cat purring."

"Can you run the amber test again?"

She nodded, murmuring "Moment." and tugged the pouch of her stones and tools out of the bag again. It rocked slightly back and forth, then settled into an even figure-8 pattern. "That's a positive result, for the Forney variant."

"Well then. If you'd give me your arm and touch the book with your other? Since we don't know what will open. Do I have space behind you?"

"What are you thinking?"

"Is there space behind you, Kate." He was insistent.

Kate glanced around, then said, "Next to me. There's open space along the wall to your right, the aisle's about a yard wide."

"I am thinking both of us introduced ourselves to the house. Perhaps we both need to open the door on this end."

She nodded, and he shifted to stand next to her, visibly realigning his sense of space. "Ready."

Kate took a deep breath, then let it out, and said "Going." She reached to touch the book, and there was a click, like something heavy shifting, and then a grinding sound, stone on stone, and the wall shifted. It was a magical construction, not purely physical. She'd half expected it to pivot, like the hidden passages in some great houses she'd been told about, but it slid down, into the floor.

"The shelves are moving down, into the floor. It must be quite a large mechanism, that's a lot of weight."

"Magical architecture later, Kate. Is there a door?"

The shelves lowered and lowered, and then she could see. "A door and windows. It's still light out, but getting on for sunset." She paused, inhaling sharply. "I can see the door handle now. Should I?"

He nodded again. "Do. Carefully, but we don't have a lot of time to dawdle."

She took just long enough for the most basic brief safety checks. Touching the door would not cause fire or ice or magical attack, at least the better known ones. Then she said "Drop my arm for a moment, just in case, and take a step to the right."

He did, with a murmured, "As you wish." He didn't like it, but she was glad he saw the sense of it.

Then, finally, she reached out to touch the door handle. Nothing happened. It appeared to be a door handle. She pushed it, down, and heard a satisfying click of the latch giving way. A moment later, and she nudged the door. It stuck slightly, but only briefly, then it swung open.

"It opened. Let's get out for the moment, shall we?"

Giles stepped back toward her, and she shifted, letting him take her arm.

"There's a lip on the door here, about two inches. Like the ground's lower outside."

Navigating through the door took all their attention, and then they were standing in the front of the house, the original front. "Let's get back, see what we can see. Then we can figure out our next step."

"Are the bookshelves moving again, or are they staying put?" It was a timely question.

"Staying put for the moment, but the door's open yet." Kate frowned. "I'm not sure if I should try to close it or not."

"I think we must. There might be rain or wind. It would be a shame for any of that to get in. Or animals, I suppose."

"Here, we're about twenty feet back now, by the wall on this side. There's no opening, it goes straight across, and about twenty feet away from the manor on all three sides, it looks like. You wait here, I'll see about the door."

Giles opened his mouth to say something, then shook his head. "Talk to me. So I know what you're doing."

Kate shifted to kiss his cheek, just once, gently. "Of course." Then she took a step back and began. "Walking towards the house, I see nothing different on the outside, now I'm looking. More plants, I suspect they're relevant. Flowers, more roses. But not just roses. And right, here I am by the door. The bookshelf hasn't come up. I'm closing the door now."

She paused, pushing the door closed, and then turning the handle slightly, hearing the click of the latch. "It seems to be ... no, it's definitely still open from this side. There must be some kind of magical trigger from this side, but I don't want to experiment with that right now."

"That takes more investigation, and more tools, and a larger supply of sandwiches." Giles called back. "Come back. We should see if someone delivered your note."

Kate nodded, but she turned away from the door feeling rather regretful. There were so many things in there they hadn't explored. Perhaps this would be her last chance at it. They'd bring in specialists now. Penelopes and theorists and historians and who knows what else. Not her.

"Kate? You stopped talking."

"You're right, Giles. We should see about getting back. And we've both got some scrapes and bruises to tend. Just." Her voice trailed off.

"You don't want to leave."

"There's still so much we don't know. I don't like... leaving it half-finished." She couldn't say the rest.

"Come back, Kate." His voice was gentle. "There will be other days for your exploration."

Her head snapped up. "You can't be sure."

Giles sounded very amused. "Patience, Kate."

She frowned, not sure how to take that, but came back to him, murmuring "Here, here's my arm." He didn't answer any of the other questions, implied or otherwise. Getting back down to the house was fortunately a lot easier. They walked down the right side of the house, so they kept going counterclockwise, across the kitchen garden, and back out the gates and through the outer walls. There was no one in the field when they came past the gates, but when they came down the path toward the house, they could hear a noise.

"What do you mean, Mrs Hitchcock?"

Kate cleared her throat. "Sir?" It was the kind of voice that was called sir. It wasn't until they got around the corner of the house that she could see Lord Edgarton on the porch, and Mrs Hitchcock in the doorway.

"Davies!"

Kate murmured to Giles. "Lord Edgarton and several of the Guard - not people I know well, specialists, I hope. And Mrs Hitchcock refusing to let them in, she's standing in the door."

A moment later, the housekeeper was flapping her apron. "You let them come in and clean up and sit down before you bother them with things, you, you people." Very flustered, and yet protective.

"Davies?" That was Lord Edgarton.

"Sir." Kate tried to pull herself a little straighter. "We have found a way into the mansion, though it's a little rough. And a way out. Possibly that is also a way in, but we're not sure yet if it will hold. But if we may, sir, it's been a long day, and we could both use a wash and a bit of bandaging up."

Giles followed that with his smooth drawling, "So if you don't mind, give us an hour? I'm sure Mrs Hitchcock can do something for tea all round, please? What time is it, by the by?"

"Going on seven. We didn't get your note until half-four."

"Tea, then. Washing up and tea. Then we'll sort the rest out."

THIRTY-TWO

OXFORDSHIRE

G iles could feel Kate tense, under his hand. He leaned toward her, murmuring "If you'd escort me upstairs." Then he raised his voice. "Mrs Hitchcock, no sign of Vale, then?"

"No sir," The answer was quick, at least. "And it looks like a bag or two is gone. His clothes, maybe other things. I've not had a chance to check the household silver, sir."

"We'll have to sort that later. Please make our guests comfortable, and I appreciate you staying on, I know you want to get home to your family."

"It's no trouble, sir. I'll go put the kettle on. You'll be wanting a meal?"

"Kate had the foresight to pack sandwiches, but soup or something warm would be a kindness. And whatever Edgarton and his people need, please."

"Of course, sir." He wondered, for a moment, what had changed in her attitude, that she was listening to what he wanted rather than assuming.

"Kate, upstairs?"

"Of course. Sir, we'll be down as promptly as can be."

Edgarton murmured something in reply, and there was the rustle of people moving, finding spaces in the living room.

When they reached the top of the stairs, he said, "I'll need a bit of help, and I'd rather ask you than anyone else."

He heard her soft "Oh," then, "Of course. No Vale. What do you need?" She sounded nervous.

"Can you run the bath in the hall bath for me, let me wash up? I'm fine once I know where things are. And lay out a suit for me on the bed, they're all interchangeable. The blue tie and pocket square, they'll be in the top drawer of the dresser. Then you can have a wash."

"And your bruises?"

"I do know where my bruise salve is. Anything showing that needs healing?"

She turned a little, to look at him properly. "A few small things. I'll bring the salve for that, heal you right up. Just scrapes."

"Then we'll feel better able to make a good show."

Running the bath was handled as efficiently as he'd hoped. He was glad to send her off to her own bathing room, with an "I can manage from here." Getting dressed was a little more complex, figuring out where she'd put things, but everything was there.

When she came back, she smelled different, fresher, some soap with bright flowers in it, sharp herbs. Not roses. It made him smile.

"Here, I've the salve. Oh. You managed." She sounded startled. He realised suddenly it must be the first time she'd seen him without the glasses. He wasn't scarred, not like some men were, but he'd been told - repeatedly, by his mother and his family - that the way his worse eye didn't focus properly was disturbing. He had to hold himself steady, suddenly worried she'd turn away from him in disgust.

"It was a long day, but you set things out well. I feel much better, a change of clothes. You?" He kept his voice light.

She snorted. "I put my uniform on." If she found him distasteful, it at least didn't dent her good humour.

"Quite proper, with Edgarton here. Will he be difficult?"

"At me? I'm not sure. I don't know the others with him. What he needs to do to make the right sort of show. Here, hold still, you've got scrapes on your cheek." She leaned in, so close he could feel her breath on his cheek. "There. That's healing up now." The touch, more than anything, reassured him. How willingly she'd offered it.

He let out a long breath. "And how are you? What can I do?"

She paused, leaving her thumb resting on his cheek. "I don't know - what we do now."

"We go downstairs, we talk to them. We send them off for the night, somewhere. There's a barn, they'll cope."

He heard her suck in her breath. "Lord Edgarton does not sleep in a barn."

"Well, no. Entirely insufficient to his lordly needs." He could tease, and he thought it would help her do what she'd never dare otherwise.

It made her laugh, and he grinned in her direction. "And then you and I come up here and rest."

"After that?"

"We figure out more about the house." He was clear on that part. What they'd found so far fascinated him, but how it got there was even more of a puzzle. He didn't want to let it go.

"We?"

"Oh, I said I'm keeping you on this. For as long as you care to. And they'll need me, I'm quite sure. Some of what you described, there's a handful of people who could do the maths about that ritual circle. Three of them are growing senile, one of them has some exceedingly distasteful personal habits, and the other is fully occupied in a task he can't be extracted from for at least six months. Come on, let's go downstairs if you're ready."

"I'm as ready as I'll be." She sounded nervous.

He stood, then listened for a moment, to her breathing, how it had gone shallow, and he bent to kiss her cheek. "And you and I should talk about what's next, us. I haven't forgotten that."

She shivered, under his hand. "If you say so."

"Focus on work right now, shall we? Until we figure out that part."

She took a deep breath, an audible one, then nodded. "Ready. Here, do you have my arm?" She slipped so quickly into the working manners, the brisk attention to detail.

Five minutes later, they were comfortably downstairs, he had settled in a chair, and could feel her standing beside him. "Go round the room, introduce yourselves, please." he said. "So I get a sense of who's here. And Kate, have a seat. You've had quite the day."

He heard a slight rustle, then he heard someone get up, and offer her a chair.

Edgarton cleared his throat, then said "You know me, Giles. One analyst, two penelopes, three guards on duty - at the gates to the site and the road in." He didn't need the names as much as the sense of where they were in the room, and Edgarton knew it, so he half-listened to the names. Most of them wouldn't say much, anyway.

"Your note was very confusing."

"Kate mentioned what she'd written. Briefly, we solved the matter of how to open the gates - the old ways are decidedly important here."

One of the penelopes coughed. "Pardon, sir. How old?" It was the older woman, he'd worked with her before. Something Althorpe, he forgot her first name.

"Before the Pact. The magics we found that worked are those that would have been familiar to the house in its day. Later magical approaches did not appear to work. It's an intriguing study in temporal thaumaturgy, and I expect the maths to be delightfully complex when we sort them out."

He paused a moment to see if there was a further question. There was no sound, so he went on. "That done, we explored the exterior of the house. There are gardens, pleasure and kitchen, more roses, but we could not get in through the kitchen door, there was a talismanic ward. Kate?"

"It seemed likely to respond to creating a replacement. The Elecampane series was quite promising. Resonances along a perfect fifth."

"You realigned?"

"Yes, ma'am. I'd run the Rigsby before that. It showed significant ongoing magical resonance, but of course not the precise applications. Also deep-seated magical construction, likely embedded in the architecture, and present for many years. Other testing suggested there was some sort of chronological interference, a hiatus of the building rather than the magic running down over centuries."

"So how did you end up in the building?"

"We were investigating a side door, facing east, on the southern half of that wall, when Major Lefton disappeared from sight. I could hear him after a moment, and we could determine he'd slipped into a part of the cellar."

He heard Edgarton's voice. "How did you end up down there, then, Giles?"

"We obviously have not had a chance to investigate. The area was, we think, designed to hold materials that would be affected by magic - Kate's light charms did not work."

One of the penelopes spoke up. "Margaret Loft, sir, I have some ideas about that, sir, when we can examine the space." He got the sense he had just given a complete stranger the best gift she could dream of.

He smiled, genially, and then said "Go on, Kate."

"After consultation, I ran back to the house to get more help. I thought, sir, that Vale would fetch what he needed, and come help. But when he didn't come to the meadow in front of the manor, I discovered he had left." Kate's voice was precise again, and he only then realised how careful she was being in what she said and how she said it.

"He gave no sign?"

Kate paused for a long time, and Giles shifted to murmur, "Speak truth, Kate. Whatever it is."

"Sir." It was entirely unclear if she meant that for him or for Edgarton, even as she continued. "I admit, sir, I had found Vale a bit discomforting. Nothing I could not handle, but several times I had suspicions he was not doing quality work, that he might be manipulating the situation for his benefit. I would not mention it now, of course, except for the situation."

"What manner of things do you mean?"

"There was a transcription of numbers he did, and it had more than one error."

"Several." Giles agreed, his voice even. "I had noticed that once Kate confirmed her measurements."

He heard Kate shift, and he nodded at her, just once. She said, carefully. "He had a few friends out to visit, sir. All men. One of them I didn't like much at all, the way one doesn't, if one is in the Guard. But I didn't catch his name, sir, so I couldn't investigate, and I was quite sure Vale wouldn't tell me even if I asked."

Giles wished she'd asked him, but of course she wouldn't have. Not without more evidence than a feeling.

"And there was the matter of the coin in my coin purse, when you needed some..." He considered, then said, "Would you grab the wooden box on the desk, please? The one with the green inlay?"

Kate moved slightly, then said, "Of course." He could hear her move to the desk and bring the box back. He pressed his thumbs in the two indentations on the sides, heard the small click, and then opened the box. "Would you count, please?"

He heard her shift the coins in her hand, and the notes, then she said "Twenty three, all in bills already made over to you. And a few small coins."

"Lord Edgarton, that charge should be burglary, then. Or embezzlement, I suppose, technically. At the highest level."

Giles kept his voice even, but he was startled. They'd only got the quarterly funds out the week before this case came up. "There should have been nearly a thousand in bills and larger coin in there."

Kate blinked then said "Oh." Her voice was suddenly extremely quiet.

K ate didn't know what to make of Giles. That was a huge amount of money. Her salary for a year and a half, give or take, before the deductions for her room and board. She didn't even have a word for his expression, his tone of voice. Mildly annoyed. Irritated. But not angry.

She shifted, pulling her hand back toward her, but he turned his palm and squeezed her arm, and said, "We'll talk shortly, all right?"

Lord Edgarton caught it, she was sure he had. He waited a moment, then said, "If you can do a brief statement when we're done here, Giles, we can get the wheels in motion."

Giles nodded and settled back in his chair. "There are other more important matters. The manor."

"The manor indeed. Davies, do continue, we will table the problem of Vale for the moment. He ran."

"When it was clear he was not coming, I packed up what I could - I'd already made some sandwiches in the house, fortunately - and set off for the manor. I let Giles know I was back, and then - well, I tumbled down the same way."

"Is it still a workable way in, do you think?"

"I suspect yes, sir. Giles explained about the space with no magic. I couldn't make a light, but it doesn't seem to have affected any of the magical tools in my equipment. They responded as expected once we were outside the area."

Giles coughed, and said. "I haven't had the time to think through this entirely, naturally, but I did some approximations in my head, while Kate was working on investigations earlier. I do wonder if the anti-magical field might not have interacted with the chronological magics. I think we should not assume it will last indefinitely. I would, of course, have to work out the sums and equations, and I'll need a bit of braille translation and so on."

Analyst Loft murmured "I'd be glad to assist, sir, if you can let me know what you need."

Kate felt a sudden surge of jealousy, entirely unbecoming jealousy. She wanted Giles to talk over that theory with her. No matter how skilled the penelope was.

She shifted her hand more firmly over his, and said, "Lord Edgarton, sir, it does turn out we make quite a grand collaborative team." Then she continued, promptly, not letting anyone get a word in edgewise. "We made our way - thanks to Giles, entirely - down a long hallway, the length of the wing, to stairs, where I could see light. The stairs led to a dining room, the plate laid out as if for a meal."

Edgarton said, "The usual precautions, I assume? Mention anything unusual, but for the moment, we'll take them as read."

Kate's voice was more certain now. "I investigated, and determined that there was more magic behind the double doors, leading into the centre of the front. We paused for a break, and then we discovered..." She paused. "Someone was in the middle of a very elaborate ritual working, sir. The initial evidence suggests it was something to do with the Fatae, both in what offerings were accepted when we made them, and the layout of the ritual itself."

"Which was?" That was the older woman who seemed in charge of the Penelopes.

"A seven-pointed star, some specific colouration, though it's possible the pigments shifted over time. I made a sketch, of course, ma'am."

It earned her a nod. "They told me you keep good notes." Definitely setting her expectations.

Kate paused, then murmured, "I do my best." Another deep breath, and she continued. "I took notes and did some rough measurements. Based on the initial survey, it looks like someone was standing in the centre of the figure holding a bottle. Whatever was in it was either dust or had turned to dust. There was no sign of anyone, a human being. No bones, no clothes, nothing like that."

Edgarton frowned. "Do you have any theories?"

"Possibly, sir." She considered, then decided to wrap up the description before they got off on theory. "We determined that the original entrance to the building must be behind some bookshelves, and investigated those first, to see if there was a way out. There were doors on the far side, but they looked like they might be locked or bolted."

"And you were successful somehow?"

"Yes, sir. There was a ... trigger, a hidden key, for the shelves. They sink into the floor. There was a door behind, with a handle, and we could unlock it with one of the common unlocking charms. We left the apparatus lowered behind us, but of course it's possible the door may lock from this side."

"No, you did the right thing, not having prepared to be caught inside. And knowing that you had need of more staff." Edgarton leaned forward, then said "I am trying to decide the next step. Giles, do you have any thoughts?"

"Additional staff." Giles was prompt with that. "But I want to be there. I must be there, for some of the analysis of the figures Kate described. And I want Kate firmly in the mix. Or you won't keep me on."

Kate was startled to see Edgarton repress a grin. "Like that, is it? Well, I suppose we can arrange that. And for the moment?"

Giles considered. "We need a good night's sleep. All of us. Are you camping out here, or something else?"

Edgarton frowned. "I think we spend the night. If there's a room for me, the rest can make do with tents, it's pleasant out and we brought the comfortable set, of course. We're not under wartime conditions."

"To what purpose?" Giles was sharp.

"An initial further survey, with enough people to do proper measurements and get the lay of the complexities. That will take a day or two, and then we shall decamp to Trellech and make long-term plans. I must arrange duty rosters and such." He was clearly laying out a grand plan in his head.

Giles nodded. "Do you need any additional information tonight?"

"It would be helpful for further discussions, if you could propose a theory as to the effect of the ritual. Obviously, you're working from only the limited initial data, but do we expect further houses to reappear, is it a method that could be used to deliberately protect spaces, and so on. You know the sort of thing I'll be asked about."

There was a long pause, then Giles nodded. "I do.

Regrettably." He coughed. "Mrs Hitchcock can sort out a room for you, I'm sure. Breakfast at eight, a look at our site at nine, then?"

"Eight it is. Are you off for the night?"

"We've had a tremendously long day, yes, and Kate will want to review her notes and such. Kate, come up, would you, I've a few notes for you to add."

Kate nodded, and stood, reflexively. She noticed Lord Edgarton watching her and he gave a nod. "Well done, Davies. I'll be writing up a proper commendation, of course, but I'm sure we'll be adding to it with what you've done here."

She wasn't at all sure what to do with that, other than murmur, "Thank you, sir." It was a relief to feel Giles slip his hand into her arm, and nudge slightly with his thumb. She nodded at the others, and they made their way upstairs, into his bedroom. "The bed's here, Giles, to your right."

"Ah, thank you. I can manage the clothing, though if you could help with a tie tomorrow, I'd be obliged. And a few things for my bag."

"Of course. Half-seven?"

"That will do well." He paused, as if trying to decide how to phrase something. "Kate, I mean it when I say I will insist on working with you. My plan is that we will do the survey they want, then settle in Trellech for a few days at least. A week, perhaps two. You'd like to do more research, I'm sure."

She nodded.

"Would you stay with me? Rather than your quarters? You can have your own rooms, of course, there's a suite on the first floor, the housekeeper will be glad to set it up. I don't want to impose, but I - I would like you nearby."

Kate swallowed and thought a dozen things. Why was

he asking? Did he expect her to? What did it mean about Vale? Finally, she said, carefully. "I'd like to know your reasons?"

"Well, I do need the help. I don't need a great deal, other than the notes, but my housekeeper doesn't live in. I expect we'll want to be consulting each other about the work frequently, of course." There was a pause, then a "And I'd like to see how we get on. When we've time in private. I won't press, I hope you know that, if it makes you uncomfortable, I understand."

Kate raised a hand, then remembered, and said, "It - it's strange. You're very strange. You know that."

Giles snorted. "I've been told, yes. Why at the moment?"

"You come from a different world. The money..." Her voice trailed off. She hadn't meant to say it, not like that.

"Very different. Does that bother you?"

"I don't know how to make sense of it. Of you."

"Ah, I'm not very sensible, often. People think maths is all logic, but it's really rather wide ranging, in places, and I've always preferred the more theoretical aspects of the field. Given the choice."

"That..." She paused, then let him hear it, the way her voice was dry, how complicated she felt. "That was obvious, yes."

He reached out a hand toward her. She looked at it, for a good thirty seconds, then she settled her own in it, knowing that it was an agreement of a kind. She hadn't expected the sigh of relief from him that followed, something layered and full of meanings she couldn't begin to interpret.

"Come stay with me. Help me sort out this puzzle. Work with me. Not for me, you report to Edgarton. But let us do this thing together, as we have all along. Let us see what we make of each other, how our equations come out. No - lasting commitment, just experimentation."

She nodded, slowly. "A trial."

"Exactly. See how I suit you."

"And you?"

"I'm already rather sure on my end. Can't make the maths come out any other way."

THIRTY-FOUR

OXFORDSHIRE AND TRELLECH

The next three days passed in a blur. They were full of discussions with specialists and analysts, everyone working fifteen hour days, with meals of sandwiches as they got five minutes.

Giles kept Kate close to him, unless she was assisting with various tests and analysis. She had learned quickly how to keep up the quiet murmur explaining who was doing what, giving him context for the conversation. It was an art Vale had utterly neglected, and other people forgot mattered.

What he hadn't expected, though, was a comment on the afternoon of the first, when they paused for tea and transcriptions. He could hear Edgarton talking to a few people, then louder, "Let us tidy up here, and take a break for a few days. Deidry, here, thinks it may be better to let the space sit for Lammastide."

Kate replied, almost immediately, "How long, sir?"

"You've been working flat out for weeks. It's Sunday. Go away. Research. Get your notes in order. We'll reconvene in one of the meeting rooms at the Guard on Friday morning and figure out our next steps."

Giles leaned closer and murmured, "We talked about that. Come back with me, yes?"

Kate was quiet, for nearly a minute, then she said, "At least for the night."

They had had so little time to talk privately. She had helped with the few things in his daily routine he couldn't do on his own. All the small things that relied on sight like matching tie and pocket square, or reading out notes. What he noticed, more than anything, was how easily she slipped into that.

She didn't assume anything about what he could do or not do, but once he explained a particular need, she followed through. He could bathe himself, and dress himself, so long as it did not need colour matching, once he knew where his clothes were. He needed someone to tell him the visual cues, the lights of the diagnostic magics. And someone to explain the gestures people persisted in making, without saying anything.

Much better than Vale. More than that, he enjoyed spending time with her. Feeling her near him, the pressure of her body against his when they were sitting.

The trek back to Trellech took the better part of two hours, even with multiple carriages. On the other end, Edgarton oversaw the Guard, who tucked his trunk and Kate's into some sort of cart, and the two of them into seats. When they arrived at the town house, he heard an immediate "Master Giles, goodness."

"My housekeeper, Agnes Meredith. Mrs Meredith, this is Kate Davies. You got the notes, I know."

The older woman bobbed. "Suite on the first floor, the best guest suite, sir. And I've a supper in progress, it will be ready at six on the dot." He was glad Mrs Meredith was not being difficult.

"There we go. Would you show Kate up to her rooms, and see someone brings her trunk up, and mine? I'll be in the office, I want to check on some things."

"That Vale?" She disapproved. He realised that perhaps she had never cared much for Vale, but had had too much loyalty to the family as a whole to say so.

"You've not heard from him?"

"No, sir. The house was locked up, like you left it, when I came back from my sister's, all the warding in place, the special ones. I saw people lurking round in the street once or twice, like someone was looking for him, but I let the Guard know, and they've had someone patrolling through since."

"Ah, that's a clever thought. I suspect he made some trouble before we left, it will take a bit of sorting out. Did you manage the appointment?"

"Mr Doyle will be along at ten tomorrow morning, sir, and Mr Nostrom at one. I thought lunch at noon."

"That will be excellent." He added to Kate, who was standing, uncertain. "Doyle is my solicitor, and Nostrom handles my accounts, beyond the day-to-day funds we take out quarterly."

"It's very different." She was clearly quite unsettled. He wondered what she was making of the house. They had removed a lot of the more delicate decorations, the antique vases and china, early in his time there. But there were still portraits on the walls, and tapestries, and various other luxuries.

"Go up and look at your rooms, settle in. I'll be fine until supper. We can talk after."

She murmured, "I'll do that." He heard them go up the

stairs, Mrs Meredith's voice carrying more than Kate's, explaining where things were. His rooms on the far end, overlooking the garden, her guest suite here, overlooking the square. The family library, here, between them. It was a standard set up for townhomes in this neighbourhood, but he suspected quite new to Kate.

He was still in the office, typing at the brailler, when she came back down. He heard her footsteps between the clicks of the machine.

"Making notes?" Her voice sounded light, but there was something under it.

"I can't rely entirely on memory. That's a terrible idea. I was considering some of the techniques to investigate."

"More research for me?" Oh, there was a moment she sounded exhausted.

"Not tonight. Possibly not for tomorrow, either." Giles replied immediately. "Tonight is for dinner, a bit of conversation, and then rest."

He heard her settle in a chair, near him. "This is a lovely home, Giles."

"Thank you. Mostly not my doing - I preferred to be up in Oxford, given the choice, but Mother thought I should have the townhouse. Smaller than our other properties, more manageable. Useful when I see specialists."

There was a long pause, as if she were trying to decide what to ask. "Is there much of that? Or is that prying? If it is, tell me, please? I don't know - what's all right with you."

"Well, that makes two of us. How about we both ask, and we both speak up if something's too much. Fair?"

He knew his grin was still charming, people told him so. Something in it this time made her laugh, but she said, "Yes, fair enough."

"The specialists can't do much. It's frustrating. More for

them than for me. But I toddle round and let them try new approaches when they think of them. In private."

"More frustrating for them?"

He waved a hand. "I see no point in fussing over what cannot be changed. I'd rather focus on what I do now. There's still quite a lot, more than any one person could do in a lifetime."

"Surely you, you miss things."

"Certainly. Bohort. Reading any book I want, when I want. Sunsets and gardens of flowers in bloom - those are rather stereotypical, but true enough. Seeing what people look like. Voices are very informative, but ..." He paused, and considered. "It's not the faces I miss, as much as the body language. The little things, how someone leans forward, or the quirk of their mouth."

Kate hummed under her breath for a moment. He was certain she didn't realise she did it. At that point, he heard Mrs Meredith come down the hall, and her "Supper's ready, sir."

The next hour they spent enjoying the food. Rather better than Mrs Hitchcock, with the delicacy of flavour and attention to detail he appreciated. If he could not have sunsets, he could at least have gravy with more to it than meat and garlic. This had a delicate balance of sage and thyme, a hint of the coming autumn.

When they finished, he suggested, "Perhaps the library, upstairs? Mrs Meredith, if you could make sure there's water in the kettle up there, we can handle the rest, you can go home when you like."

"Of course, sir." She bustled off, and Kate stood.

"You don't need my arm here, do you?"

"Oh, no, I'm quite clear on where I am." He made his way up the stairs, letting his hand brush against the wall once or twice to get his bearings. Then up and to the right, into the library. He drew the locket off his watch chain, and held it in his hand, using it to navigate between the points they'd set up, to find the sofa and settle into it.

"This doesn't feel real." Kate's voice was behind him, near the door.

"Come, sit, where you like. And I suppose it wouldn't."

She ended up perching on the other end of the sofa, he could feel her weight shift it. That was promising. There were other chairs, solitary, and she had not picked one of them. "I don't know where to start."

"You've been on duty rather a long time. I told you the heart. I find you fascinating. You seem to like me, which is rather appealing on my end, mind. You've made it quite clear you don't know what to make of me. Are there particular concerns I might..." He wasn't sure how to finish that sentence.

"What do you want out of this? A passing thing? I don't... you wouldn't want me to stop working, would you?"

He couldn't help laughing. Not a simple, polite, amusement, but a guffaw that went on and on, until he got out "Goodness, no." He had to wait until he caught his breath. "You're a fine skilled woman, Kate, and I've no wish to tether you. I'd much rather see what you come up with."

"Won't your family..." Again, she let the sentence fade off.

"Oh, they'll throw half a dozen fits. They throw fits about everything. I don't talk to them much, and I promise you, however we end up, I will keep that away from you, as much as I can. And I have rather a lot of ways."

"Why me?" This, oh, this was baffled, and now they were getting to the core.

"My blindness hasn't... some people deal with it badly.

Most people, honestly. They let their own fears get in the way, or they assume that what they know, closing their eyes, is what I know, and..." He shrugged. "You're not like that."

"It's bad strategy. Assuming you know things you don't."

It made him smile. "So. Will you give me a trial? See how it goes?"

THIRTY-FIVE
TRELLECH

Kate watched, as Giles held out a hand to her, like he had three days ago, in his bedroom. "Please?" He was leaning forward, earnest, and she realised suddenly how easily she could break him. Not with magic, not with words, even. It would be as simple as not taking that hand.

This time, she was much faster about slipping her hand into his. "Show me," she said, then winced. He must have caught the movement, it flickered across his face, but he said, "Come this way."

He was leading her now, hand in hand, navigating the space easily. It was different, watching him somewhere he knew intimately. She only then realised how much of a challenge their entire time in Oxfordshire must have been, how much constant work he had been doing invisibly.

He drew her through a door at one end of the library, into a large suite of rooms. They were decorated in heathered blues and greens, like standing in the mists on a seashore or moor. He gestured at two doors at the end of the room.

"Dressing room on the left, bathroom and lavatory on

the right. Please, be at home." There was a little hitch of his breath, then he murmured, "I mean, please don't move things around I might need? But other than that."

He stood there, by the end of the bed, and released her hand. She watched his face, an intensity there he tried to dampen. He failed, there was something eager, boyish about him again. Hoping. She hadn't seen him hope for much, so far, just his relentless thoughtful logic.

She let out a breath and then said, "Show me what's on offer, then." It came out as more of a challenge than she'd intended.

Something shifted in his face, and then he grinned, suddenly. "Oh, I shall." He paused and then said "May I - may I touch? Will you tell me if something is too much? I don't even know what you like."

Kate closed, and something in her wanted to answer that vulnerable hopeful spark of joy. Despite how she'd kept a great wall around herself for so long. "I'm no virgin, but it's been a while. I'm careful who I bed."

He reached out then, finding her shoulder, using it to sort out where the rest of her was, by the way he then cupped her cheek. "You're unique, Kate. Not the sort to give yourself away cheaply." He leaned to kiss her. It was like the kiss in the dark cellar, that rush of him being close. And it was the smell of him, of pine soap, a spray of herbs, and an inescapable hint of roses. She felt his other hand come up, against her waist, and she moved a little closer to him.

"Mmmm." He pulled away to nuzzle at her ear. "I do hope you're not wearing boots. I'm not sure I'm up to getting those off you."

She laughed, and arched against him, feeling his body against hers, and oh, yes, a quite clear sign of his desire.

That none of this was feigned. "Slippers." she said cheerfully. "And a dress. You gave me time to change before supper."

Giles nibbled at her ear, his arm tightening as she shivered. "Well, then." He was still in shirtsleeves and trousers, the jacket somewhere downstairs, she assumed. She moved enough to get her fingers to undo his shirt. He gave her a few moments, then his fingers moved. "You don't mind the touch?"

"Like you exploring," she murmured, as the side of his hand brushed the top of her breast. "It turns out." He was absorbed in it, his fingers finding the large buttons down the front of her dress, undoing them. Their hands moved lower, the clothes slipping from shoulders, the sleeves dropping away from wrists.

She'd not been naked in daylight with someone before that she could remember, not as an adult. She was trying to decide what she felt when his hand stroked down her side, the arch of her ribs, the curve of her hips, and he murmured. "What do you like in bed? Gentle? Fierce? It's been a while for me, too."

Something in the tone made her lean in to kiss him, but it came out as another challenge, something fierce and demanding. "Try me."

He took a breath, and then he was backing her up against the bed, pressing himself against her, between her legs. She could feel his cock hot and hard against her stomach, his hands coming down to cup her hips. He paused, as if considering. "In the bed, you. On your side. Facing the windows."

She blinked, but obliged, as soon as he pulled back enough to let her move, settling on her right side with her head on a much softer pillow than she was used to. He kept one hand trailing along with her as she moved, anticipating where she went, curling over her hip with something that wasn't possessive as much as a compass always pointing north.

A moment later, he was climbing into bed, pressing his body up against hers, that hand curling around to stroke at her, making her even more damp than she already was.

The voice in her ear, though, that got her, almost immediately. It was warm, purring, punctuated with nibbles at her ear. "Here we are, then. In my arms. This is not the time for it, not when we're getting to know each other, but I have hopes of so many things with you."

He rolled his hips against her, she could feel how he was slick, needy. "You feel me, don't you, my gorgeous Amazon. Choosing to take me as a lover. You could have anyone, I'm quite clear on that, the way you're strong and shining when you are given your head. And the way you're loyal and careful and thoughtful, all those things most people don't notice."

She shivered suddenly at that, at the intimacy of him saying it. Laying out her heart piece by piece, all the places she'd hidden away for years in service of her career, protecting herself. He hugged her tighter for a moment, turning words into kisses, continuing to press and rock until she let out a breath again.

"There, there we go. Nice and easy, today. Enough to convince you to give me plenty more times. So many things to show you. I want you laughing in bed, my Kate. I want your strength. I want to show you my skill. How delicate my touch can be." He changed the angle of his wrist, and she arched hard against him, sensations like fireworks going off in her body.

"That..." It came out as a gasp.

He chuckled in her ear. "You've not had a man with my skills, no. People taking their own pleasure, not so interested in yours. Mmm. I'll spoil you for that, forever. You don't mind, do you?" The drawl in his voice, the self-assured confidence he'd been bred to, that got her even more than the touch. It amazed her how where once it had irritated or even scared her, now it intrigued her. He had been so careful to build her up, she could not imagine he would stop now.

Kate shook her head, trying to figure out what he was doing, spreading her legs slightly. Giles moved his hips, one hand adjusting the angle, so his cock slipped between her legs. The hand against her front did something she couldn't describe, and she could feel the head of his cock pressing inside her. Not fast, not hard, but very present.

She was breathing shallowly, she realised, like any movement, any shift might spoil it, might shatter the delicate bubble they were curled into. He nuzzled against the back of her neck, at her hairline, breathing her in, but his hands were strong and sure. She ventured a deeper breath, and he pressed more deeply into her, rocking deliberately, in and out.

"There, oh, yes, do you like this too? You feel grand, oh, yes," It was a steady murmur, nearly a babble, of his pleasure, and something about it aroused her as much as the sex itself. She could feel herself, something in her unfurling, blossoming. Something long neglected, now encouraged.

They fell into an easy rhythm with each other, none of the missteps, the awkward angles, she'd had other times in other places with other men. As they kept going, he let out breathy sighs, into her ear, between the murmurs of praise and pleasure. "Oh, want to try so many things with you." He sounded almost drunk, his words slurring slightly. "Toys and magic, the sparks that feel so good, warm you and bring you joy, make you cry out with it. Oh, yes." The more he talked, the more he rocked, the more she responded, until they were both breathless, climbing to something together.

She crested first, into a shower of pleasure much stronger than she expected, clenching around him, her eyes snapping open as she felt him thrust behind her. His arm had slipped up to cup one breast, bracing himself against her body. And his voice in her ear, oh, that was urgency and need and unabashed pleasure. It built and built, and then she could hear a sharp cry. He pressed and held, nothing but the warmth of his pleasure, the shudders of his body and pure response.

They took a long while to recover, long enough the light outside shifted to twilight then to darkness except for the lights from nearby homes. Just the two of them, alone, together. She wasn't sure if he had drifted off, but then he moved, brushing his lips against her shoulder. "Will you keep me, then?"

She let out a long sigh. "Let me kiss you."

His arm released her, long enough for her to settle on her back, and tug him close, a more equal embrace. Then she kissed him, breathing in the warmth and the affection, taking her time, reassuring him with actions, not words.

When he finally pulled back, she murmured. "More of that, yes." Then, laughing, let her hand drift down to stroke him, and feel how he was recovering, before she added "Soon. Please."

G iles ran his hands through his hair. "Where are we?"

"Trellech, your club, in a private meeting room." Kate's voice was dry, but then she patted him on the hand and he heard the chair scrape as she got up. "Lord Edgarton will be here in about an hour. Should I go see about something to drink?"

"Gin and tonic, please."

"Already?" She paused, not quite reaching out to touch him this time, but he could feel her body an inch or two from his shoulder.

"I have the beginnings of a headache. Some of those interviews were awful."

"Better than yesterday. Let me get some refreshments, and then we can talk them through. Five minutes. Do you need the loo? A potion for your head?"

He shook his head.

She said, "Back shortly," and then he heard her step away, the sound of her shoes on the wood floors brisk and purposeful. He ran his hands over his face again, feeling all the aches and minor pains rushing through. He was exhausted from trying to track the conversations, even with Kate's excellent help.

Half a dozen times, she had saved him by sharing some key detail, the way someone sat or moved, whether they looked interested. There were things he was sure she had not mentioned, and he'd need to get it out of her. He hoped that wouldn't be a great deal more work.

Once they had needed to pause for Edgarton to assemble additional specialists, they had been limited in what they could do. Giles was certain there had been endless machinations behind the scenes, over drinks at the club and the supper table in various private homes. Whatever Edgarton had done, it had worked. Eventually. The shift from needing answers yesterday to endless mysterious delays was wearing on them both.

Giles and Kate had spent their time sorting out which research questions got the greatest priority. And being begged for access, which was not on their agenda, but which was apparently on everyone else's. He rather missed the time when the entire thing was classified.

It had been handy to have her seated beside him. After the first day of interviews, they had worked out a few simple cues, that she could offer with her left hand, while taking notes with her right. Hints of position, or attitude. It was very rudimentary, yet, but promising, it almost gave him enough information to work with properly.

The thoughts kept him more or less occupied until she came back. When she did, her lighter steps were followed by a heavier set. "Right here on the table, Sean, thank you." Kate's voice was crisp.

She was doing better around staff, he'd noticed. In the manse, with Mrs Hitchcock, she had been rather deferential, as he'd expected of someone who'd grown up serving tables herself. But here, she was polite and clear, letting the staff do their work so she could do hers. If she felt self-conscious about it now, he couldn't hear a hint of it.

Then he felt her settle down beside him again, the quick brush of her hand on his leg. "Gin and tonic for you, and a cream tea, with sandwiches, for us and for Lord Edgarton. Sandwich? There's cream cheese and cucumber, salmon paste, and cheddar and chutney."

"Leave the chutney for Edgarton, he likes those. If there's a scone, I'll have that and the salmon."

"Moment." There was the scrape of a plate being set in front of him, her left hand resting on his right as she set things up. "Sandwich on the right, scone has pots of clotted cream and jam at the top."

"Best." It was a simple endearment, but her fingers twitched on his wrist for a moment before she moved her hand. "It wasn't inappropriate, earlier?"

"The cueing? Good grief, no. Very helpful. The leaning forward and back, that helped quite a bit. Odd, how something simple makes such a difference. Do keep it up."

"I do wonder what they think."

"Well, you are certainly not taking advantage of me under the table." His voice turned amused, teasing.

"Certainly not. I have professional standards, you." The mock-outrage delighted him, particularly how she was more comfortable teasing him. He then took a breath. "We do have work, though. Which of those were least awful?"

Kate let out a long breath. "Do we sort them by who was awful, or by who seemed competent in regards to the research?"

"Ideally, we would have a manageable set of people who are both competent at research, and not awful. But I suppose we won't be that lucky."

"Professor Osrian had some interesting ideas about wanting to examine the printing and publishing methods of the books." Her voice slowed on the last few words.

"But?" Giles wasn't letting her duck that.

"I didn't like the way he looked at me. It might be nothing, but ... "

"Kate, out with it."

"Some men undress you. Or are thinking about it."

"Well, that's not compatible with a cohesive and productive research team, is it, now? I want you to be able to walk the entire house, not have to duck whatever room he's in because he's being tedious."

"Or worse than tedious?"

"I am entirely confident in your ability to defend yourself, dear Kate. But it might be hard on the furnishings, so that's another reason not to let him near delicate historical materials."

"I don't know he's like that."

"Kate, dear brilliant Kate, you are a grown woman, who grew up in an inn, for Merlin's sake. You have likely known how to spot that sort of man since you were five, even if he wasn't going to bother you."

She went silent, and Giles worried that he'd pushed too far, too fast. She still couldn't think of herself as worthwhile. It bothered him, enough that he worried he pressed too hard when he corrected her. Then he heard her inhale, and murmur, "You keep saying so."

"Who else, then?"

"Mr Ruggles. He had some very interesting ideas about some of the construction of the devices in the house. That one that isn't a printing press, but it's designed to do something, that lever."

"Quite. Some sort of alchemical preparation, perhaps? Flattening, drying?"

"That is why we need an expert." Kate pointed out.

"True. Put him on the list."

They worked their way through the other five people they had met with today. One they definitely wanted, one they absolutely did not, and two they were both conflicted about. When Kate got to the last name, she said, "There's something about Mr Aelfdene that doesn't quite sit right."

"He's very accomplished, isn't he?"

"And charming."

Giles leaned back. "To you, in particular? I thought he was pleasant, but nothing unusual."

Kate paused, then cleared her throat. "He did the thing where a man reaches to kiss your hand, a little click of his heels, the precise angle of the bow, and the - gleam in his eye. Not the sort who'd push you into a convenient dark corner for his own pleasure, but the sort who uses his charm to get what he wants."

"Ah, that sort." Giles tapped his fingers on the table. "All things I wouldn't spot. Could you work with him?"

"That rather depends on what he actually wants."

"Can you take a look at his references? Find out a bit more about him? I suppose we should do that for all of our final candidates."

Kate seemed about to say something, he heard the little inhale, when there was a knock at the door. Giles called out "Come in?"

"Lord Edgarton, sir, ma'am." That was Edgarton, moving quickly. He felt Kate shift next to him, straightening, pulling her professional self back into place instantly.

"Edgarton. We have sandwiches and scones and tea, do let them know if you want something else." Giles knew his part in this particular dance. He and Richard Edgarton were near enough peers.

"I see you've been driven to drink. I've another meeting after this, I'd better not. How did the last interviews go?"

Kate slipped in, easily. "We just finished discussing. We'd like to check some of their references and details. May I have access to the Guard archives, just to see if there's anything there?"

"Certainly, Davies. How long do you expect you'll need? There's some pressure to get the research in motion."

Giles heard her flick through her notebook. "Three days." She tapped her fingers. "Two, if I can get priority access."

"I will put in the request before the end of the day."

Giles snorted. "They are pressuring you, aren't they?"

"When are they not? Now that the house is open, all sorts of people want to use it as a ball in the middle of a bohort match, no worries about the consequences. Fortunately, the senior ministers agree that too many cooks can spoil the broth, but the sooner there is a team sorted for a thorough investigation, the better for everyone."

"Sibley still a problem?" Giles kept his voice even.

"Sibley became much less interested once we pointed out that the method is both not reproducible, and also not at all controllable. He has been directed elsewhere. Do let me know if he's a bother. When can you be ready to go back there?"

"Kate, two days plus time for the report?"

"I'll need the evening to write it up."

Giles heard Edgarton grumble under his breath, one of those habits he hadn't quite dropped. "Today is Friday. Wednesday morning?"

"Wednesday." Kate agreed so easily Giles knew she had some particular plan. "Nine on Wednesday morning."

"I'll have a room reserved for the afternoon." There was a scratching of his pen, making a note. "And what will you be up to, Giles?"

"We're still puzzling over the initial calculations. The challenge, of course, is not just where the planets were, but what planetary alignments he thought he was working with. Seven distinct points, of course, and at least three are planetary alignments. It is, however, deucedly hard to track down books from the right period in a form I can do much with."

There was the sort of uncertain pause Giles rather liked causing, of people not sure what to do with that.

Kate took pity on Edgarton after a short pause. "By which he means, sir, that his Middle English is more rusty than he'd like to admit. Though he does have a point that it goes into braille abysmally. I've ended up reading a lot of it aloud, and he will mock my accent."

"You do that odd thing with your vowels."

It made Edgarton laugh. "So you're managing just fine, then."

Giles waved a hand. "As you see." He felt Kate's hand on his thigh again, reassuring and easy.

"So. Meet Wednesday. Davies, get me the list of anyone you have particular questions about or that need delicate handling on Monday. I'll have the authorisation for you by eight in the morning."

"Sir." Kate's voice was a contented, confident agreement. That, at least, he could feel smug about.

"Giles, later. Monday afternoon, for tea? I'm interested in your theories, you can expound at length."

"You may regret that. The townhouse, then I can demonstrate on the sandtable."

He heard Edgarton laugh. "Oh, well, yes. Monday." He stood, then paused. "I do have some news, Giles. About that cousin of yours."

"Do you." Giles kept his voice even, but he had been worried about the lack of any leads.

"He's been tracked onto a ship to Burma. Not one of the first places we checked, what's in Burma besides opium fields?"

Giles felt Kate before he heard her, the clenching of her fingers on his leg. Then there was a soft explosion of a swear, something in Welsh he could barely follow, and he suspected directed at herself.

"In Flanders fields the poppies grow!" It came out rather like an expletive itself.

"Kate?" He shifted his hand onto hers. Giles heard her take a deep breath, and another, but thank the magics, Edgarton wasn't making it worse, rushing her.

"There were women, in the garden shop. When I got the blood and bone meal for the roses. Well-born women, who'd been at the Healing Temple garden party. They were talking about someone - Phil, no last name, but I believe it was Vale they meant. One of them said something about how she'd be glad for him to take her to Flanders any time. It made no sense, of course. I thought they perhaps meant some private club."

"Do you know who it was?"

He felt Kate gather herself. "One dark haired, very sharp bone structure, about my height. The other was more striking. Taller, auburn hair, in quite a short bob, I'm sure not with much magic? They mentioned that Phil had shown up with..." She paused, rummaging in her memory. "Gordon was the last name. Delen Gordon, and a name that began with Alc. Alcyone, Alcestis... Alcmene. Something like that."

"That will give me plenty to be going along with, thank you." Edgarton was eager now, a terrier off after a rat. "Do have a pleasant evening, let me know about anything else you think of, see you Monday, Giles."

Kate waited until he had gone, before she said, "I didn't overstep, Giles?" She was hesitant, now.

"Goodness, not at all. I want to know where he went. And I suppose opium would explain more than a few mysteries. Dealing, I think, not just taking it himself."

"But it's illegal now." Kate sounded offended. "And you associated with the Guard."

"He did not like the fact I chose you at all. I suspect he thought Byles would look the other way, or not notice in the first place, and Peck would be entirely focused on her work. You, on the other hand, were much more of a threat." He paused, then said "What an awful phrase. Going to Flanders. Tawdry." He felt her hand move.

"That was where you..." Her voice trailed off.

"My eyes, yes. Good men died there. Thousands. Tens of thousands. Far better than him." His voice went bitter at the end, and he had to stop and swallow.

She went quiet then, for a good minute, before she took a breath. "So. The next few days."

"You have a plan, I assume?" They were both rather clinging to some hint of normality now.

" I'd already asked the library staff about some help tomorrow, assuming you can manage without me." She offered it like a tentative gift.

"Library on Saturday, work through our notes on Sunday, and you have a plan for your research on Monday?"

"Precisely." Then, softly, she said. "Tonight, could we ignore the world for a bit? Please?"

"Oh, definitely. I wish to indulge your every whim, dearest Kate." The fact she asked, the fact she was turning to him for that support, he would treat that like the treasure it was.

THIRTY-SEVEN

THE MANOR

"Kate? Where are you?"

She turned from where she'd been looking at books on the shelves, trying to make sense of the way they were organised.

"Bookshelves, Giles, north east corner."

"Right of the central front door." She heard him pause, the way he did when he was thinking about how the room was arranged. "Can you get on your knees there? Is there space?"

She blinked at him, startled. "My knees?"

"Is there space?" The question was more urgent.

"Yes? All the way up this side to the entry door, there's about - three feet, maybe four, between the shelves and the furniture."

"Hands and knees, please. Then I'll need you to help me."

She felt ridiculous, but she did as he asked. He likely had a reason. Scratch that, he certainly had a reason, even if he wasn't explaining himself, yet. She backed up into the furthest part of the corner, calling out, "Starting now. What am I feeling for?"

"You tell me. I don't want to prejudice your results."

She grimaced, but bent, putting one knee down then the other, running her hand along the floor, touching lightly. Giles had been teaching her how he had learned to use his hands, how different objects felt, if you touched them when you weren't bearing down. She was doing it mechanically, by rote, until she reached, and felt something. She couldn't quite suppress the gasp of recognition.

Across the room, she heard Giles laugh, full-throated and delighted. "Keep going."

She felt a crack in the floor, angling up toward the centre of the room. No, not the centre. It went somewhere in the inscribed circle, but not to the centre of the room. A crack, like a crack in the world, but not deep. She ran her fingers along it as far as she could without getting under the furniture, and then moved up, along the rows of shelves. One foot, two feet, a yard, two yards, as deliberately and carefully as she could.

Halfway up the side of the room, she felt another crack, not quite horizontal, but at an angle. "Second one, Giles."

"Keep going."

She got up to the door, and then had to stand, and push it closed. "Langdon, keep the door closed for a minute, please. Don't let anyone through." The junior Guard on the other side nodded. "Yes, ma'am."

She found two more of those mysterious ridges, one right by the door, one up in the south eastern corner.

"Four cracks, Giles, that I could feel, that came all the way to the edge of the room."

"There's three on this side. Radiating."

He sounded gloriously smug. And he should, they'd

been trying to figure out why the room felt subtly off for weeks now, and finding nothing obvious. Cracks like that, they meant something, she was sure of it.

"What are you thinking, Giles?"

"We need the tent and the sandbox."

She grimaced. Not her favourite tools, fussy as they were, but he had a point. There were things he couldn't explore here, not safely, and things they couldn't model and experiment with. The Penelopes had set up a magical device, a broad sandbox, as big as the magician's primary workroom, with precise measurements of the inscribed circle.

"I'm going to need measurements for the cracks."

"Call them out, I'll write them down. All four sides, please."

"Let me get Langdon for the other end."

Getting the measurements was rather fiddly. They had to avoid walking in the circle, which involved rather a lot of holding long measuring sticks with plumb bobs over the inscription from safely anchored furniture. It felt ridiculous, and it only didn't look ridiculous because the only observer was Giles. When she and Langdon were finally done, Giles was fairly bouncing on his toes.

"Davies, I need you right away." The voice came from the far door, into the side room.

It was Professor Warrington, and she looked up and said "Not right now, sir."

He looked offended, and then worse, came out with it. "You are supposed to be assisting me, you can't possibly know what you're doing, what are you doing there, you're risking the furniture."

She heard Giles, behind her, the way his body shifted. He was not bouncing with anticipation now. She took a risk, and said, "Giles, ten left." He pivoted precisely ten degrees to his left, so that he faced Warrington straight on. They'd been working on that. It made people take him more seriously. Ridiculous, but necessary. And it passed easily enough for a measurement she was finishing up or some other note.

That left the problem of Warrington. She couldn't eviscerate him verbally. He did not rank her on this project, but he could make things very difficult for her with the Guard, and that wasn't an option. Warrington was the sort of person who would be particularly awful if she bested him.

Solving this puzzle was harder than in her bohort matches, but she took a breath, steadying herself. "We are investigating a particular theory of Major Lefton's, requiring some precise mathematical measurements. Could I offer you Langdon's help for the moment?"

It didn't disarm him, but it was hard for him to argue with. She watched him splutter for a moment, then she heard Giles speak behind her. "We do need to get these down, I'd like to check the angles of the sun as well."

"You're not moving the furniture. Or ... using it?"

The furniture was all roughly as sturdy as it had been when the manor disappeared, it had not aged or suffered from termites. Or wood rot or damp or carpenter ants or any number of other dangers. But Warrington could not get that through his head. He was a rather limited sort of academic, really.

"Nothing outside the parameters of the project, sir. Langdon, go lend your hands to Professor Warrington, please. I'll check in when we're done, but we may be quite a while."

Langdon, bless him, was competent enough at stepping smartly forward, and waiting for Warrington to order him around. She thought he'd do quite well in the Guard, he had a good sense for when to shut up.

They both waited until Warrington had retreated, Langdon trailing in his wake. She heard Giles behind her. "Clear?"

"Clear."

"He doesn't like you very much."

"Teach your mother to suck eggs." It came out immediately, before she flushed then laughed. "Well, I suppose not your mother."

"Not her style at all." There was the long drawl of the aristocrat. "Still. He doesn't like you."

"I'm too smart, and you're too competent. And you make him uncomfortable."

"We're both too competent. Ah, well. We all have our burdens to bear, and competence around him is his. Now, would you escort me, so we can explore what these cracks mean?"

It took them just a few minutes to move outside, to the tent that the penelopes had set up. "There are some new points to investigate - can we clear the sand table of everything except the inscription?" When Kate spoke, half a dozen people came over. One lifted her hands, and the sandtable rearranged itself, the powder-fine grains forming into a flat surface.

Giles shrugged. "You'll have to set it up, Kate. Nice and even, like we measured it."

"Read me the numbers, then."

Doing it in reverse was fiddly, finding an end point, then the next point in, then another. Then she had to raise each one with a tiny touch of magic, lifting it from the base layer. The entire design was some obscure form of magic, a particular speciality of just one family, but

Giles had used it before for some of his other investigations.

The base pattern, once set, would stay there until the entire design was destroyed, and then points could be raised or manipulated to create a sort of tactile map for Giles to use. Kate had found it rather useful to see the inscription without the interference and distraction of furniture, to be able to examine it from every angle.

The process was tedious, exacting. She had to stop and take several breaks, to stretch her hands and keep them from cramping.

Giles, curse him, was lounging with a bottle of lemonade by the time she got all the points laid out.

"Grab something to drink, Kate, your voice is going raw. Then we'll have a go."

It took her a long breath to get her patience back. "High standards." It came out a bit tight, she couldn't get her jaw to unclench enough.

He winced visibly, and said, "Pardon, I know I'm pushing."

She would give him that, he did realise promptly, when he'd pushed her a bit too far.

"Get a drink, stretch." His voice was softer, now.

She nodded, and did as he'd suggested, moving to work out the kink in her back. The others made quiet conversation, something she couldn't quite make out. A couple of minutes later, she said. "Right. What am I doing with this?"

"Whoever's on duty, could you bring those lines into sharp relief, and give me some sort of texture on the scuff marks, where they start? And the fallen powder."

This required some discussion, but after another minute or two, Kate heard "Ready, sir."

Giles stood, making his way carefully to the edge of the

sand table, then he took a breath. "Now is for being undignified. I'm going to need to crawl around. I may need your eyes to sort out what is what."

"Of course." Kate took two steps back, to let her look at the whole thing with a bit more perspective, to see how the lines angled. They weren't straight, they weren't compass directions. They didn't even meet in the centre of the inscriptions. She frowned, trying to make sense of it. Giles had settled, feeling his way, getting a sense of the width and the angles.

"These aren't centred." It wasn't a question, it was a demand for information from the universe.

Since the universe was unlikely to answer, Kate responded, "No."

"And this is where the powder was. Wait, let me move, so you can see." Giles rearranged himself, to the other side of the inscribed circle, so that the convergence point was more visible. It was, to be precise, more like a gap where the convergence should be.

Thinking aloud, Kate said, "The cracks stop at the edge of the inscribed circle. Which implies they were some form of energy, buffered or adjusted or flowing with the inscription. But they clearly aim at a point that isn't the centre of that inscription, where you would think the caster would be standing. Certainly if he were any kind of well-trained magician."

"That may be a rather large assumption. After all, well-trained magicians do not generally do highly individual ritual magic work. Not without a spotter."

Kate circled, slowly, then joined Giles in sitting on the surface itself, running her fingers along. "If the powder was here..." She reached for his hand, putting it where she meant. "And here's one of the cracks. Is it possible - the cracks are related to where he was? Not a defect in the casting, per se?"

Giles tapped his fingers. "Bring me my abacus, would you?" He had that highly distracted air now, about to launch into cathedrals of mathematics inside his head.

Kate let out a small sigh, and went off to claim the best abacus from the work tent.

G iles settled back, listening to the small sounds of people finding their seats. He brushed his fingers over his own brailled notes to one side, but he trusted Kate would cover everything needed, and take notes for both of them, besides.

"Right, let's get started. Names, please, clockwise around the table." Edgarton was a tad impatient this morning, an edge to his voice. The introductions were a concession to Giles, so that he knew where everyone was, and one he couldn't bring himself to give up. It was entirely too helpful.

"Giles Lefton, one of the chief investigators."

"Guard Katherine Davies, the other chief investigator."

The names went around. Two new observers this time, both specialists in the time period, one focusing on architecture, the other on the prevalent magical theories of the time. However, they were down to just one penelope, reporting for the lot of them, which would make this meeting much easier for him to follow. Half a dozen besides himself, Kate and Edgarton.

"Walk me through the latest, please." That was Edgarton, off to his right.

Kate cleared her throat, then began. "As my interim report noted last week, Giles was able to identify some crucial information for us. There is a subtle series of cracks in the floors, flowing toward a particular point in the work room." She obviously caught some half-asked question. "To clarify, we refer to the large room with the inscription as the workroom and the room with the long table as the great hall. The room on the other side is the solar, or family quarters."

There had not been much there, once they'd investigated. Kate had described how everything was rather faded, with a single bed and reading chair close to the fireplace.

Kate continued, evenly, even though he hadn't been paying attention for a few sentences. "Once we had the model in the sandtable, Giles was able to do extensive mathematical modelling. We are now quite certain that the cracks all point to the caster of the working, or more precisely at the place where his body fell. We feel confident, as well, with suggesting that the lines intersect where his heart was at the time of his death."

There was a pause, and Giles was sure there was another gesture he couldn't see. Kate, thankfully, spelled it out for him. "Master Franklin, you had a question?" The magical theorist, that would be, then.

"May I ask how you came to that conclusion, given the lack of physical evidence. I've not had a chance to examine the space directly, of course."

"First by careful measurement of the cracks, determining where they fell. Second, by using non-invasive methods. The radius for Ptolemy's Arc was quite small, a matter of an inch or two. Based on the distance from two shadows on the floor that look like the remnants of items in the caster's hands, it seems very likely to be his heart, rather than his head. We do, of course, appreciate further investigation."

There was only mild grumbling from Franklin. Sensible of him. Giles knew him far more by reputation, as a man who knew his own subject quite well, but who thought he knew other people's specialities better than they did.

Kate, however, was doing wonderfully, holding firm. She had been working long hours with the penelopes to map every possibility. He knew her knees were more than a bit bruised from getting up and down off the floor once everyone had decided she was the closest in height to their caster.

Edgarton broke in, his voice smooth. "Do continue with the implications, please, Davies."

"Sir." That was prompt and immediate, for all Kate was more comfortably relaxed with the others in their team. "Before I suggest our current theories, I would like to visit a few details."

Giles leaned forward. There were questions Kate had asked no one else had touched on, and he had encouraged her to raise them here. He heard Edgarton's easy "As you wish, Davies."

"One question that has been nagging at me, sir, is whether there were other people in the household when our caster did his working. Even if he was the only member of the family, a manor like that would have half a dozen staff, at least, in that time."

That brought a series of mutters around the table. Apparently not a thing most of them had bothered to think about.

"First, I should say that research from the librarians in Temple Court has given a name to our caster, or at least a likely one. Ralf Mannering, whose family had inherited the property from a relative - an aunt, we believe - earlier in the 1400s." Kate paused, and Giles was sure she was glancing at her notes.

"I must give credit to one of the librarians, here. Asenath Finlay. She is the one who realised the calendar dating system had changed between the disappearance of the manor and the reappearance. We felt there was some consistent pattern, based on some of the astrological calculations, but it took us quite a while to sort it out."

One of the voices from down the table said, "What do you mean, the calendar changed? Ridiculous." That was one of the senior members from the Ministry.

Giles coughed, and he felt Kate's fingers flick against his hand, encouraging him to go on.

"It is easy to think that we have counted days the same way since time immemorial. In reality, our current system, the Gregorian calendar, only came into wide-spread use in the 1750s. There was, by that time, a difference of some ten days between that and the Julian calendar previously in use."

He paused, letting them catch up mentally. "I'll spare you the lecture on how that works, and how they became out of sync. When I ran the calculations for the models of what had happened, the inscriptions in the workroom kept suggesting it happened at the summer solstice. But other indicators we found - such as when the manor reappeared - suggested something different. A skewing, somehow, between the human sense of time and the magical."

Kate slipped in. "Asenath was able to find some records that suggested there was a fair nearby for the solstice. Not as well known as the Midsummer Fair in Cambridge, in that era, or the St. Giles Fair, in early September. But fairs of that kind were quite common and widespread. So far as we can tell, the house was empty of all except Ralf Mannering when he set about his working."

Another voice, a woman's this time, said "What does that have to do with the date?"

Giles spoke, again. "The solstices are not a matter of the calendar, rather they are points around which the calendar revolves, you understand. It was Asenath who thought about the change in the calendar. Once I applied the appropriate offset, the places we thought were errors or gaps were no longer an issue."

That lead to a babble of voices Giles couldn't sort out. Edgarton's voice broke into them. "A summary of the details is being duplicated, you'll have copies by tomorrow. For now, we will proceed assuming that Giles is correct. He generally is."

Giles couldn't restrain himself from a mock salute, fingers to just above his eyebrow, then waving off. He then said, amiably, "I am open to other hypotheses, of course, that fit the data so far."

Someone down the table asked, "Can you describe the details that make you sure there was no one in the house?"

Kate tapped his wrist, and he let her speak. "We've investigated the entire house carefully, doing our best to disturb nothing. The chamber pots had all been emptied and cleaned. There was no food cooking, as we said, but also very little left out. We do suspect the original property was larger, including a dairy and stables."

"So you are saying that some land was taken, but only - the walls?"

"We suspect that how the space was defined is a similar issue to the calendar. Something common then, but not to modern ways of looking at things. But as can be seen, the manor and the walled gardens, with a margin of some twenty to thirty feet in each direction beyond that."

"What happened to what was there?"

"Ah, that's a good question. All the records we can find since then just ignore that patch of ground. Rather thoroughly, from what we can tell. Again, additional research is needed. There was no nearby manor or country home - the ones closest by were in use at the time of the Pact, and since, and no one apparently sought to build between them."

"Any signs of other magical interference?"

"There is some local folklore about ghosts, but we think that is just an effect of the magic. There is clearly a lot more work to be done, even before the investigation of such a well-preserved historical building."

"Do we know why?" That was the architect, Giles thought.

"Master Belridge, we again only have suppositions. It will likely be years before even the contents of the library can be fully examined and inventoried."

"You have a thought, though, yes?"

Kate paused, long enough that Edgarton said, his voice even, "Go ahead and theorise ahead of the evidence, Davies."

"Sir. Master Franklin, of course, please add anything I'm missing." Giles could feel her gathering herself.

"We know that a number of people were overset at the idea of the Pact, an agreement King Richard III made apparently quite suddenly in 1483 in a last attempt to preserve magic in Great Britain." She was using the geographic names quite precisely, and Giles approved.

"There were a number of ways people acted on that disagreement," Kate continued, her voice even, but Giles couldn't help but remember the outrage in her voice when she'd read various historical accounts to him, curled up in the library at home. "We feel Ralf Mannering was one of them, and that he wished to maintain a connection with the Fatae despite the restrictions of the Pact."

"Which were that the Fatae withdrew, touching no part of mortal magic for these people and this place." That was the penelope, quoting one of the most traditional songs about the Pact.

"Exactly so." Kate took a deep breath, and then said, "And so he came up with an idiosyncratic magical ritual to force open a gate. As he died, he wedged it open. We presume that the Fatae or the magic of the Pact itself made the manor disappear while it was an active breech in the agreement. Only once the gate closed, could the house reappear."

There was another burble of commentary, until Giles heard Edgarton's "Silence, please." Everyone quieted, and he added, "The implications?"

"This project will take a long time, sir. Years. Possibly decades. All we have right now are guesses and suppositions, enough to propose a direction for research and investigation. This isn't a simple puzzle." Then, a tiny pause, and she was brave enough to add. "Even if Giles makes the maths and calculations look easy."

Giles grinned openly, then gathered himself and said, "There are rather a lot more calculations to do, the effects of the magical workings. We will be interviewing additional historians, theorists, and other specialists in the coming weeks." He had to return to Oxford, at least part of the time, and Kate would also eventually have other duties. "There is a list in your packet."

"That brings us to the next steps. Thank you, Davies." Edgarton coaxed the group through the practical issues, and confirming the priorities. Everyone else thankfully followed along easily enough, and the meeting ended promptly on time.

Giles waited for everyone to clear out of the room before he turned a little toward Kate. "Tea, and discussion?"

Edgarton coughed, and Giles realised he hadn't left. "Edgarton?"

"Oh, just rather pleased at how you both handled yourselves. Clear and precise."

Giles laughed. "If you expected anything else from us, you have not been paying attention at all."

"I've a bit more social news for you, Giles, and a few things you should know from the Guard, Davies. Drinks at the club?" Giles had rather wanted to take Kate home in private, but she tapped his hand, one of their personal signals. Of course she wouldn't want to turn down the chance to look good in front of Edgarton.

K ate rubbed her face. She'd been back at Guard headquarters for a fortnight now. The work of the house was in the hands of historians, no longer her domain to oversee. She found she missed it painfully, an ache she couldn't bear to talk about, even to Giles. And he was about to dive back into the commitments of Trinity term at Oxford. They would have much less time together. Worse, they'd be working on different things entirely.

Her superiors had set her to reviewing old reports for inconsistencies. It was far better than portal or river duty, and she'd found several issues that needed better follow up than they'd got. But it was nothing like the glorious work of figuring out the house's secrets.

"Guard Katherine Davies."

Looking up, she spotted the captain's insignia. Not someone she knew, but she promptly replied "Sir."

"Your presence has been requested. Come with me, please." His tone and manner gave her no hint of what to expect.

She took the briefest moment to set the papers in order,

slipping the folder she had just finished back into the locking file drawer. Then she stood, taking a moment to make sure her uniform jacket was hanging correctly, reaching a hand to tuck a strand of hair back into the loose bun.

He led her, not speaking, her up to the Appointments room. Opening the door, she looked down the long wood panelled room, with the rows of seats along each side.

It was used for official reprimands as much as anything else, and she could not keep herself from thinking about where she might have failed, and how badly. But then she heard Giles in her head, felt his hand on her arm, the clear way he'd made certain she could see her own worth, and she knew better. Whatever she was here for, it wasn't for a reprimand.

The captain led her briskly up the centre aisle, so briskly she couldn't look around to see who was in the side benches. Fifteen people, maybe twenty. He then bowed precisely. "Officers of the Guard, I present Guard Davies, as requested."

Kate bowed, the formal bow that had been trained into her during her apprenticeship, then stood to attention. When she looked up at the dais, she found three of the senior officers sitting there. One was Lord Edgarton, who had his unreadable face on. The other two were both quite senior, she'd only seen them before at formal parades. Lady Donovan had a rather distinct appearance, with her grey hair pulled back tightly and a privately tailored uniform, but Kate had to work for other man's name. She only placed him as Colonel Judling when Lord Edgarton spoke.

"Guard Davies." He paused, just long enough to worry her, then said "Stand at ease. You have recently finished an extended assignment, working on a complex problem. We have read your reports in detail, but please summarise the relevant information for those assembled."

Kate could recognise a spot examination when she heard one. She settled herself into a more steady position on her feet, took a breath, and looked up, keeping her expression as clear and pleasant as she could.

"Of course, sir. Major Lefton was assigned to investigate a manor house that had reappeared in a rural area of Oxfordshire. Specifically the reasons for its reappearance, any magical effects or concerns to be aware of, and the contents of the manor with an eye to determining the sequence of events, causation, and results. We were able to gain access to the manor after significant experimentation and determined that it disappeared in 1484."

She paused, trying to figure out how to sum up the rest. "The owner of the house had endeavoured to make his own arrangements with the Fatae in the wake of the Pact, and it ended unexpectedly for him. The house reappearing turned out to be due to the effects of that complex ritual magic finally reaching their conclusion."

"More specifically, we feel the most likely scenario was that the Folk were claiming his remains through the barrier of the Silence, and once that was completed, the house, for lack of a better phrase, fell back into place, with minor structural damage resulting from its suspension." There had been discussions about whether or not the man had been dissolved or pulled through, which had been dropped as both insoluble and really quite disturbing to contemplate.

Taking a breath, she continued. "We examined the house in detail, making sure it was safe for historians and other specialists to study, and there is now a proper rota for further investigation. I was reassigned to Trellech at the completion of the initial phase, two weeks ago."

"Thank you. What was your precise role in the work?"

"Analyzing wards and protections so that Major Lefton could proceed in his work, as well as providing appropriate assistance with the physical tasks of investigation. Once we were able to enter the house, I was the Guard responsible for overseeing the additional staff - three analysts, three penelopes, and two clerks - as well as coordinating the work of various historians, art historians, and magical theorists investigating the house itself."

"This differs from work you've done before, yes?" That was Lady Donovan.

"Yes, ma'am. I found I enjoyed it. Especially figuring out the best sequence for the work we needed to do at a given time, and which talents were the best fit for the needed tasks."

"We gather from your previous superior officers that you have a reputation for assisting junior staff." That was Colonel Judling. He sounded like he might approve of that, but his expression was so neutral that she could not be sure.

Kate was not sure what he wanted her to say, and went with the truth. "Yes, sir. People helped me when I got started. I wanted to pass that on." The noise he made was difficult to interpret - it could be a laugh or a dismissive snort.

Lord Edgarton looked at the others, raised an eyebrow, and said, "Satisfied?"

They both nodded promptly, and only then did Edgarton smile. "We are delighted to be the ones to tell you that you have earned promotion to Captain. We intend for you to receive additional training with an eye to leading a small group assigned to deal with unusual problems. You have been tenacious when dealing with complex puzzles, treated others well, and kept your primary goals well in line. Step forward."

She took several moments to react. This was not at all what she'd expected. Then she bowed slightly, and took the steps forward to the front of the dais, for Edgarton to come down and pin the new insignia on her jacket. "You have leave through Monday as a reward for your excellent work. And I gather there are evening plans arranged for you, as a celebration." Now he was beaming. "There are people here to congratulate you, of course. Ladies, gentlemen, fellows of the guard, I present to you Captain Davies, who has our trust and our thanks for her service."

Kate turned around, she knew that was her cue.

There were a number of faces there. The Healer she worked most with. Two of her previous commanding officers. Adria was there, somehow, she'd thought Adria was posted to London at the moment. People came up, and pressed hands into hers, murmured things in her ear. She smiled and nodded, letting it wash over her, letting them see her honest pleasure. At the tail end came Lady Donovan and Colonel Judling.

"You'll be doing stints with both of us, to learn." said Lady Donovan. "Enjoy your days off. I will send along where to report on Tuesday morning, and I expect you to work quite hard."

Kate had to smile. "You have a reputation, Lady Donovan, for high standards. I will do my best to keep up with them."

It earned her a broad smile, and a "I knew I liked you. Tuesday." She swept off, the colonel going along with her.

She heard a cough, then, and saw Lady Alysoun, with Giles on her arm. She hadn't seen him, they must have been behind others. Her face lit up, she knew it, even if he couldn't see it. But Lady Alysoun could, and it made Kate flush, terribly embarrassed.

"Oh, goodness. Don't worry. I realised it as soon as I saw you with him when we visited the site. I am quite glad you've found someone suitable. And that he has the good sense to keep you close. Here you go, Giles, we'll see you later."

Giles released her arm and took several steps forward. Kate reached out, slipping her hand into his. She barely heard Lord Edgarton offer his wife his own arm, and the sound of their steps on the wood floors moving away, toward the doors.

"Captain Davies, that has a fine ring to it."

She took one last look around the room, making sure everyone was gone, before she slid her arms around his waist and kissed him. "Did you know? When did you know?"

"A week ago, after they read the reports, they called me in. I had to admit a positive bias mind you. Your work fortunately speaks for itself, and the comments of the others on the project."

Kate let out a long breath. "I had no idea. I thought I would be back on portal duty, or escort, or ... something."

"And instead, you get a glorious lot of new puzzles to keep you sharp. Mmmm." His voice was a contented purr. "Possibly some we can work on together, Edgarton says."

She laughed and kissed him again. "You are so smug."

"I think I've rather earned it, don't you? Life is going wonderfully. Now, I do have plans this evening. Supper out, a private little restaurant I believe you'll enjoy most thoroughly, and then there's a small garden party being hosted by a few friends of mine. I would like to introduce you around properly, make it clear we're together."

Kate felt overwhelmed. "I don't have a thing to wear."

"Oh, don't worry about that. Alysoun made sure you had something suitable. They'll be there. Home to change, then we'll have a grand evening."

"Indulging me again?" He just grinned at her, unrepentantly. "I thought you didn't do parties?"

"You may have changed my mind. You are superb, Kate, at telling me what I need to know. Say yes?" There was an edge to his voice, something much more energetically hopeful than his usual.

"You know I can't resist when you suggest something in that tone." She considered, then said "Something else today?"

"Oh, they finally got Vale back here, and I saw the list of charges. So did his parents, and they've fully disowned him. Cut him out of the family, or they will have by now, the old rituals. With rather a lot of apologies to me. He'll be seeing significant prison time, yet to be determined." He sounded relieved, more than anything, and she moved to look at him, straight on, taking both his hands.

"So no one's fussing about who you hire at the moment?"

"Nor about you. Especially not with the promotion."

"Well." Kate paused and swallowed. "I'll just have to live up to all these expectations then. Right. You said something about getting ready."

"Lead on, my captain. Do lead on."

IF YOU ENJOYED *Wards of the Roses* and would like to read more of this series, please sign up for my mailing list to get all the latest news and fun extras. As a thank you, you'll get a copy of *Ancient Trust*, a prequel novella taking place in 1922 when Lord Geoffrey Carillon inherits his title. Giles makes a key appearance.

Your reviews (on whatever review site you use) are much appreciated, too!

Kate first appeared in the series at the end of *Outcrossing* (several years later than the events of this book). She and Giles also are very helpful in *On The Bias* at a key point in the plot.

Read on for more historical details about this book and an excerpt from *In The Cards*.

AUTHOR'S NOTES

Thank you so much for picking up *Wards of the Roses*. This is my favourite title in the series so far. As always, I owe a great deal of thanks to my editor and to my early readers. Any remaining errors are of course entirely mine.

I knew I was going to write a book about Kate as soon as she appeared in the final chapters of my first book, *Outcrossing*.

You can find more about Giles and Kate, a little further along in their relationship in *Country Manners,* found in the *Winter's Charms* collection.

Going more or less chronologically through the book, here are my notes and inspirations. If you have a question not answered here, please do email me at celia@celialake.com. I'll be glad to answer you.

Bohort is a magical game based on a mediaeval game designed to train people for fighting. The magical version is played by teams of five players who need to solve various puzzles (magical and otherwise), and complete one or more tasks. Think of it like capture the flag only with more things throwing coloured powder, creating a highly localised ice storm, or repelling you from the goal like two poles of a magnet. There's a mounted variant called pavo.

As you've likely figured out by now, **The Guard** serve as the police force of the magical community, providing assistance and dealing with violations of the law, but also investigating odd situations and figuring out if they pose a danger to people around them. Women can and do serve (and in high-ranking positions), but there tend to be fewer in active service than men.

The 1920s were a fascinating turning point for people who were **blind**. Guide dogs and the long white cane many people use today actually came out of rehabilitation work with soldiers who were blinded during World War I. They weren't yet in use in the United Kingdom in 1920. People commonly used the sighted guide method that Giles has Kate use (taking her arm just above the elbow), also still in use today.

Poison gases were the cause of a significant amount of blindness during the war - mustard gas, chlorine, and phosgene were some of the major ones. Giles was blinded by a magical gas which had many of the same effects. Use of these chemical weapons was hotly debated during the War.

St Dunstan's, the place Giles got initial rehabilitation training, was founded in 1915, after the earliest cases of war blinding came home. It's now known as Blind Veterans UK. There's an excellent book about the history by David

Castleton, *In The Mind's Eye: The Blinded Veterans of St Dunstan's*.

(The Refuge, the magical equivalent, is something I made up, but it taught similar skills in independent living and navigation using magical techniques. The locational tool Giles uses in his townhome is a magical version of some current locational technology.)

The issues Giles deals with are based on my conversations with a number of people who are blind (as well as additional reading). There can be a tremendous amount of vulnerability in relying on someone else to handle business affairs, or in navigating interactions with strangers (such as when Giles holds out his hand, and isn't sure if Kate will take it.) The constant effort to keep track of the space or who is speaking in a group can also be exhausting.

People sometimes wonder about whether one capitalises **braille**. The common convention in the blindness community is that you use a lower case when talking about the method of coding text, and a capital when referring to the original creator, Louis Braille.

Giles mentions there are half a dozen variants of braille in use (the United States didn't standardise on one until 1919, and the United Kingdom had a lot of books in different versions floating around.) The other method he mentions, and my favourite of the raised type methods, is called Moon Type. It uses symbols that are easier to read for some people (and easier to learn for many people who become blind later in life.)

Many people are really afraid of becoming blind - it's reliably one of the top fears people list. Giles quite reasonably points out that there are skills that help, and many of them aren't that hard to learn, they just take practise. The method he teaches Kate for navigating an unfamiliar room without hurting your fingers is one of those. If you'd like more resources about blindness and what people get up to in the present day, the website Blind New World has great resources.

~

As my bio mentions, I'm a librarian, so I'm delighted I got to include a chapter or two in a magical **library** with helpful librarians.

The **composer** Giles insists on playing in chapter 13 is Arnold Schoenberg, born in Austria and who emigrated to the United States in 1933. He was extremely influential because of the number of composers he taught. Schoenberg was just beginning to explore twelve-tone composition techniques when this book happens, but they are heavily rooted in mathematical structures and patterns.

I'm fascinated by lost languages, and the Guard have one all of their own, known as the **Lost Tongue** which they use to discuss orders and practical issues and ensure no one can overhear them.

The Pact (and **The Silence**) are given context in the book, but I admit I have a particular fascination for the Wars of the Roses and for Richard III. There's a little more background in the guide on my website, and I expect to be revisiting what brought Richard to that point in future books. We will definitely be hearing more about the Fatae (that's for book 7, *Seven Sisters*).

I could not resist naming the people who unweave magical workings **penelopes** in honour of Penelope, wife of Odysseus of Greek mythology. She kept her home and herself safe from outrageous suitors while her husband was taking the long way home. She refused to pick any of the suitors until her weaving was done, so she would weave during the day and unweave it at night.

Kate quotes from *the Mabinogion* when she's reciting all the Welsh names. It's a collection of stories compiled from mediaeval Welsh in the 12th and 13th centuries. Lady Charlotte Guest did a widely read translation in the mid-1800s that distorted some of the myths. Patrick Ford's translation is considered one of the best modern ones, and I've been reading interesting things about one recently done by Sioned Davies. The list of names comes from the beginning of Kihwch and Olwen (also called Culhwch and Olwen.) In the story, the names go on for a couple of pages.

As Giles notes, they were still discovering planets in the 1920s. (**Planet X** was Pluto.)

Opium became illegal in the United Kingdom in early 1921- right around the time of the book. It was illegal in the magical community slightly earlier.

The newsletter (https://www.celialake.com/newsletter/) and my social media accounts will have all the details about new and upcoming releases. If you sign up for my newsletter, you'll get a copy of *Ancient Trust*, a prequel novella taking place in 1922 when Lord Geoffrey Carillon inherits his title. Giles makes a key appearance.

Thank you again for coming along on this journey with me. Check out an excerpt from my next book, *In The Cards*, that tells the story of Laura Penhallow (younger sister to Lizzie, from *Goblin Fruit*.)

EXCERPT FROM IN THE CARDS

November 1925, a large party

Laura finally found a corner of the terrace. The party was large, many more people than she had been expecting, and she could feel the flutters of anxiety again. Too many people, wanting too many different things, and Laura wasn't sure whether what they wanted was a good idea for anyone involved.

From her position, though, she could begin to pick out the little groupings. She remembered her brother-in-law's comments, as he was coaching Lizzie through some of the formal social events they had to attend.

He had said people would make their own groupings. In a group of mixed age you could expect a group of older folks tutting over the foibles and miseries of youth. You could expect a cluster of bright young things, certain they were going on to rule the world. Or at least comment cynically about it.

Somewhere around the edges, there would be the more interesting people, the ones with particular hobbies or passions or intrigues. That's where he spent his time. Well, with Lizzie, now, who had taken to his hobbies of diplomatic conversations and occasional investigations like a fish to water.

They had just left on a belated honeymoon, though, and were no help here. Laura had got the invite on the strength of Lizzie's marriage. She was too old to be much threat to the daughters just coming out, and too young to cluck over things with the aunties and grandmothers. The War had taken many of the men who might have been her age. It left her with youngsters, or people long since married off, usually with two or three children walking and talking by now.

Even with all of that, it was better to be at the party than home alone. Here, she might meet someone interesting. She wouldn't at home with the chickens. In fact, she'd already been asked to a house party in a fortnight out on an island off Cornwall.

A smaller gathering, Madam Amberly had said, perhaps a dozen people, with a larger party on the Saturday. She was pleasantly lost in thought about what that might be like, if it might lead to something more, to friendships, when she heard someone calling across the terrace.

"Laura? Laura Penhallow?"

It was a young woman she'd met at one of the many parties Lizzie and Lord Carillon had thrown, trying to rehabilitate the Penhallow name a bit. He had hoped to make it clear that the two sisters were not their father and uncle, whose ill-fated explorations had lost many people a lot of money.

It had mostly been a failure. Oh, people were pleasant enough to both of them, and they weren't excluding Lizzie now. But there was a difference between the big public invitations and the private ones, the ones where you actually made friends.

She nodded and waved a little. "Psyche, over here." Psyche Donovan was from one of the better-off families. However, her family had mostly earned their money by being clever and good at magic, rather than the more distasteful approaches. Psyche was very earnest, very fluttery, and prone to having her nose in a book, but she also had a kind heart. Laura had found that more rare in these circles than she liked.

"Did you know? There's a fortune teller. Do come, I don't want to go by myself. That's a lovely dress, is it from Meaning, in town? The pale blue, it really brings out your eyes, and that edging, it looks so sharp. Quite the mode! But you still haven't bobbed your hair."

Laura smiled. "My sister would have my head. And I'd miss it. I fought too hard to keep it long for years." It was pinned up fashionably, though, with the help of one of the maids at Ytene. "I'm not sure what I think of fortune tellers, but I'll come along, at least."

Psyche grinned, and reached for Laura's hand, tugging her along like a rather speedy tugboat guiding a larger ship through a harbour's traffic. They went off to the right into one of the smaller drawing rooms on the first floor.

Laura's first impression was that someone had worked to set quite the spooky mood. There were dim charm lights glowing in the corners of the ceiling and throwing shadows everywhere. Streamers of fabric in deep reds and purples and blues, sparkling with other charms that made the colour ebb and flow.

In the centre, at a round table, sat a woman, her hair tied back in a scarf, wearing a rather dated dress. It was nearly

Victorian, though it was rather less modest around the decolletage than that usually implied.

"Come in, come in. Which of you shall I read for first?"

Psyche hung back, suddenly shy. Laura glanced at her and said, "My friend was curious. Can you tell me more about..." She paused, looking for the diplomatic phrase. "Your approach?"

It earned her a chuckle. "An open mind but a cautious one, I like that. Did you by chance study divination in school?"

Laura blinked. "No, ma'am." She almost offered something more - that she'd left school before the years it was an option, that she's not sure she'd have taken it anyway. "I've known a few people who read cards, though."

"Then you may know something of these. I use a French deck, an ancient deck, the Tarot de Marseilles. Not so old as the Sforza or some of the Italian, but it is a good friend, a helpful friend. Come, sit." The woman had a slight accent, one Laura, with all her experiences in Europe, couldn't quite place, with a faint hesitation between words.

Laura paused for a moment "Is there a fee?"

"Most cautious and practical!" It seemed to delight the reader. "No, no, I read here by arrangement with our hostess, a little space away from the noise and the strutting of young men and the grumbling of old ones."

That made Laura smile, and Psyche bumped her with her hip. "Go on, you go first."

"Come, sit down here." The reader gestured at the chair across from her. "Your friend may stay if you wish, or I will read for her next if you prefer a private reading."

Laura frowned, sitting down and letting her skirt settle. She didn't really believe it would turn up anything she wanted hidden.

"Psyche, do stay, it will be more fun that way."

The reader beamed at them. "Now, then, you should take these cards, spread them before you, and then draw the cards and place them here, as I tell you."

Laura nodded, and begin to spread the cards in an arc, keeping them close enough to her side of the table to reach them easily.

Psyche settled down in a chair beside her, peering at the backs. "They're beautiful. Mistress. Um. What should we call you?"

"I am Madam Bertilak." It was like she was giving a gift. Laura frowned, considering the name, then the woman gestured again. "Find your cards, dear one. Begin there, move right to left, as the sun passes over the earth. Face up."

Laura could just hear her sister's likely lecture on how that wasn't how it worked at all, but she did as instructed, placing five cards.

"Your foundations, the distant past." Madam Bertilak indicated the card on the right. "The recent past. The present. The near future. The more distant future, prone to change." Her finger moved from card to card.

Laura nodded. That seemed sensible enough, if one thought bits of card could tell you anything. She leaned to peer at the cards, brightly coloured.

"The magician. It can indicate a lingering illness, especially of the lungs. Something where there is a certain amount of - how does one say it?" Madam Bertilak paused, tapping the table with a fingernail. "Show. Smoke and mirrors. Performance. There may also be real skill, but it is hidden behind the show."

Laura frowned, and shook her head, the image of several of the doctors she had met at various sanitaria suddenly dominating her thoughts. They had smiled, shaken hands, and charmed her mother. None of them had much to offer except the usual; the endless fresh cold air, the surgeries to inflate or deflate the lung, the specific foods. How if something did not work, it was a flaw in her, not in their treatment. She shivered, suddenly cold, and the reader glanced at her.

"An uncomfortable past, my dear? I am sorry, but you have had a bad time of it, haven't you? This is the eight of cups, and I find it often in the readings for young women, betrayed by men. Betrayed in the... heart, you say, not just in the body."

Laura frowned, and said "Psyche, would you be a love and fetch me something to drink? Wine, or - if they have a mulled wine, or cider?"

Psyche bobbed up. "Oh, of course, and a shawl? You seem to be taking a bit of a chill."

"That is so kind, yes. My shawl's in the cloakroom, here's the token."

She waited until the younger woman had left, curling her arms around herself at her waist, willing the tension out of her shoulders without success.

"They cut close, then?"

Laura had been looking down the cards, but she looked up, to meet Madam Bertilak's eyes, which were a curious blue-green. The expression was kind enough. A real kindness, not the false kindness Laura had long since learned to recognised. Like fake kind doctors.

"Rather, yes, madam." She paused. It would give too much away to explain, at least yet. "The next card, please?"

"There is a gift here." She tapped the second card again. "A sign - there are plenty of cups, to be filled. You may take things away from what you have learned in this betrayal. And I am sorry for it. You seem a kind woman."

Laura ducked her head, but said nothing.

After a few moments, Madam Bertilak went on. "The next card, ah, that is - you have had many changes in your life, yes? This is the wheel of fortune, it explains itself, the way that life changes, swinging us up and down, up and down. You have been down, here, so perhaps now it is time for up."

Laura looked up and smiled, more hopeful now. At least this one had not cut so much like a knife. "That would be welcome, yes."

"This, oh, goodness." The woman tutted over it. "This card, it scares many people. It is Death, you see, the reaper who comes for us all in our turn." A skeletal figure, holding a scythe, grimacing, with parts of bodies and heads strewn on the field at his feet.

Laura peered at it and then took a breath. "I've seen enough of death that - what I feel is more complicated than fear."

The woman raised an eyebrow and said, "A most unusual young woman. Mature for your years and wise. But you should not fear for yourself, for see, this last card?"

She indicated the last card, on the left, "Les Amoreux. The lovers. In this deck, it is about choice. You see that it is a young man, with two women. One older and wealthy, but the look on her face, perhaps she is not so kind? And the younger, gentler, beautiful, but not near so well dressed. He must choose. But see, there is Cupid, with his arrow, a sign from the heavens about which way will bring blessings."

"And you think that is for me?"

"Ah, but the other cards, in your past, those have been true enough, yes?"

"You said..." Laura paused, "You said this was only a possible future."

"Yes. You will have to live a little longer to find out. My advice to you, wise young woman, is to think carefully about what you choose, how it will last."

Laura was about to say something else, when Psyche came back with a mug of mulled wine, and a shawl. She was glad of the excuse to give her seat over, and fuss about warming herself up.

Need a mystery and romance on a remote island off Cornwall? You can get *In The Cards* from your favourite source for books.